Dear Reader,

I haven't had so much fun writing
popped up out of nowhere and took
even just half as much as I have.

Things have been hectic around here, healthwise, for both my husband and me. Thank you all for your prayers and warm wishes, and your friendship. My readers are very much my extended family. I don't do newsletters or video chats, or all the other things I really should be doing to keep in touch with you. I apologize for that. I will try to do better next year. That's going to be my one New Year's resolution.

Meanwhile, I am taking it one day at a time and not thinking too far ahead. I will be working on new books after the holidays, one of which will be about Cal Hollister. His former love interest is mentioned in this book, and if you've followed along in previous books, you'll be familiar with him already. I'll leave you to guess the identity of the young blonde woman he meets in Fernando's. (Hint: she was introduced in one of the Wyoming books).

I hope you all have a happy and prosperous 2021, and may it be with far fewer terrible things than 2020 gave us—issues of health that almost crashed the economy and took many lives. Of course, on a lighter note, we had the great toilet paper shortage...

Take care, stay well, keep safe. Much love. Many hugs from your greatest fan,

Diana Palmer

Author of more than one hundred books, Diana Palmer got her start as a newspaper reporter. A *New York Times* bestselling author and voted one of the top ten romance writers in America, she has a gift for telling the most sensual tales with charm and humour. Diana lives with her family in Georgia.

NOTORIOUS

DIANA PALMER

MILLS & BOON

Mills & Boon
An imprint of HarperCollins*Publishers* Ltd
1 London Bridge Street
London SE1 9GF

www.harpercollins.co.uk

HarperCollins*Publishers*
1st Floor, Watermarque Building, Ringsend Road
Dublin 4, Ireland

This paperback edition 2021
1
First published in Great Britain by Mills & Boon,
an imprint of HarperCollins*Publishers* Ltd 2021

Copyright© Diana Palmer 2021

Diana Palmer asserts the moral right to be
identified as the author of this work.
A catalogue record for this book is
available from the British Library.

ISBN: 978-1-84845-871-0

MIX
Paper from
responsible sources

FSC
www.fsc.org   FSC™ C007454

This book is produced from independently certified FSC™ paper
to ensure responsible forest management.

For more information visit: www.harpercollins.co.uk/green

Printed and Bound in the UK using 100% Renewable Electricity at
CPI Group (UK) Ltd

For a complete list of titles available by Diana Palmer,
please visit www.dianapalmer.com

NOTORIOUS

ONE

Gaby Dupont glanced again at the paper in her hand. She hesitated to do this, but her grandmother had pleaded with her. They needed to know something about this noted Chicago criminal attorney, Nicolas Chandler, and his very famous law firm, Chandler, Morse and Souillard. Gaby was the only one of the family who lived permanently in Chicago, where he did. If her grandmother hadn't been so upset, and so insistent, perhaps Gaby could have found another solution. But this might be her best option.

She pushed the doorbell and stood nervously waiting for someone to open the door. This apartment was in a swanky area of Chicago, overlooking the lake. It was as expensive as the place where Gaby lived. She knew this man by reputation, and also because the law firm he headed had represented her grandfather in a criminal action that still made her sick to her stomach to remember. There was an appeal being threatened in the case, and Gaby's grandmother wanted to know if this attorney was going to consider representing her ex-husband again. She needed to know. So did Gaby.

Gaby had done masquerades before, mostly in an attempt to avoid a greedy cousin who was stalking her relentlessly for some property willed to her by a mutual great-aunt, which she wasn't willing to give him. She'd never understood the passion some people had for the almighty dollar. Gaby would have been happy with less. It was attitude, she considered, more than what happened to you.

Gaby was twenty-four and she didn't want to get married. Her grandfather, Charles Dupont, had sold her like a prize mare without her knowledge when she was sixteen. Her innocence had a monetary value, and without Gaby's knowledge—or his wife's—he'd arranged a party, during which he took Gaby into a room with a foreign businessman to whom he owed a lot of money and three of the businessman's friends. Gaby was to be his payoff, since Madame Dupont had refused to pay his gambling debts.

The man was strong and Gaby couldn't get away from him. But Gaby's screams had brought her grandmother running. Two men at the party, Madame's chauffeur and bodyguard, had busted the lock on the door and saved the barely clad teenager from further assault at the hands of her grandfather's colleague. One of the men had taken photos with his cellphone just as Madame Dupont went in the door and saw what had been done to her only grandchild. The photos were used in a criminal complaint. There were a few assorted bruises and lacerations on the foreign businessman before the assaulting parties managed to escape, just before the police arrived. Gaby's grandfather, the perpetrator of the cowardly assault, had been left to face the music.

Gaby had been transported to the hospital, her grandfather to jail. Gaby's grandmother had filed for divorce the very next day, leaving her immoral husband penniless and furious at his changed circumstances. Sadly, Gaby's assailant was a foreign diplomat, and he used his diplomatic immunity to escape any charges. His three friends vanished like smoke. Gaby's grandmother had been furious, but her attorney had been forced to relinquish the criminal charges against the diplomat. Gaby's grandfather, however, had been arrested and tried and convicted. Thanks to a friend, an influential and rather shady judge, his sentence had been lessened and the penalty also reduced. Now a mutual acquaintance had told Madame that Charles Dupont, who'd lost his law license, was planning to demand a retrial due to new evidence so that he could get his license reinstated. What new evidence he had, the acquaintance didn't know. It was enough to panic Gaby's grandmother, nevertheless.

Her grandfather's nephew, Robert Matthews, a business colleague, had also been left out in the cold financially as a consequence of his uncle's arrest. He was claiming that property given to Gaby in a will from their mutual great-aunt was actually his and he was planning legal action. The property was Gaby's only real means of support. Well, her grandmother would never have let her starve, of course, but the property was rented to a large corporation that established an agricultural operation on it, and the profits were enormous. Gaby was wealthy in her own right because of that inheritance.

So the two of them, Gaby's grandfather and her cousin, posed a danger to Gaby and her grandmother. In fact, Madame Dupont had hired a new bodyguard, a former mercenary named Tanner Everett, just for Gaby. She was that afraid for her. Gaby had insisted that her bodyguard be invisible, especially when she went to see the attorney. She had more trouble than she could handle already. He agreed, but he had that amused smirk that made her want to hit him.

She'd never really liked her grandfather, whose obsession with material things had left her nauseated. Her grandmother, Melissandra Lafitte Dupont, came from titled French aristocrats, although she'd lived in Chicago since she was a girl. She owned a palatial estate in France where she always went for the grape harvest, because Dupont wines from her winery sold all over the world. When Gaby's adventurous parents, Jean and Nicole Dupont, had died while on an archaeological dig in Africa, Gaby had come to live with her grandparents at the age of thirteen. She'd always loved her grandmother. But her grandfather had been a different story. She had more to fear from him now. He was asking for a retrial, charging that the evidence was sketchy at best, and that some of it had been manufactured to convict him. He had an attorney, a small-time one, who was just starting out in the business and, therefore, less expensive. But gossip was that he was going to ask Nicolas Chandler's firm to represent him once more. Since Chandler was the best criminal attorney in the city, Gaby had a great deal to lose if he took the case. But he wasn't, from reputation, the sort of man who could be approached about a potential client. He was incorruptible, arrogant and afraid of nothing on earth. So Gaby was going to try a soft approach. Perhaps he could be reasoned with by the victim of a client he might be considering.

Gaby waited outside the apartment after she rang the bell. She hoped that she could get Mr. Chandler to speak to her about his firm's involvement in her grandfather's case. She wanted a private chat, hence her trip to his apartment rather than to his office. It took a long time before the door finally opened.

A girl of about fifteen with spiky, purple dyed hair and piercings everywhere, dressed in a short skirt and slinky blouse with overdone mascara and popping bubble gum just stared at her.

"Well, what do you want?" the girl asked insolently. She gave Gaby's gray pantsuit with its pink camisole and her unmade-up face in its frame of upswept thick, red-highlighted brown hair an insulting scrutiny.

Gaby's pale blue eyes twinkled. "My goodness, I thought an attorney lived here," she said. "Is it an agency? You know, for escorts…?" She added a speaking glance of her own at the girl's attire.

The younger woman's eyes almost popped.

"Who's at the door, Jackie?" a deep, curt voice called.

"I have no idea!" the girl said, dripping sarcasm. "Maybe she's selling magazines or something."

"Not likely. I don't read those sorts of magazines," Gaby returned pleasantly.

The girl's indrawn breath was interrupted by the arrival of a big, husky man. He looked like a wrestler. He had wavy black hair with a few threads of silver, a leonine face with deep-set dark eyes and a sexy, chiseled mouth. He was wearing slacks and a designer shirt in a shade of beige that emphasized his olive complexion.

"You're late," he said abruptly, and looked at his watch. "I specifically told the agency no later than 1:00 p.m." He glared at her. "Do you want this job or not?"

She was lost for words. She'd come to ask him a delicate question and he was apparently offering her a job. Her heart jumped at the unexpected opportunity.

"I thought it was for one thirty," she improvised.

"One," he returned curtly.

She almost gasped. "You are a very rude man," she said.

His eyebrows arched. "And you are one step away from the unemployment line," he shot back. "I need someone to organize my library and catalog my books again." He gave the young girl an angry, speaking glance as he spoke.

"I just knocked over a bookcase or two," the girl muttered.

"On purpose and with help." He took a breath. "Well?" he shot at Gaby. "Can you do it?"

Her degree was in anthropology, but probably it wouldn't take a scientist to rearrange books. "Of course I can," she said confidently. "I minored in library science." It wasn't quite the truth, but she didn't expect that he'd go that deep with a background check.

He gave her a brief scrutiny, obviously saw nothing that interested him and opened the door wider. "Do you have references?"

"Oh, yes," she replied, and offered up a silent prayer of thanks that she actually did have them in her purse, because she'd just come from an interview for a job she didn't get at a local museum. She had a nice income from the legacy her great-aunt had left her, the one Robert Matthews, her cousin, was trying to get away from her with a proposed challenge to the will. She wanted to do something useful with her life, not sit in a luxury apartment all day and do nothing. That was a one-way ticket to insanity.

"Don't hire her, Uncle Nick," the wild girl said angrily. "She's got a mean mouth!"

"Look who's talking," Gaby returned. "And at least I'm not in danger of septic infection from dozens of piercings and that colorful tattoo down your arm. How do you blow your nose with that ring in it?" she added. "And how in the world do you eat soup…?"

"If you say one more word…!" the girl threatened.

"Jackie, go back to your room," the man said curtly. "Now." He never raised his voice, but the raw power in it could have backed down a mob.

Gaby would have known that he was an attorney just by the way he used his voice. He headed a prestigious law firm in Chicago, Chandler, Morse and Souillard, and he had a national reputation as a trial lawyer, famous for celebrity cases.

"Mr. Chandler?" she asked politely.

He nodded. "And you are...?"

"Gaby Dupont," she said with a polite smile. The name would mean nothing to him. There were dozens of people with her surname—no need to make up something that might come back to haunt her later.

He cocked his head. "And why do you want this job?"

"I'm starving?" she replied hopefully.

He didn't smile, but his eyes had a faint twinkle. "Come in."

He led the way back to his library. The apartment was huge, done in tasteful dark Mediterranean furniture and cream and brown curtains and carpets. The library had a burgundy Persian rug, an oak desk and a library that covered all three walls from floor to ceiling. The floor was full of stacked books, boxes and cartons of them.

"I've just moved in," he said, indicating the disorder. "I don't have the time or the patience to catalog and place all that, and the assistant I hired decided to go back to school and study architecture," he added gruffly.

"Hence, the job opening," she mused.

"Exactly. Put the books on the floor and sit down." He'd indicated the seat in front of the desk. Impressive. Burgundy leather and hand-tooled wood. Expensive. She moved the pile of books on the chair to the floor, then sat down.

"Your qualifications?" he asked.

She handed him a sheet of paper. It outlined her college degree and her hobbies.

He looked up at her curiously. "Are you married?"

"I am not."

"Engaged? Involved? Living with someone?"

Her eyes almost popped. "Mr. Chandler, I hardly think any of that is your business. This is a job interview, not an interrogation."

He gave her a long-suffering look. "I want to know if you have entanglements that will interfere with the work you do here," he returned. "I also need references."

"Oh. Sorry. I forgot." She handed him another sheet of paper. "And no, I'm not involved with anyone. At the moment." She smiled sweetly.

He ignored the smile and looked over the sheet. His eyebrows arched as he glanced at her. "A Roman Catholic cardinal, a police lieutenant, two nurses, the owner of a coffee shop and a Texas Ranger?" he asked incredulously.

"My grandmother is from Jacobsville, Texas," she explained. "The Texas Ranger, Colter Banks, is married to my third cousin."

"And these others?"

"People who know me locally." She smiled demurely. "The police officers want to date me. I know them from the coffee shop. The owner…"

"Wants to date you, too," he guessed. He stared at her as if he had no idea on earth why any male would want to date her. The look was fairly insulting.

"I have hidden qualities," she mused, trying not to laugh.

"Apparently," he said curtly. His eyes went back to the sheet. "A cardinal?" He glowered at her. "And please don't tell me that he wants to date you."

"Of course not. He's a friend of my grandmother."

He drew in a breath. Her comments about men who wanted to date her disturbed him. He studied her in silence. He was extremely wealthy, not only from the work he did but from an inheritance left to him by a late uncle.

"You don't want the job because I'm single?" he asked bluntly.

Now her eyebrows lifted almost to her hairline. "Mr...." She glanced at the paper in her hand. "Mr. Chandler," she continued, "I hardly think my taste would run to a man in his forties!"

His dark eyes almost exploded with anger. "I am not in my forties!"

"Oh, dear, do excuse me," she said at once. She had to contain a smile. "Honestly, you look very much younger than a man in his fifties!"

His lips made a thin line.

The smile escaped and her pale blue eyes twinkled.

He wadded up a piece of paper and threw it at her.

She just grinned.

He sat back in his chair. "Well, you can obviously deal with Jackie, which is a plus. She drives me crazy. Her mother's in Europe with her latest boyfriend and unlikely to return until her daughter's grown or married or in prison."

She laughed.

He shook his head. "And you have qualifications." His dark eyes narrowed. "You aren't connected with any foreign spy service?"

"Not unless I joined in my sleep," she assured him. "Honestly, I'm just a plain working girl."

"Working at what?" he returned with a cold smile. "You don't cite any previous job experience. How old are you?"

"Twenty-four." She thought fast. "I worked for my grandmother as a social secretary after I got out of college."

"You don't list her on your sheet of references."

"Why would I list a relative?" she asked.

"You did list a relative. The Texas Ranger."

"Oh. Him." She sighed. "Well, a man who's married to a

distant relation is less likely to lie for you than a close blood relative, right?"

He laughed. "I give up. All right. We'll try it for a couple of weeks and see how you work out. You can start by cataloging the library. Can you take dictation, answer the phone, make appointments...?"

"Well, yes," she began, hesitantly.

"We'll add all that into the job description, then. You can be my private administrative assistant. It's getting harder to avoid bringing work home as the business expands, and I do need someone in that capacity. Can you handle it?"

"Of course," she said without hesitation. She'd done all that for *Grand-mère*, after all, without pay.

He mentioned a figure that was a little surprising. It was a great deal more than most people could expect for the services he'd outlined, and her face betrayed her.

"You'll be living in. Did I forget to mention that?"

Oh, dear. Complications. However, it would be convenient. Her grandfather wouldn't know where to find her. Neither would the cousin who kept trying to force her to give up a fortune in property that he swore rightfully belonged to him—despite the concrete will that left it to Gaby. The cousin, Robert Matthews, was disturbed. Very disturbed, to her mind, but Gaby had heard that he intimidated his mother to the point that she avoided even speaking to him. Probably, she reasoned, his ties to the Outfit—an unofficial title given to the criminal organization in Chicago—made his mother nervous, as well.

"Living in will be fine," she said after a minute. "Do I have to room with the Goth Girl?" she added with raised eyebrows.

He chuckled. "No. You'll have your own room. And please don't call her that to her face," he added. "I have too many breakables in here that I'm fond of."

"I'll restrain myself," she promised.

He got up. "Well, it will be interesting, if nothing more," he said. "You'll start Monday, how's that?"

Today was Friday. That gave her the weekend to organize things. Since she owned her apartment, she had no worries about the rent going unpaid. "I'll be here first thing Monday morning," she promised.

"I leave the apartment at eight in the morning to get to the office on time. You'd better be here before then. Or you might not be able to get in," he added with pursed lips.

She took his meaning. The Goth Girl would probably lock her out once she knew Gaby was going to work here. She chuckled. "Okay. I'll be here before eight."

"Do you have other relatives besides your grandmother?" he asked curiously.

Her face closed up. "No," she said, without elaborating.

That expression made him curious. But there would be plenty of time later to dig deeper, if he wanted to. He needed an employee. Her private life was no concern of his. "Monday, then. Good day."

He let her out of the apartment and closed the door.

She was fumbling in her purse to put away the sheets of paper he'd returned to her when she heard an absolute feminine wail come through the door of the apartment she'd just left.

"She's going to work here? No!"

Gaby smiled to herself all the way to the elevator.

Her bodyguard was waiting downstairs beside a black limousine. It was a sedan, not the stretch limo he usually drove for her grandmother. Gaby had wanted to be discreet, although the last thing she'd come here for was a job. She lived near her grandmother, who was one of the wealthiest women in

the country, and Gaby was her only heir. The job was an opportunity, though, and she was going to take it.

"How'd it go?" Tanner Everett asked with a smile.

She looked up, trying not to stare at the black eye patch
over the blue eye that had been damaged beyond repair in
some foreign country while he was plying his former trade
as a mercenary.

"I got hired."

His black eyebrows arched. "Hired?"

"Well, he was expecting someone to interview as a personal administrative assistant. I let him think I was the person. And I got cold feet about asking him questions when the
Goth Girl answered the door."

He put her inside the sedan and got in behind the wheel.
"The Goth Girl?"

"You had to be there." She laughed and shook her head as
he cranked the steering wheel and pulled cautiously out into
traffic. "It seems that Mr. Chandler has a niece with enough
tattoos and piercings to put her in line for a job making license plates in some big federal facility."

It took a minute for that to penetrate, and he roared. "She
sounds like a handful."

"She is. I'm going to be Public Enemy Number One." She
grinned. "I love the sound of that. I've led such a quiet, un-
eventful life with *Grand-mère*," she added.

"You didn't get to talk to him about your grandfather, I
gather."

"No. He isn't the sort of man you approach directly with
such questions. I almost made a fatal faux pas," she told him.
She leaned back against the seat. "I hope my grandmother isn't
going to be mad because of what I did. It was an opportunity
I didn't feel I could overlook. If I get to know him, I can find
out all sorts of things without having to beg for information."

"That way lies disaster," he said quietly, glancing at her in the rearview mirror. "Lies catch up with you."

"This is just a little white lie," she argued with a smile. "And nobody's going to get hurt. Honest."

"If you say so."

"I do."

Her grandmother, small and wizening and fierce for all her size, gave Gaby a severe stare when she was told about the position. She gave Everett one, too, but it just bounced off him.

"I did not tell you to get a job," she told Gaby firmly, her faint French accent coming out as she grew angrier, her pale blue eyes throwing off sparks.

"But it's the best way to find out," Gaby argued. "I won't have to stay long. Meanwhile, I can learn about him and his law practice. I can find out which attorney in his firm represented grandfather and how he felt about what…what happened to me."

Everett made a face. "Your grandfather should have had ten years for that."

"His best friend is a judge," she said on a sigh. "Justice is largely a matter of money these days," she added cynically.

"Not always."

Madame Dupont made a gruff sound in her throat and turned away, resplendent in a taupe silk pantsuit that took ten years off her age. It made her short, wavy silver hair brighter, too. "My granddaughter, working at a menial job. What is the world coming to?"

"I'll learn to catalog books as I go," Gaby replied with a wicked smile. "And I'll turn Goth Girl inside out as a personal favor to Mr. Chandler."

Madame turned, her perfect eyebrows arching. "Excuse me?"

"Mr. Chandler's niece lives with him," Gaby explained.

"She has more piercings than a soldier during the Napoleonic Wars, and tattoos that would grace a prison cell."

Madame looked toward the ceiling. "What perils are you placing yourself into?" She turned. "You should go back right now and tell that attorney the truth of why you went to see him."

"I will not," Gaby said softly. "It's a terrific opportunity."

"Lies come back to bite you, my sweet."

"These won't. It will be all right. Really."

Madame came forward and drew Gaby into a warm embrace while the delicate fragrance of Nina Ricci's *L'Air du Temps* wafted into her nostrils. It was the only scent Madame ever wore. "If you say so, my darling." She drew back and touched Gaby's soft hair. "You must not put yourself in any more danger than you already face."

"I'm not in danger." She pointed to Tanner Everett. "Ask him."

He chuckled. "She isn't in any danger," he parroted in his faint Texas accent. "I give you my word."

"Well, that is something, at least. But you have to live in? I shall die of boredom here alone," Madame wailed. "You won't be here every day doing these little chores that make my life so much simpler!"

"You could invite Clarisse to stay," she suggested. "She loves you, too. And she can answer the phone and keep up with appointments and do letters for you."

"Clarisse." She made another gruff noise under her breath. "She and her fiancé drive me almost mad. I have found them making out in every room of this apartment. Even the bathroom!"

"They'll be married in two weeks and she'll settle down."

"Not in time. No Clarisse." She sighed. "Well, perhaps I can tolerate Sylvie for a few days."

Sylvie was her cousin, a sweet and gentle older woman who loved soap operas and swashbuckling movies.

"She'll drive you mad with old Errol Flynn movies," Gaby commented.

"Oh, I like pirate movies," Madame said absently. "I'll nap while she watches those vulgar soap operas, so that I don't offend her with commentary."

"Good idea," Gaby said.

Madame sighed. "When do you move in with him?"

"With them," she corrected, and smiled. "Monday morning, so I must go back to my own apartment and decide what to take with me." She moved forward, embraced her grandmother and brushed a kiss against the beautiful skin on her cheek. She drew back with a sigh. "You know, you have the most perfect complexion I've ever seen, even at your age." Her grandmother was seventy-two, going on seventy-three. There would be a huge party to celebrate that birthday in the summer. There was always a crowd of dignitaries, because *Grand-mère* knew film stars and soccer stars and TV stars and a great many other famous people. Even someone in the president's cabinet! She was respected and loved by all her acquaintances, and she had friends who didn't have money. She chose the people she had in her life, and they weren't all wealthy.

Madame beamed. She touched Gaby's face. "Which you have inherited, *ma chérie*," she replied, her voice as soft as the fingers that brushed over Gaby's face.

"I have only your skin, not your beauty," Gaby said, and without rancor. She glanced at the youthful portrait of Madame Melissandra Lafitte Dupont over the mantel. She had been debutante of the year in her class, wooed by princes and minor royalty all over Europe, but she chose to marry instead a fast-talking salesman of a business executive with grand ideas and no money. As people said, there was no accounting for taste.

"You were so beautiful," Gaby remarked, staring at the portrait.

"The artist was blind." The elderly woman chuckled.

"He was not. He captured the very essence of you," Gaby argued as she moved closer to the portrait, so that the pale blue eyes were large enough to divine that they were alive with humor and love of life. "Grandfather never deserved you," she added in a cold, angry tone.

There was a sigh behind her. "We live and learn, do we not?" was the sad reply. "He could have been anything he liked. But he was greedy, and you paid for his greed, my baby." She hugged Gaby close. "I would give anything if you could have been spared that."

Gaby hugged her back. "I had you," she said softly. "So many people have less. I was lucky."

"Lucky." Madame made a curse of the word. She drew back. "I cannot convince you to give up this mad scheme?"

Gaby shook her head, smiling.

"Ah, well. At least I can make sure that he is your shadow." She nodded toward Everett.

"I already am her shadow," he chuckled.

"True enough," Gaby returned. "Heavens, he can squeeze into the most incredible places. You never even notice him."

"Which is why I'm still alive," came the sardonic reply.

"So you are. Make certain that no harm comes to my granddaughter," Madame told him. "Or I will find the deepest dungeon in my estate outside Paris, and you will rot there." She even smiled when she said it.

"Did I ever mention that I always carry a nail file?" he replied, used to her threats, which he found more amusing than threatening. She knew he was good at his job.

Madame chuckled. She loved their repartee. "Very well. Good luck to both of you."

"You mustn't recognize me if you see me on the street," Gaby cautioned her.

Madame made a face. "And what about my birthday party month after next?" she asked haughtily.

"In two months I'll either have what information we need, or I'll be suspended from the window of a penthouse apartment by a stocking with a gavel in my mouth."

At which statement, everybody broke up.

Her suitcase packed with enough to keep her going for a week, Gaby took a cab to Mr. Chandler's apartment. Everett was behind it all the way, in a black sedan.

She rang the doorbell at precisely 8:00 a.m.

There were voices muffled behind the door. One was deep and loud, one was high-pitched and loud. Abruptly they ceased, and the door was opened.

Mr. Chandler looked at his watch. "Well, Ms. Dupont, at least you're punctual."

"So she can read a watch," the Goth Girl said sarcastically. "But can she catalog books and answer the phone?"

"I have many talents, one of which is alligator wrestling," she said with a straight face and looked directly at Mr. Chandler's niece. He muffled a sound that could have been laughter. The girl glared at both of them and stomped off into her room.

TWO

Chandler led the way down the hall and showed Gaby to a room.

"It's next to Jackie's, but she doesn't usually make too much noise," he muttered as the occupant next door suddenly turned her stereo playing a rap song up high enough that the walls shook.

"Turn that damned thing down!" he shouted.

There was an immediate response. Gaby hid a grin.

"She'll try you," he said.

She shrugged. "I got through four years of college. I'll cope. Besides," she murmured, "I brought a whole library of my favorite tunes."

"Which are…?"

"Drum and bagpipe solos," she said with a straight face.

He started to speak, thought better of it and laughed instead. "Put your stuff down and I'll show you what I want done today. I don't have long, if I'm going to make it to the office on time."

"You're the boss, though," she pointed out as she followed his long strides down the carpeted hallway to his study.

"I have to set an example. If I show up whenever I please, the staff might follow suit." He glanced at her with twinkling eyes. "Chaos would ensue."

"I guess it would. Okay. What would you like done?"

He outlined several tasks that he wanted completed by the end of the day.

"And we employ a daily woman who also cooks for us," he added. "Tilly comes in at nine. You'll like her. Tell her what you want for lunch and she'll fix it."

"Oh, I'll eat anything, I'm not picky."

"Don't tell Jackie that, or she'll have the cook make you fish stew. Trust me, you never want to eat it." He made a face. "I told Jackie she couldn't go out late dancing with her boyfriend one Saturday. Dinner that evening was forgettable. Really."

She laughed. It was nice to know the Goth Girl's ways of getting even so that Gaby could forestall her. She knew her way around the kitchen, too. She'd just get to the daily woman first. She had an idea that there would be no truce even from her first day on the job.

She was right, in fact. She went into the kitchen at eleven, just after the Goth Girl had gone out with an airy description of her destination and a secret smile.

"Can I ask what Jackie ordered for lunch?" she asked the older woman.

The matronly cook and housekeeper, Tilly by name, just grinned. "Fish stew...?"

"Do you like quiche?" Gaby asked.

"Oh, I love it, but I can't make it."

"I can. I need a few things," she added with a conspiratorial smile. The cook laughed and went to get them.

Gaby made an impressive quiche Lorraine, complete with delicate crust. The cook, invited to share a slice, was enthralled with the result.

"You cook beautifully," Tilly said.

"Thanks. My grandmother had me sent to a senior chef and taught to cook. She never learned, so I had to." She didn't add that the reason her grandmother never learned to cook was that she was filthy rich and employed a chef—in fact, the same chef who taught Gaby how to cook.

"Well, this is delicious. Should we save some for Jackie?"

"Oh, yes, we must," Gaby said with impressive faked concern. "If she didn't get anything to eat while she was out, she'll be hungry."

"I agree. I'll make sure it's put up properly."

"Thanks."

It was after dark when Jackie came home. She went right to Gaby's room and opened the door without knocking. Gaby was sprawled across her bed in sweatpants and a T-shirt, with her long hair loose around her face, reading a book on her iPhone. She looked up, surprised.

"Well, I guess you've settled in," the girl said haughtily. "Did you have a nice lunch?" she added wickedly.

"Very nice." She got up and took Jackie by the arm. She pulled her to the door. "This—" she pointed to it "—is called a door. When you go to someone's personal room, you knock." She took Jackie outside and demonstrated. "Then the person inside can decide whether or not he or she wants you to come in." She gave the girl a blithe smile. "We had quiche Lorraine for lunch. There's some left, in case you didn't have time to eat."

"Quiche…? But Tilly can't make quiche," she faltered.

"I can." She smiled again, went back into her room, closed the door and locked it audibly.

Curses ensued from the other side of the door.

Gaby just laughed and went back to her book.

Supper that evening was a subdued affair. Jackie glared at Gaby and picked at her food, which was a macaroni and cheese casserole and asparagus, cooked by Tilly.

"How was school?" Chandler asked his niece.

"Boring. Tedious. I hate it!"

"Well, cheer up, when you're seventeen or you graduate, whichever comes first, you can leave."

Jackie glared at him, too. "I miss my old school!"

"You can always get on a plane and join your mother wherever she's living in Europe," he said, barely noticing her as he made notes on an iPad for court.

Jackie put her fork down and actually looked sick. "I'm full."

He looked up. "Then you're excused."

"She's not eating, either," Jackie muttered, noting Gaby's apparent lack of appetite.

"Oh, I'm still full from lunch," Gaby said with a big grin.

"Were you here for lunch?" Chandler asked Jackie suddenly, looking up from the screen with hostile brown eyes.

"No," Jackie said shortly.

Chandler looked at Gaby. "What did Tilly feed you?"

"She was going to make fish stew," Gaby said, with a wry glance at Jackie, "but I suggested quiche instead."

"Tilly can't make those fancy dishes," he began.

"I can," Gaby replied. "I made the quiche."

"You can cook?" he asked, startled.

"My grandmother had me professionally trained when I was

about the age of the Goth Girl, here." She indicated Jackie, who fumed and stood up, angrily.

"I am not a Goth Girl!" she almost screamed.

Gaby and Chandler both stared at her. She was wearing black pants and a black camisole. She had tattoos on both arms and pierced jewelry from her ears to her nose. She was wearing black nail polish and black lipstick.

"I can call you a beatnik instead, if you like," Gaby said pleasantly. "They wore black and hung around coffee shops playing bongo drums and reciting poetry. In fact, I know of such a club, right downtown."

"That's The Snap, right?" Chandler asked.

Gaby chuckled. "Yes, it is. The owner said that everybody snaps instead of claps, so the name just seemed right."

"It actually does."

"I do not play bongo drums," Jackie growled. Not for worlds would she admit that she knew the place and loved to go there.

Gaby looked at her. "The original beatniks didn't wear tattoos," she remarked. "Did you know that they have actual tattooed human skin in one of the larger museums in the city?" she added.

Jackie made a horrible face. "I'm going to bed."

"It's just eight o'clock," her uncle said.

"TV. I'll go watch TV," she muttered.

"There's a new series about women in prison," Gaby called after her. "It might give you some pointers."

There were horrible curses, followed by a slamming door.

Gaby burst out laughing. "Sorry," she told her boss contritely. "Couldn't resist it."

He shook his head. "You've got her standing on her ear. I haven't been able to get so much as two words out of her since she's been here."

"She's hurting," Gaby said suddenly.

He scowled. "Excuse me?"

"Something or somebody has hurt her badly," Gaby said simply. "Have you asked her why her mother wanted her to stay with you?"

He hesitated. "It wasn't her mother. Jackie asked to come."

"That must have taken a lot of guts, at her age," was the soft reply. "I imagine her mother was insulted by it."

His firm, chiseled lips opened on a breath. "She was. How did you know?"

"We all have tragedies in our pasts," she said simply. "At a guess, her mother's boyfriend did or said something inappropriate, or she'd still be with her mother. Tilly said she loved her mom."

"She does. Not the new boyfriend, however. Frankly, I think he's the worst kind of layabout, and he's got a roving eye. I don't know what the hell my sister sees in him."

"Who can understand the leanings of a hungry heart?" She sighed and smiled.

"Have you ever felt them, Miss Dupont?" he asked pointedly.

She grimaced. She couldn't tell him about the trauma that had kept her chaste for so many years. "I was too busy being educated to hang out with wild crowds. My grandmother paid for my education, but insisted that I not go to any, as she referred to them, party schools. So I ended up in one known for its academic excellence and I never went to a keg party or even dated much."

He just stared at her, incredulous. "How old are you?"

"Almost twenty-five," she replied.

"And you don't date?"

She cocked her head and stared at him. "Frankly, I find most men lacking."

"Lacking what?"

"Manners, decorum, intellect, compassion, that sort of thing. Well, I did find it in one truly kind man, but he was gay." She smiled at him.

He let out a breath and shook his head. "At least you won't be after me."

"Mr. Chandler, I do not stalk fifty-year-old men!" she exclaimed haughtily.

He burst out laughing, recalling their first meeting, because she certainly knew he wasn't yet out of his thirties.

"Just as well," he commented after a minute. He sipped coffee. "You wouldn't know what to do with me, anyway."

"You can put a rose on top of that," she agreed. "I've never indulged so I don't know what I'm missing. That's my explanation for my lifestyle. You'd be amazed how often I have to use it in the modern world."

"Modern." He made a face. "I was raised by traditionalists."

"Me, too. It makes it hard to fit in. Even harder, because I don't own or watch television."

"You reactionary," he accused.

"Guilty as charged."

He finished his coffee. "I have briefs to work on." He stood up. "If you want to watch any of the new movies, we have most of them on Prime Video," he said. "Feel free."

She shook her head as she, too, stood up. "I read in my spare time."

"Read what?" he wanted to know.

"Right now, it's Arrian."

"Arrian?"

"The Greek philosopher. And there's Quintus Curtius Rufus," she added.

"Alexander. You like to read about Alexander the Third, called the Great," he replied.

She nodded. "It truly fascinates me that you can read something written almost two thousand years ago and feel what the author felt when he was writing it." She paused. "It's almost like having them speak to you, across the years."

He nodded slowly. "That's how I've always felt about it. I read the classic authors, as well."

She smiled. "I wish more people did. They might have less pessimism about the future."

He smiled back. "Yes. They might. How's the cataloging coming?"

"Slowly," she said. "But I'm getting them in some sort of order so that I can start. You have an impressive library."

"It was more impressive before Jackie pitched a temper tantrum and overturned two bookcases," he mused.

"We all have our issues. Perhaps a course in anger management...?"

"Please don't suggest that where she can hear you," he said with mock horror.

She grinned. "I'll try not to. Good evening."

He nodded. "Good evening to you, too."

Gaby went back to her room, pleasantly surprised by her boss's laid-back attitude. But once she closed the door, through the walls came the loudest, most explicit song Gaby had ever heard.

She reached in her closet for her recently purchased boom box, extracted a CD from its case and inserted it, placed it against the wall that adjoined Jackie's and maxed the volume. The exquisite strains of "Scotland the Brave," played by a magnificent bagpipe band, almost shook the walls.

Within two minutes, the music was abruptly turned down.

Gaby turned off her stereo. She waited, poised over it, but the music didn't reoccur. So Gaby got into her silk gown, crawled into bed with her iPhone, turned off the light and read herself to sleep.

The next morning, the boss was missing from the breakfast table.

"Had to go in early to meet some important client." Tilly sighed as she put delicately scrambled eggs, bacon, sausage and biscuits on the table. That was followed with jars of preserves, all homemade.

"Tilly, this is wonderful," Gaby told the cook, smiling.

Tilly glared at Jackie, who was picking at her food. "Nice to know that somebody appreciates my efforts," she said, and went back into the kitchen.

Gaby took another bite of her eggs and sipped black coffee. "What happened?" she asked the girl.

Jackie glared at her. "I beg your pardon?"

"What happened to you, with your mother's boyfriend?" Gaby persisted.

Jackie was so flustered that she dropped her fork. "Why… why would you think…"

"Oh, give me a break," Gaby muttered, staring at the girl. "You might as well be wearing a sign. Come on. Talk about it."

Jackie put her fork down. Her whole face tautened. "He backed me into a wall and I couldn't get away," she said gruffly.

"Did you tell your mother? " she asked gently.

"Yes. I told my mother." Her eyes lowered. "She said I was lying, that he'd never do anything like that."

"How did you get away from him?" Gaby asked.

She drew in a long breath. "I watched this movie. It's about a female FBI agent, and she taught this lesson about SING, about how and where you can hit a man for the best effect. I did the groin pull. Oh, boy, did he let me go. I ran into my room and locked it, and he cussed for five minutes straight. Then Mama came home and I told her. And she didn't believe me."

Gaby felt her anguish. "Something similar happened to me," she said tautly, not going into details. She didn't add that it was her own grandfather who'd sold her to the foreign man, or the details. That would have been much too personal at the moment.

"It sucks, the way some men are," Jackie said.

"It does," Gaby agreed. She looked up. "Your mother will come to her senses one day and she'll apologize."

"Yeah? Well, it doesn't help much right now, does it?" she muttered.

"No. It doesn't." She studied the younger woman and saw beneath the flashy black makeup and the piercings to a basically shy and introverted person who had a sensitivity that she carefully hid.

Jackie drew in a long breath. "I've been a horror. My uncle Nick has the patience of a saint, but he should have thrown me out."

"You're his niece," she said. "He'd never do that."

She looked up. Her dark eyes were full of pain and bad memories. "It wasn't the first time," she said, and averted her gaze. "I just didn't tell her about the others. She was getting over my dad dying, and I figured she was trying to hide her grief in a new romance."

"Your father died?" she asked gently.

Jackie nodded. "He drowned one summer when we were at a resort on an island in the Caribbean. There was a red flag warning about riptides, but he ignored it. He was depressed about his job. He was about to lose it, and it hurt his pride that my mother had all the money on her side of the family. She said he did it on purpose. I missed him…"

"My father and mother died together," Gaby told her. "They were on a dig, in Africa. Their jeep overturned."

Jackie grimaced. "How old were you?"

"Thirteen," she said. "I went to live with my grandmother. She's the kindest person I've ever known." She cocked her head. "How old were you, when you lost your father?"

"Ten." Jackie looked at her with sad eyes. "My uncle is nice. I just don't want to be here," she said harshly. "I want to be with my mother, and I can't. She said she loved me, but she didn't believe me, and I was telling the truth!" She bit her lower lip and tears welled up in her eyes.

Gaby got out of her chair, pulled Jackie up and hugged her, rocked her, while she cried.

"We all have storms," she said to the weeping girl. "They pass. Life can be sweet. You have to learn to sip it. Not gulp it down. You live one day at a time and live it as if it was the last day you had. I find that it works very well, as a philosophy."

"I guess it's not such a bad way," Jackie said after a minute. She pulled away and looked embarrassed. "Thanks," she added huskily.

Gaby just smiled. "Sometimes all you need to get a new perspective is a hug," she teased.

Jackie laughed. She wiped her eyes, smearing her makeup down her cheeks. "Mom isn't the sort to hug people. Neither is my uncle. When my daddy died, Mom went off with a new boyfriend. I felt lost. I still do."

"Your uncle loves you," Gaby said. "Even if he doesn't go around hugging you. But you have to meet him halfway."

Jackie made a face. "I guess so."

Gaby cocked her head and looked at the young girl. "You know, you really do have a unique look. It's not at all bad."

Jackie flushed. "You really think so? I mean, most boys think I'm weird."

"I'm weird, too. I don't care what people think."

Jackie laughed for the first time since Gaby had arrived on the scene. "I noticed. Bagpipes?" she asked, eyes very wide.

"My forebears on my mother's side were Highland Scots who migrated to America. You might say that bagpipes are my music."

Jackie replied, "Well, to each his own." She looked up. "I really hate bagpipes."

"I really hate what you listen to. So we're even," she teased.

Jackie smiled. "I suppose so." She turned away and then turned back. "Thanks. For listening. Nobody else ever did."

She went down the hall to her room before Gaby could say another word.

Nicolas Chandler came home late and in a temper. Jackie had long since gone to her room, and Gaby was in hers. She heard the boss muttering curses in the living room.

She put on a robe, her long hair trailing down her back over it, and padded barefoot into the living room.

"Good heavens, what bit you?" she asked.

He turned. "What the hell are you doing up?" he shot at her, and he looked fierce, with his dark eyes blazing.

"It's hard to sleep with people turning the air blue. The walls aren't that thick."

He glared at her.

She held up both hands. "I didn't do whatever it is that you're raging about."

He put down his briefcase, hard. "My firm is representing a millionaire whose wife attempted to kill him for his inheritance." His lips made a thin line. "So tonight, she came to his front door all in tears, begging for forgiveness, and he let her in."

She let out a breath. "So, which hospital did they take him to?"

He glared at her.

She lifted her hands and let them fall. "Simple deduction. Was he raised by morons?"

"No. By a saintly woman who taught him that anything can be forgiven."

"And most everything can, but some things shouldn't," she replied. "I guess she didn't tell him that."

"He's on life support," he said thinly. "There were no witnesses, and she says he had a horrible fall, all by himself, from the second-story balcony."

"Did they look for fingerprints on his back?"

"This is not funny!" he bit off.

She lifted both eyebrows. "No, but it's predictable. Will he live, do they think?"

"He was doing well until someone disconnected his oxygen."

"Let me guess. She was the only person in the room."

"Her and three hospital personnel. Just not all at the same time." He ran a hand through his thick black hair. "I should have been a vacuum cleaner salesman."

She burst out laughing.

Her twinkling eyes drained some of the fury out of him. He shook his head. "You think reasonable people will act reasonably," he said. "They never do."

"You should hire him a bodyguard."

"I just did," he replied. "She's going to spend every night and day in his room until he dies or gets released."

"You hired a female bodyguard?"

"Men are too easy to get around," he pointed out.

She laughed. "I'm so glad you said that instead of me."

"It's sadly true." He went to the bar and poured himself a scotch, with one cube of ice from the small fridge that flanked it. "It's been a hell of a night."

"Who called you?" she asked. "Not the ex-wife, I assume?"

"No. The police detective assigned to the case. He's a distant cousin. We keep in touch."

"Probably saved his life," she guessed.

"No doubt." He sat down, one big hand going to loosen his tie and the top buttons of his spotless white shirt.

"I don't suppose they could arrest the ex-wife on suspicion?"

"She's not an ex," he pointed out. "And not without probable cause. It's a he said, she said situation."

"I'm truly happy that nobody has tried to kill me yet," she said, hands in the pockets of her thick, very concealing bathrobe.

"Why would they want to?" he asked, and seemed really curious. "You're obviously not rich or you wouldn't be working for me."

Appearances could be deceiving, she almost said, but then she smiled instead. "Right on," she told him. "I guess money brings its own issues."

"It does. I avoid parties like the plague unless I'm required to go to one. I'm on several spinster most-wanted lists around town."

"Obviously because of your intensely seductive and pleasant manner," she murmured.

He glared at her. "You're not my type," he said at once.

Her eyes opened wide. "I'm not? Thank you! I was really worried!"

The glare got worse.

"Well, if you're quite through turning the air blue, I'm going back to bed."

"You might as well," he returned with a surly glance. "Unless you think Prince Charming might ring the doorbell looking for you."

"Princes are a figment," she pointed out. "Besides that, they live this regimented, routine life that shackles them to public appearances and charity causes. I'd never be able to adjust to that sort of imprisonment."

He wondered how she knew about the lives of princes, but then he realized that the internet was a great source of information and he dismissed it from his mind.

"You don't want to be a princess and have servants and a Ferrari and your very own couture house of design to dress you?"

"I'm quite happy in old blue jeans, taking care of myself," she pointed out. "People who marry for money, earn it."

"Wise, and so young," he chuckled.

"I'm not that young," she returned. "I hope your bodyguard sleeps light. The victim's wife sounds like a determined assassin."

"The room is wired like dynamite," he said with a faintly smug glance. "If she tries anything, she'll be doing some very hard time, whether he lives or not. And I got a warrant, to make sure it would hold up in court."

"Good for you. People who kill for money are even worse than people who marry for it," she said solemnly, and she knew more about that than he might realize. She'd been sold for money by her own grandfather, who would do anything for it, like the cousin who was after her inherited stocks and bonds. "Money is of so little consequence in the scheme of things," she said absently. "I never understood the obsession some people have with it."

"You'd have fit right in with those beatniks you were telling Jackie about," he pointed out.

She laughed. "I actually prefer coffeehouses to restaurants. There is the matter of radical politicism that the beatniks were famous for. I don't want to blow up things."

"I wish the world at large shared that sentiment. We've had far too many people who think violence is the answer to any problem."

"Too much television," she said, standing erect. "Fie on video games and wrestling matches and other provokers of radicalism!"

"Go the hell to bed," he muttered.

"Just quoting the pundits," she said defensively, and with a grin.

"Like they know anything," he scoffed. "Opinions are like…"

"Yes, I know," she interrupted, "and everybody's got one." She chuckled.

"Aren't your feet cold?" he asked, frowning at her bare feet under the long concealing gown and robe.

She wiggled her toes. "A little, but I love shag carpet," she said. "It feels so good to walk on."

He laughed. "I'll bet you stand outside in thunderstorms."

"How did you know?"

"It takes one to know one," he said simply. "I was driving from Jax to St. Augustine, my mind on a case, and I didn't realize that the only vehicles I was meeting were cable and phone trucks and emergency personnel. It wasn't until I parked at the courthouse in St. Augustine that I realized why. There were gale force winds."

She laughed. "I've done that, too," she said. "Stood on the beach and felt the wind whipping through my hair while the waves slammed against the shore, whitecaps foaming. I loved it."

He cocked his head, studying her. "What beach?"

She had to think fast. It had actually been on the Riviera. "Biloxi," she fished up.

"That's not how you pronounce it," he pointed out, and now he looked suspicious. "It's pronounced 'bi–LUX-ie' by the natives."

"Well, I'm not a native and I can pronounce it how I like," she said with a grin.

"I guess."

"Anyway, I liked the beach at Panama City best, anyway. Such a shame how much those cities on the Gulf of Mexico have changed after all the devastating hurricanes."

"Everything changes," he pointed out. "It's the only real constant in life."

"I like change."

His dark eyebrows rose.

"Quarters best, but I'm partial to dimes, also."

He glared at her.

She held up both hands. "Right. Bed. Please, no more nonstop cursing. And I hope your client survives, if for no other reason than to see his wife being shredded by the prosecuting attorney."

He chuckled. "Our DA would have her for lunch, without ketchup."

"I expect he's a friend of yours," she said. "You know, sharks congregating together…? Going away now!" she added quickly, turned and made a beeline back into her room.

He waited until the door closed before he started laughing.

THREE

Gaby had hoped that a new relationship was forming with the Goth Girl after their talk the day before, but Jackie had withdrawn right back into her surly shell. She picked at her breakfast, glared at the adults and left the table without asking.

"I guess it was too much to hope for," Gaby sighed.

He glanced up from his coffee cup. "Excuse me?"

"The momentary truce," she said.

He thought about that for a minute and then nodded. "She has moods. Usually they come after she's spoken with her mother." He frowned. "I wonder if they've spoken recently."

"No idea."

"Well, I need to go by the hospital and check on my client," he said, rising.

"I'll get back to work on your book collection," she replied.

"There are some notes on my desk that I took out of my briefcase. Can you knock them into some sort of order for me when you get time?"

She nodded. "I'll do it first thing."

"Thanks."

"That's what you pay me for, boss," she pointed out.

He frowned slightly. "I suppose so, but you were originally hired just to catalog and sort books," he added.

"A job is a job." She gave him a blithe smile.

He cocked a thick eyebrow. "Just for the record, the temporary agency I called said that their candidate came down with the flu and that's why she never showed up here," he said, pursing his lips.

She flushed.

"Which leads to a question. Why did you come here in the first place?"

She thought fast. "I have a friend who knows someone at the temporary agency," she lied. "She told me about this job and said that if I hurried, I might beat their candidate to it." She leaned forward. "Their employee is twenty-two, has green hair and has body piercings everywhere."

"She and Jackie would have gotten along," he said, and broke into a laugh.

"I guess so." She grimaced. "So. Want to fire me for interviewing for a job I wasn't really asked to take?"

He waved it away, fortunately without questioning her lie. "You can cope with Jackie and you're not likely to help lead her into more trouble than she normally gets into," he said. "I don't mind."

She grinned. "Thanks."

"What would you do if I said it did matter?" he asked out of curiosity.

"There's a great job going at the local gyro sandwich place," she said, wide-eyed. "I can cook goat."

He did burst out laughing then and went away shaking his head.

★ ★ ★

He was an easy boss most of the time, but Gaby learned the hard way that he could be temperamental. It was mostly when he was working on a case that disturbed him. She got the fallout.

"I told you," he began in a blistering tone, holding up one of the books she'd catalogued that was in the wrong place, "that the *Illinois Compiled Statutes Criminal Offenses* book Volume One goes next to the Volume Two book. Can't you count?"

She stared up at him worriedly. So many thoughts raged in her mind, most of them to do with her grandfather's reopened case and this man's part in it, not to mention what was going to happen when he found out who Gaby really was.

"I am truly sorry," she replied. "It was the dragon."

He stopped in midtirade and stood just staring at her blankly.

"The dragon?" she continued. "You know, on that television series that just ended last year?"

He blinked. "The dragon."

She pulled out her iPhone and showed it to him, screen first. "I was watching the last episode while I cataloged the first of the law books. I was very upset." She lowered her eyes and looked miserable. "I mean, the poor dragon. There he was, his mistress dead, his siblings dead, nobody to hug him and pet him and tell him how wonderful he was." She stopped and peeked up at him, to see if he was buying it.

"It's not a real dragon," he said after a minute, his dark, deep-set eyes as unreadable as his face.

She frowned. "It's not?" She let out a whistle. "Well, that's a relief. I mean, I kept wondering all those weeks how they kept the dragons from eating the actors!"

He burst out laughing, his bad mood over, just like that. It was a real laugh, too, deep and uninhibited. She hadn't heard it since she came to work for him.

She grinned. "So," she said. "What's eating you? Another man who wants to let his wife kill him because he's too polite to mention it to the police?"

He chuckled. "No. A financier who had inside information about some stock and wants us to defend him in court, even though he's guilty as sin. I refused the case and he spent ten minutes questioning my parentage and most of my ancestors."

She cocked her head. "And what did you do?"

He grimaced. "Gave him a good case for assault, if he wants to press it."

"Excuse me?"

"I took him by the collar and propelled him out of my office into the hall and locked the door behind him," he elaborated. "You could hear the curses all the way to the elevator. When I was fairly certain he was gone, I told my secretary she could unlock the door if she could stop laughing long enough."

"We don't have secretaries anymore," she reminded him gently, feeling an unwelcome surge of jealousy for the woman who worked closely with him at his office. "They're called Administrative Assistants."

His broad shoulders shrugged. "Anyway, it was a hell of a day."

"What about the man whose wife is trying to kill him?"

He pursed his lips. "Interesting conclusion. She sweet-talked him into firing the bodyguard."

"Oh, the poor man," she exclaimed.

"The poor man?" he asked, surprised.

"He'll blame himself for whatever happens."

He scowled. "How do you know so much about human nature?"

"I've never been sure," she said simply. "I just sort of see into people."

He looked down his straight nose. "See into me. I'm curious."

She drew in a breath and stared at him for several seconds. He was incredibly handsome, she thought, and quickly dismissed the unwanted sensations he kindled in her.

"You're temperamental," she began. "Once you start a fight, you won't quit until you win it, no matter how long it takes. You're fair and honest, but you have a nasty temper. To your credit, you only lose it over injustices, especially those committed against people you care for." She frowned, because she was getting tidbits of information from a source she could never quite comprehend. "You were married," she said softly, watching the shocked reaction in his leonine features. "You loved her very much. She died—"

"That's enough," he snapped, his dark eyes glittering dangerously. "Who told you that—was it Jackie? Or have you been doing some discreet investigating on the internet about me?"

She shook her head. "I don't know where it comes from," she said honestly. "I've had it my whole life. It's a gift. But sometimes," she said, recalling her bad experience, the one that had destroyed her as a woman, "it fails me, when I really need it."

He studied her openly, his dark eyes curious and exploring on her slender, perfect figure, her pretty face in its frame of thick chestnut hair in a complicated braid down her back. She had the bluest eyes he'd ever seen, pale blue and piercing, and a mouth that was soft and bow-shaped and inviting. He jerked his face back up to her eyes.

"I'm sorry," she added quickly. "I didn't mean to offend you."

"I was married," he said, and with some little resentment.

He had no real close friends, and he never spoke of his marriage to outsiders. He had an occasional lover, very feminine and undemanding, but even she didn't bring up the subject, ever. His eyes betrayed a little of the pain of memory. "Leave it at that. And never mention it again or you'll be back at the employment agency." He glared at her and turned away, concealing the agony the memory brought with it.

He never spoke of it. The images that flashed through his mind were the ultimate torture and he had nobody in his life. Well, there was Mara. He couldn't imagine Mara giving a damn about his private hell. She liked his money and, occasionally, his body. But she had plenty of lovers. She couldn't get close to Nick. Nobody did, not even his longtime associates in the law firm. His one close friend had died in a plane crash several years ago. Except for his flighty sister and his wild niece, there was no family.

"Do you have anybody, besides your sister and your niece?" Gaby asked suddenly.

He turned, far too close to her, towering over her. She was aware of the masculine cologne he wore, the soap clinging to his skin, the aftershave on his cheek. He smelled clean and good and manly, and she'd have bet that he'd feel like heaven in a woman's arms.

She pushed that last thought away quickly. She'd only tried to date one man, and the experience had been a major failure. Her date became amorous at her apartment door and she'd actually screamed. The man had been insulting and she'd never seen him again. Even months of therapy hadn't helped her deal with her remembered horror very much.

But now here she was, feeling sorry and connected, and attracted to a total stranger and it felt like...coming home.

He was staring down into her pale blue eyes, his mind trying to cope with a sudden very sensual response to the compassion in her eyes. He drew in a long breath. Her body stirred him. It was unexpected, and not very welcome. His dark eyes narrowed as he registered her flush. She was shy. It touched something lying dormant in him, and he wasn't pleased. She wasn't like the women in his life. Well, not like the present one. His mother had been kind, gentle, concerned for anyone in pain or trouble. Like Gaby here.

"You're staring," he said shortly, and suspicion hardened his face.

Her eyebrows rose. "I have lots of money," she said at once. "I went to this lovely casino in Las Vegas and broke the bank. And you should see my yacht! I have it moored on the coast of Switzerland!"

Humor bubbled up in him suddenly as he noted the twinkle in her blue eyes. "The coast of Switzerland," he mused. "Are you aware that Switzerland is landlocked?"

Horror claimed her features. "You mean my new yacht is moored on land? However will I get it to the ocean?"

He threw up his hands. "And I was in a bad mood." He shook his head.

"Bad moods are awful for your health," she pointed out. "You should laugh more."

He glanced at her and smiled. "Maybe I should."

"You never talk about things that haunt you from your past, do you?" she murmured absently. "Nobody gets that close."

His head turned. His eyes narrowed under a scowl. "How do you do that?"

Her shoulders raised and fell. "I don't know," she said honestly.

"It takes a little getting used to."

"So my grandmother says," she replied with a smile.

"Your grandmother. You said you were her social secretary. She's well-to-do, then?"

She nodded. "And I inherit. So I wasn't lying about the yacht—well, not exactly. She's not that rich," she said, stretching the truth. "But even if I had the money, I wouldn't."

"If you inherit her fortune, what will you do with it?" he asked, expecting a delighted response about clothes and cars...

"I'd contribute to an outreach program for homeless people," she said, smiling. "Whole families live on the streets," she added sadly. "Not all homeless people are drug addicts or mentally challenged. A lot of them lost jobs, and then they lost everything that went with those jobs. One little boy had a serious chest infection. I made sure he got medical care. We do have it for indigent patients through taxes, you know, even though it puts a burden on the hospitals." Her eyes narrowed in thought. "We're one of the richest countries on earth and we have people living outside in the freezing cold, on the streets. It's a disgrace."

He'd been listening patiently. He was surprised. "How did you know about the boy?"

She moved restively. "I help out at one of the shelters from time to time," she confessed.

He was fascinated. She dressed well. She was educated. If she was telling the truth, she came from a wealthy background. But she helped out at a homeless shelter.

"You're a conundrum, Ms. Dupont," he said finally.

She grinned. "Thank you."

He rolled his eyes and turned away, briefcase in hand. "Put the damned criminal code anywhere you like," he muttered.

"How about in your bathroom?" she asked. "I mean, don't you need some reading material in there... That's assault!" she accused when he threw a wadded-up sheet of paper in her general direction.

"Call the police," he said helpfully, and kept walking. "I'll have Tilly make coffee for them."

She just shook her head. But at least his bad mood was gone, for the moment.

The joke about the police seemed to come true several hours later. There was a knock on the door.

Nick answered it. Gaby was still in his office, organizing hundreds of books into related stacks.

"Mr. Chandler?" a strange voice asked. "I'm sorry to tell you that your niece has been charged with simple assault. She's in a holding cell. She'd like you to come and bail her out."

There was a truly pregnant pause. "What?" he burst out. "Who did she assault?"

"Two of our officers," came the bland reply.

"Why?"

"Well, there was a demonstration. She was carrying a sign, and she had a violent verbal disagreement with a protester on the other side of the issue. She started to hit the other protester with her sign, two of our officers interceded and she hit them with the sign instead."

"Two felony charges right there," he muttered. "Assault on two police officers, in addition to the other assault?"

"I'm afraid so. I'm truly sorry, Nick. I thought you'd want to know before the press gets hold of it."

"Thanks, Harvey. I owe you one. Which precinct is she gracing with her presence?" he added facetiously.

He was told. The caller left.

Nick poked his head in the door. "I'm going to bail Jackie out of jail," he said with a sardonic pull of his mouth.

"I wouldn't," she advised.

Both dark eyebrows went up. "What?"

"If you do it, you'll give her the impression that all she has to do is call you, no matter what she does, and it's a get-out-of-jail-free card for life."

"She's my niece. Despite her faults, I love her," he replied belligerently.

"Then leave her there overnight."

He harrumphed. "Sure. Great advice. I'll be back when I can." He went out and slammed the door behind him.

Gaby sighed. One day, she thought, he'd realize what a mistake he was making. One of Gaby's friends in her school days had a parent like Jackie's uncle Nick. He bailed her out every time she got in trouble. At least, until the day she decided that she could get out of anything by calling her daddy, who was quite rich. She knifed a boy she was dating, in a drunken rage. Her father couldn't help her. The boy's parents filed a lawsuit and egged on the prosecution. All her father's money couldn't save her. She went to jail for attempted murder.

Jackie might not be that bad, not yet. But Gaby always remembered her friend, and what had happened to her. She still wrote to the woman on a regular basis, but at every parole hearing, the boy's parents were there to remind them of what the young woman was capable of doing when she drank. So far, four years after the fact, the woman was still in prison.

Nick came home with a belligerent Jackie.

"Those idiot cops," she muttered, tossing her black hair. "I wasn't going to hit that old lady with the sign. It slipped, that's all!"

"Really?" Gaby asked with a blithe smile. "I heard that you hit the police officers with it, after."

"Who said that? It's a lie! And this is none of your business anyway—you're just an employee!" Jackie raged at her.

Gaby noted the signs of drug use in the girl's bloodshot

eyes and tiny pupils and raging emotions. "True enough," Gaby conceded. "How did you like jail?"

"Are you kidding?" Jackie burst out. "It stank and there were crazy people in there!"

"I'm sorry you were disappointed," Gaby replied. "Jail isn't quite like those TV series that glorify life on the inside, is it? It might help to remember that you'll be living a long time with people like that if you aren't a little more careful about joining social movements."

Jackie glared at her. "Uncle Nick can get me out of anything," she said with a sarcastic smile. "He's the best lawyer in Chicago."

Gaby glanced at Nick, who was putting his coat in the closet. He didn't hear, or didn't want to hear, what his niece had just said.

"I'm going to my room," Jackie said haughtily. "I don't want to be disturbed."

She huffed off down the hall and slammed her door behind her.

Gaby glanced at the boss. "You can get her out of anything," she repeated, and her blue eyes were sad.

Nick glared at her. "Weren't you working?"

"Oh, yes, indeed, I was. But it's five o'clock and I'm off now," she said. "I think I'll go to my own room and play a little bagpipe music…"

"You do and you're fired," he said flatly. "I've had quite enough attitude for one day."

"Anything you say, boss," she agreed, wary of his temper. She smiled and went to her own room.

Her grandmother called that night.

"And how are things going with you?" she asked in a deceptively casual tone.

"Better than things are going with you, I assume," she teased. "What is it? You never phone me this late."

There was a sigh. "Our Mr. Everett has been digging into the background of my great-nephew."

"Yes?"

"It seems that he has become friends with the son of a prominent politician. The politician has ties to a minor crime boss in the city."

"Well, the property is in my name," Gaby said shortly. "And filed in court. There's no way Robert can get his hands on it!"

"This is the issue—he says that he has a will that was written just before my sister died, and after the one you filed. He is planning to challenge the will in court."

"How lovely," Gaby sighed. "And here I was thinking how dull my life had become."

Grand-mère laughed. "I have my own attorneys working on this. You are a blood relative, my darling. Robert is only related to us through marriage. Meanwhile, Mr. Everett is talking to a private detective he knows. There may be a simple solution to this issue. But I thought you should be aware of it." There was a pause. "You have not spoken to your employer about my ex-husband's plans to challenge his conviction?"

"No," Gaby replied. "Mr. Chandler is…well, difficult. He's volatile."

"Not dangerous?" came the immediate reply, concern in the elderly voice.

"Nothing like that," Gaby replied at once. "He's not violent. Just, well, he erupts from time to time when his clients have IQs the size of a grape."

There was a soft chuckle. "You like him."

Gaby flushed and was glad that her grandmother couldn't see that. "Yes, I do. He's one of those deep people who don't speak of personal issues. A complex personality." She laughed. "It's his niece who is the main issue. She's a handful. Her mother's off in Europe with a boyfriend who got a little too friendly with Goth Girl. So she's stuck here with her uncle, doing her best to drive him mad."

"*C'est vrai?* How?" she asked.

"She got arrested today for hitting two Chicago policemen with a protest sign," she said.

"Poor child," her grandmother said quietly. "She has no one except her absent mother and her uncle?"

"That's the way it seems. She acts out because she's so alone. I feel sorry for her. She's belligerent because she feels that she isn't loved."

"And there is that strange sixth sense you have always had, in play," her grandmother said softly. "My daughter-in-law had the same gift. She saw the accident, years before it happened. It was why she and my son left you with me so very often, so that we would become close."

"Mama knew?" Gaby exclaimed.

"*Oui.* We had coffee in my parlor one day. You would have been about ten, at the time. Nicole had awakened from a nightmare, so vivid that she said she could smell the air, the desert air, in the North African dig site they would go to. She said that she and Jean would be killed..." She paused. The memory hurt her. "She told me that I must take you, and raise you, because she had no family except for a third cousin in Jacobsville, who was much younger than she and her great-aunt Rose, of course," she added curtly, "although she has nothing to do with the family at all!" She sighed. "Anyway, I promised your mother that I would do this, to ease her worry. I did not believe her, of course," she added softly. "I thought it was just a nightmare, a thing most people have at one time or another. I thought that, right up until I had a phone call from the director of the archaeological institute to which they both belonged." She took a deep breath. "Your grandfather hardly reacted to his son's death. Jean and I were very close, but he and his father, not so much. I had to handle everything. You were only thirteen, and even then, my treasure. You are still my treasure," she added gently.

Gaby took a breath. "You never told me that."

"I waited until I thought it was the right time. Your gift has become quite apparent."

"It pops out at unexpected times. It can be embarrassing, as well," she added, thinking of the shocked and fairly angry expression that had claimed Nick Chandler's face when she spoke of his late wife.

"I imagine so," her grandmother replied.

"We have another relative in Texas, don't we?" Gaby asked suddenly. "I mean, besides cousin Clancey?"

"Yes. Clancey has a brother, Tad, who is also our cousin. But your maternal grandmother's sister makes her home there, as well, Mrs. Rose Bartwell. She lives in Jacobsville, Texas, in a boardinghouse, and she avoids any relatives like the plague. She is very much self-sufficient. There is some small gossip that she has ties to a New Jersey mobster," she added amusedly. "Of course, we still own the small ranch near Jacobsville, where we have a competent manager. I do not want it to go out of the family. Your mother loved it, because her parents lived there. It is such a shame that your mother's parents died so young."

"I wish I'd had more time with them," Gaby replied sadly. "Texas is a long way away, and Mom and Dad were always away on some exciting new dig." She laughed. "I guess that's why I took my degree in anthropology. It was something they both loved."

"I hope that you do not plan to spend your life with a toothbrush, cleaning dirt from ancient pottery."

Gaby laughed. "Well, I have no plans to marry..."

"My darling," her grandmother said very gently, "it would be such a waste. You love children. You would never have them. Not unless you plan to go to one of those clinics and have a child by a man you would never even know, from a sample in a test tube!"

"Oh, no," she replied quickly. "I could never do that!"

"It is kind of you to reassure me. But there will still be no great-grandchildren," she said wistfully. "You are the last of our line. It would be such a pity."

"There are cousins to carry on our lineage. In fact, Clancey is pregnant. She and Colter are expecting their first child a few months from now. I had a card from her before I started to work for Mr. Chandler."

"They must be pleased. He still works as a Texas Ranger, yes?"

"Yes. It's so exciting to have a family member in such a job," she laughed. "I put him down as a reference."

"My only granddaughter, working as a common secretary." Grandmother was outraged. "No Dupont has ever had to work for a living!"

"Grandfather did," she reminded her.

"Your grandfather was a minor member of the Dupont family, in fact, my eighth cousin or such. He had no money of his own, and he married me to get access to my fortune, although it was not apparent to me at the time, I was so besotted with him. He had never even been to France until after he married me." She sighed. "If I had only known the sort of man he truly was. But then, *ma chérie*, there would have been no Jean to marry your mother, and thus no sweet Gabrielle to brighten my life in my twilight years. You give me such joy!"

"You brighten my life, as well, *Grand-mère*," Gaby said with feeling. "I don't know what I would have done without you. Two tragedies in my life, and you got me through them both. If I didn't love you already, I would love you for the kindness you showed me, and the affection."

"It is not hard to love someone as kind and sweet as you. This girl, this niece who lives with your employer, she is a bad girl?" she asked.

"Jackie isn't bad. She's acting out, hoping somebody will care, even just a little. I feel sorry for her. She loves her mother, but it seems that her mother has no time for her. Since I've been at the apartment, there hasn't been a postcard or even a phone call from her mother."

"It is very sad, for a child to have nothing from its parents. Her father is dead?"

"Yes. And her mother has run wild. Perhaps she loved him very much and is looking for him in other men," she said, trying to be kind.

"Or perhaps she simply likes men," came the dry reply. "It is late. Try not to worry about your cousin. Mr. Everett has many friends in odd places, and he is a wizard at digging out information."

"Which is a very good thing, for us," Gaby said. "Sleep well."

"Bonne nuit," her grandmother replied softly, and hung up.

Gaby put her cell phone on silent, climbed under the covers and turned out the light by her bed. Life was becoming very complicated and not just because of her cousin who wanted the property she'd been willed. Her reaction today to Nick Chandler was both disturbing and unwelcome.

She knew, from tidbits that Tilly had dropped, that Nick had a lover. A beautiful woman, Tilly had told her in confidence, with a possessive attitude toward Nick and a haughty disinterest in anybody else. Nick also wasn't her only lover. It was an indication that he didn't care if his lover roamed, because he had no emotion invested in the relationship. Gaby thought that he might be the type to become insanely jealous of a woman he loved.

She remembered the odd feeling she'd had about his late wife, about his torment because of her death. She couldn't understand where these flashes of insight came from. She didn't like them, most of the time. It had been a revelation that her mother, also, had strange insights into her own future. Somewhere in our family history, Gaby thought as she fell asleep, there must have been some very strange people.

FOUR

After a largely unremarkable week, with Nick working all hours on a case and the Goth Girl more out of the apartment than in it, Gaby's grandmother phoned her again early on Saturday morning. "Wouldn't you like to come for brunch?" she asked.

"I would," Gaby replied. "Are you missing me?" she teased.

"I am, of course. But I have more news. I must speak with you."

Gaby's heart jumped. She could only think of one reason that her grandmother, usually unflappable, would sound so concerned. "I'll be there in thirty minutes."

"Very good. Mr. Everett is parked at the curb. Do you want him to come up for you?"

"No, that wouldn't be wise," Gaby said at once. Nick Chandler was home today for a change, and she wasn't eager to have him confronted with Tanner Everett. It would require more explanation than she was comfortable giving.

"I understand. I will expect you, *ma chérie*," she added, and hung up.

★ ★ ★

Gaby put on a white turtleneck sweater with black leggings and ankle-high boots and threw her wool coat over it. She left her hair in a ponytail and disdained makeup. Her grandmother was none too fond of it, and neither was she.

She grabbed her purse on the way out.

She tapped on the office door. Nick was in there, going over briefs. He looked up curiously.

"I have to go see about my grandmother," she said. "Is it all right if I take off a couple of hours?"

"It's Saturday," he pointed out. "We don't work weekends and holidays."

"You're working," she replied.

He made a face. "The staff doesn't work... Scratch that, Tilly works. Never mind. Go away." He flapped a hand at her and went back to his reading.

She chuckled. "Okay, boss. I won't be too long."

He didn't reply.

Tanner Everett was standing beside the sedan her grandmother liked to ride in. It wasn't flashy, although it was a luxury car, one of the top-of-the-line Jaguar sedans. He opened the back door for her.

"Wow," came a dry voice from behind her. The Goth Girl was standing there with her lips pursed, wearing an outrageously colorful outfit. "Fancy."

"It's my grandmother's," Gaby said, but she looked guilty.

The Goth Girl gave tall, handsome Tanner a bold look. "Your grandmother's not bad-looking, either," she taunted, and took off down the street without another word.

"Oh, dear," Gaby said under her breath as she let Tanner help her into the back seat. "That's going to complicate things."

"I wouldn't worry about it," he drawled. "From what

you've told your grandmother, I assume that your boss doesn't pay his niece much attention."

"He tries not to. But she'll be boiling over with enthusiasm to tell him this."

"It's really none of his business what you do in your private life," he pointed out. "You're an employee, not a servant."

She laughed. "Thanks, Tanner," she replied. "You always know what to say."

"I do my best, Miss Dupont," he replied with a faint smile.

Her grandmother was pacing the floor when she arrived. She took time to hang up her coat before she went into the smaller woman's arms to be hugged.

"I am sorry to pull you away from your work on a Saturday," the little woman said as she led the way into the dining room. "But I have some disturbing news."

"What sort of news?"

"A rumor that my ex-husband has a friend in the underworld who is gathering witnesses to dispute our testimony as to what happened to you," she said quietly.

They sat down at the table. Gaby felt her heart racing. "That would be found out," she began.

"My sweet, you have no idea how dangerous these people can be, or what they are capable of doing. Our Mr. Everett has been an ongoing fountain of information on what they call the Outfit in Chicago."

"But we have witnesses, as well," Gaby said stubbornly.

"Witnesses have families, my darling," came the quiet, sad reply. "They can be threatened, or bribed, or even harmed, out of sight of the courts."

Gaby just sat, her mind whirling around this new development. "What can we do?" she asked the older woman.

"For the moment, very little, I'm afraid. However, I have

prevailed upon Mr. Everett, who has, shall we say, unconventional contacts in Chicago, to see what he can find out for us."

"That was a good idea," she replied.

"And something else, quite amazing. Your great-aunt in Texas, Rose Bartwell, has a passing acquaintance with someone very high up in the ranks of organized crime in New Jersey."

"Mob families are territorial," Gaby said quietly. "I've read about them. As a rule, they don't interfere in each other's business."

"However, they do have contacts in those other families," Madame Dupont mused with a smile.

"Contacts who might be able to find out things for us?" Gaby asked.

Her grandmother just smiled.

Gaby stayed long enough for excellent coffee and finger sandwiches before Tanner took her back to Nick's apartment.

Nick was gone, but there was a note on his desk that left her with enough work to keep her busy until supper. He'd mentioned that employees had Saturday off, which led her to wonder if he'd had a conversation with the Goth Girl about Gaby's ride.

Not that it was any of her employer's business who she saw or what she did outside working hours. At least her boss didn't have any interest in her and had made it clear that any attention from her would be unappreciated. It was nice to have a working relationship that stayed in its place, she decided.

But inwardly, she had to confess that her employer was very sexy and it took a little effort not to let her eyes linger on him. She had enough complications in her life at the moment.

Gaby seemed to be the only one at supper. Tilly just smiled when she asked if the rest of the household was out for the evening. She'd long since figured out that if Tilly smiled, it meant she didn't know.

She'd just finished her small meal and was starting on a slice of excellent cheesecake that Tilly had made when the door swung open with a disturbing violence. It slammed, as well.

Nick Chandler strode to the table, jerked back a chair and sat down. "Coffee, black. I had supper with a client." He glanced at Gaby. "And a slice of cheesecake."

"Yes, sir," Tilly said, and quickly made herself scarce.

He didn't speak until Tilly had served him and went to hide in the kitchen. She knew her boss very well. Something loud and unpleasant was in the works. She had no wish to be caught in the cross fire.

Nick sipped black coffee and stabbed his cheesecake with subdued violence.

"The cheesecake is innocent," Gaby remarked, watching. "It hasn't moved all night, so it can't be guilty of anything that deserves capital punishment."

He would usually have laughed at the comment. This time, it brought only a scowl and an angry glance.

Gaby withdrew into her own thoughts. Maybe he was working on a tough case and didn't want to have his thought processes interrupted.

She was just about through with her cheesecake when she felt his dark eyes on her.

"You told me you had no romantic entanglements," he said shortly. "You lied."

She dropped her fork. The accusation was that unexpected. She fumbled it back into her hand and gaped at him. "I beg your pardon?"

"Jackie told me about your handsome escort. I believe you referred to him as your grandmother?" he purred, while his eyes resolved into something resembling an ax over a bare neck.

Her eyebrows arched. What a cheap shot, Jackie, she thought irritably. She couldn't tell the truth. So what could she tell him.

She decided on a partial truth. "He works for my grandmother," she said. "He drives her. She never learned to drive a car."

"He was driving you," he pointed out.

"Yes. To my grandmother's apartment," she said calmly, and looked straight into his accusing eyes. "It's much less trouble than trying to find a cab."

"Don't tell me. You can't drive, either."

"Actually, I can't," she confessed.

"A genetic trait?" he drawled.

She flushed. The Duponts had never driven themselves. They'd always had chauffeurs, for several generations. They were fabulously wealthy. But she couldn't say that, especially not now, when she and her grandmother were living in fear of her grandfather and what his mob connections might be willing to do for him.

"I can't afford the upkeep and insurance on a car," she said finally.

"Your grandmother obviously can. It was a luxury sedan, I believe...?" His deep voice trailed off.

"Yes. My grandmother is well-to-do. I am not," she lied.

His dark eyes narrowed. He was thinking. He didn't like what he was thinking. Jackie had told him about the handsome man squiring Gaby around and he was resentful. It wasn't jealousy. Of course it wasn't. Gaby was too young, and she just worked for him. He resented that she was keeping things from him.

"Are you sleeping with him?" he asked curtly, and then ground his teeth together at the intimacy of the question, which he'd never meant to ask.

"Mr. Chandler!" Gaby exploded. She stood up, glaring at him.

Her instant outrage was what settled the question in his mind. No. She wasn't sleeping with him. In fact, she seemed insulted that he'd even had such a thought.

"Is it that you don't sleep with the hired help or that you don't think of men that way?" he taunted.

She was glaring now. "I hate men," she said, prodded into indiscretion by his blatant accusation.

"You like women?"

The glare grew hotter. "Not in the way you're insinuating."

"You have me at a disadvantage," he began.

"Good. Let's keep it that way, shall we?" she asked with hauteur that would have graced a castle. "I'm going to my room. The work you left for me is finished and on your desk," she added with a hot flush on her cheeks.

He scowled. "What work?"

She stopped and turned, puzzled. He didn't sound as if he'd left her any.

"The letters to congressmen and the ones you wanted sent to your managers about the software updates for new equipment, and the personal notes to friends you wanted addressed."

"I never left any damned letters to be addressed!" he exploded.

"Well...well, there was a note..."

He was storming off toward his office. Just as he reached it, the front door opened and Jackie breezed in.

She stopped short at the look on her uncle's face. She glanced at Gaby, who was standing by the table, looking perplexed. Jackie didn't speak.

But her uncle did. "What sort of note did you leave for her?" he demanded, pointing to Gaby.

Jackie cleared her throat. "I was just helping out. You wanted those letters done."

"Monday," he said shortly. "I wanted them done Monday! Nobody works weekends here, except me...and maybe Tilly!"

"Oops," Jackie said with a blithe smile. "Sorry."

"I left no note asking you to do work on a Saturday," he emphasized to Gaby.

"Did you have fun riding around with your granny?" Jackie asked Gaby. "He sure was a hunk! Could you ask him if he has a younger friend?"

"He's my grandmother's driver," Gaby said quietly. "The car is hers, as well."

"Uncle Nick has a chauffeur. He doesn't look anything like your granny's. He must do weight training and stuff, to have a physique like that," Jackie commented, piling wood on the fire of her uncle's irritation.

"Mr. Everett was involved in security work before he drove for my grandmother," Gaby said. "He was required to be physically fit."

"Well, he makes my mouth water," Jackie sighed. "What a guy!"

"If there's nothing else, I'll excuse myself," Gaby told Nick.

"There's nothing else," he said in a voice like ice water.

"Then good night." She didn't include Jackie in that. She walked down the hall to her room and closed the door.

Out in the hall, there were muffled voices, one deep and angry, one lilting and apologetic. Gaby paid them no attention. Her boss thought she had a lover. How ridiculous was that? After her experiences, she'd rather have had a dog, quite honestly.

When Gaby went in to breakfast the next morning, Jackie and Nick were already at the table.

"If I'm late, I'm sorry," she said as she sat down. Her grandmother wanted people at table at precise times.

"We don't have meal schedules here," Nick growled. "It isn't the Army." He frowned when he saw how Gaby was dressed. She had on a very becoming navy suit with a lacy pink camisole, hose and high heels. "Where are you going?"

"Out with the sexy driver, I'll bet," Jackie said under her breath.

"Enough!" Nick bit off.

Jackie hunched her shoulders and dug into her eggs.

Gaby hardly tasted what she was eating. She felt like the entrée at a banquet.

She'd just finished when the doorbell rang.

Gaby got up and went to fetch her long coat and her purse. She knew who it was.

Tanner Everett, in a dark suit, stood at parade rest outside the apartment door. "Is Miss Dupont ready to go?" he asked politely.

"Ready to go where?" Nick demanded.

"I'm here," Gaby said before things could escalate. She paused at the doorway. "I won't be back until after lunch. *Grand-mère* and I have lunch together after church," she added, and flushed when she realized that she'd used the French for grandmother.

"Church." Nick looked stunned.

"I'm ready when you are, Mr. Everett," Gaby told her bodyguard. She didn't look back as he escorted her to the elevator.

"I told you he was handsome," Jackie said cattily. "I'll bet he's a wonderful lover…"

Her uncle gave her a look that sent her quickly on the way to her own room. Talk about putting the cat among the pigeons, however. She was amused at his reaction. And, honestly, she felt just a twinge of guilt at the way she'd taunted Gaby with the man. Gaby had been kind to her, unexpectedly kind after the mischief she'd made.

But she had a boyfriend of her own, and Gaby was likely to interfere. She'd been delighted that they'd moved here, so close to her boyfriend. She knew her uncle was frequently away, and she'd have the apartment to herself. Well, to herself and Keith. But then her uncle had hired Gaby, and she was in the way. No Gaby, no more worries about privacy. It wasn't nice, but she loved Keith and he'd already said he couldn't take her to his mother's place, because his mother went to church and she'd have a conniption if she caught him with a girl in his room. So it was up to Jackie to find a place where they could be completely alone.

She wanted Keith. She really wanted him. He wasn't a particularly nice boy, and he ran with a rough crowd, but she ached for him. She'd never been with anybody. She wanted to live with Keith. She was in high school, but Keith was in his early twenties. He didn't work. He was frequently involved in protests, one of which had resulted in Jackie's arrest—luckily for her, Uncle Nick had managed to get the charges dropped. He had charm, when he liked to use it.

He wasn't affectionate, though. Well, Keith wasn't affectionate, either. He wanted to sleep with her. After that, he said, they'd make decisions. Other girls had warned her that he just wanted sex and nothing more, and that he'd done something pretty bad a few years ago to a girl. But Jackie didn't believe them. She was sure it was different with her. After all, those other girls were experienced, so maybe Keith hadn't liked them being so sophisticated. Maybe he'd been waiting for an innocent girl, like Jackie. She was sure it would be heaven to let him have her. She was equally sure he wanted her for keeps. But she had to get rid of Gaby first.

Sure, there were motels, but Uncle Nick had her watched. He hadn't come right out and said it, but he knew she was going around with Keith and he knew about Keith's drug habit. If she went to a motel with him, or even to a friend's home, her uncle would know and he'd send her back to her mother. That would be a fate worse than death. She'd been pawed and chased and threatened by her mother's casual lovers too many times already. *Never again*, she vowed.

But Keith would save her. He'd be true to her. She knew it. Keith loved her. He was the only person in her young life who did.

Gaby, unaware of Jackie's plotting, went to church with *Grand-mère* and then to lunch at a local five-star restaurant. They had quiche and fruit and casual conversation. They weren't comfortable discussing their worries where they might be overheard.

Afterward, Mr. Everett drove them back to the apartment.

"And how does your job go?" the little woman asked Gaby as they lounged in her spacious, beautiful living room, full of priceless antiques.

"Well enough, I guess." Gaby sighed. "The Goth Girl told her uncle that I was having it on with Mr. Everett, however," she added with a gamine grin.

"Having it...on?"

"Sorry. Sleeping with."

"But, no!"

"Of course, no," Gaby muttered. "He's very nice, but you know how I am about men, about any men." She wrapped her arms around herself.

"We should have tried another therapist," the older woman said quietly.

"Therapy doesn't erase what happened." She closed her eyes

on horrible memories. "If I'd been older, perhaps it wouldn't have been so traumatic."

Her grandmother got up and embraced her warmly. "My darling, it would have been traumatic for any woman," she pointed out. "I just regret that your assailant could not be prosecuted."

"He had diplomatic immunity. I wonder if grandfather knew that?"

Her grandmother made a rough sound. "Of course he did. He always planned well. Him and his obnoxious ideas, his grubbing for money. I have always had it. But it never owned me, as it owned him. He wanted more, always more." She threw up her hands. "Why? I have never understood why."

"Greed," Gaby said simply.

"I suppose that is so."

There was a long silence.

"Your employer," her grandmother said softly, "he was disturbed that you left with Mr. Everett?"

"Fuming," she said unconsciously. "I don't know why. Well, he'd already said that nobody worked on Saturdays except himself, and his niece left me a huge lot of work to do that I thought was from him. He'd got over that. But this morning when Mr. Everett came up to get me, he was in a red rage."

The older woman lifted a delicate eyebrow, but said nothing else.

"What will we do about Grandfather?" Gaby asked as she stood by the door, waiting for Everett to bring the limo around and come up for her.

"I will speak to our attorneys," she replied quietly. She made a face as she studied her granddaughter. "I should have had them approach Mr. Chandler, instead of letting you do something so...so beneath you as to work for him."

"It isn't beneath me." Gaby burst out laughing. "*Grand-mère*," she teased, "most young women work these days. And I have never been one for cocktail parties and ballrooms."

"Yes, I know," came the sad reply. "My fault, all of it. If I had been more observant…"

Gaby went to her and hugged the smaller woman close. "Life happens," she said gently. "And there is a purpose to everything, even if we never know exactly what it is."

The little woman hugged her back, fiercely. "Yes, and we go to church to make sure that we remember those things, but I worry so, and I forget." She drew away, her eyes tender. "You were always a sweet child. I do not like having you in danger."

"The only danger I'm in is a court case, and we're going to win it," Gaby said firmly.

"You think so?"

"I do." She hesitated. "When I know Mr. Chandler a little better, I'll sound him out on Grandfather." She sighed. "I would rather face a lion across a courtroom than face him," she confessed. "He's…volatile."

"He is not dangerous to you?" came the quick query.

"Oh, heavens, no!" Gaby said at once. "He gets angry at injustices," she explained.

"Such as?" her grandmother asked with twinkling eyes.

"I'm not allowed to talk about things he mentions," she said primly. "I'm an administrative assistant, and the law is serious business."

"Yes, to some," her grandmother said wistfully. "But you be careful. And if there is trouble, you call Mr. Everett. You have his cell phone number on speed dial, yes?"

"Yes. Also the Chicago Police Department," she said in a loud whisper, and grinned. "But I think it would be a very stupid man who tried to get past Mr. Chandler," she added with a chuckle.

There was a tap at the door and Tanner Everett came in. "Ready to go, Miss Dupont?" he asked.

"Yes, indeed." She kissed her grandmother. *"Bonne nuit."*

"Bonne nuit, ma chérie."

Everett insisted on walking her to her door.

"You have an overabundance of caution," she said as he helped her out of the car.

"Force of habit," he replied. He scowled. "Isn't that your employer's niece?" he asked suddenly.

It was. Jackie was leaning against a wall down a side street, and a tall, rough-looking boy, obviously much older than the Goth Girl, was leaning against her in a sexually explicit way and his hands were tugging at her jeans.

"Excuse me," Gaby said in a tight voice and started walking toward the girl, unaware that Everett was close behind her.

"What are you doing?" she exclaimed shortly.

Jackie jumped, although the boy, dressed in expensive clothes, with tattoos and piercings everywhere, moved away with a cold nonchalance.

"Mind your own business," he told Gaby.

Gaby started to speak. Everett moved in front of her and dropped into an easy combat stance. It wasn't blatant, but it made the older boy tense and move back.

"She's fifteen years old," Gaby told Jackie's rough-looking companion. She smiled coldly. "Do you know the sentence for statutory rape? And I believe her uncle is a noted attorney...?"

The man spat out an obscenity and walked off in a huff.

"Keith, come back!" Jackie cried. "Please!"

He threw a gesture at her and kept walking.

"Now see what you've done!" she raged at Gaby. "He'll never come back, and I love him!"

"Lucky for you," Everett said curtly. "He's probably got a rap sheet as long as my arm."

"You shut up," Jackie yelled. She was crying, tears of rage that melted her excessive black eyeliner. She glared at Gaby. "I'm going to tell my uncle and he'll fire you!" she added.

"Good idea," Gaby said. "Let's go see him right now. It's raining."

Jackie's mascara was running down her cheeks, black and streaky. She sobbed all the way into the elevator, almost up-ending an old man with a cane. Everett righted the little man with a gentle smile and apologized for the girl.

The old man gave her a sad appraisal. He shook his head. "In my day, young people were held to a higher standard of conduct. I suppose it truly is the apocalypse," he mused with twinkling blue eyes. "Have a good evening."

"You, too," Everett replied.

Gaby, who'd been holding the elevator for him, stepped back as he came into it.

He gave Jackie a hard look, and she seemed to flush, but he didn't say a word.

They paused at the door to Chandler's apartment. Jackie had a key, which she used, and she shut the door loudly in Gaby's face.

"I hope you have a key," he commented as the sound of a lock being thrown came loud on the silence.

She smiled. "I don't. But no worries. I'll just sit down here on the floor until someone notices me." She hesitated. "Thanks. For what you did. I rush in without thinking."

"I noticed." His blue eye narrowed. "I'm going to have him checked out."

"How?" she asked simply. "You don't even know who he is."

He just smiled.

She sat down against the wall and leaned her head back against it. Everett stood at parade rest beside her. "You could go back to *Grand-mère*," she pointed out.

"Certainly. The minute you're allowed inside."

Not three minutes had passed when heavy footsteps and a growling deep voice came close. The door was thrown open and Nick Chandler's angry, unsmiling face went from Everett's to Gaby's.

"What the hell are you doing out here, sitting on the floor?" he asked shortly.

"Jackie locked me out."

"I can see that. Why?" He glanced at Everett and his eyes narrowed. "And what the hell are you doing out here?"

"Bird-watching," the younger man said.

The older man wore an expression of disbelief.

"Through the window." Everett nodded with his head. "I believe it's a peregrine falcon. Too far away to tell if it's a male or female."

"If it's perched precariously on a ledge with one claw between itself and eternity, it's female," Nick said with icy politeness.

Gaby choked on stifled laughter. Everett's eyes twinkled, but he didn't smile.

"Good evening," Everett said to both of them and sauntered off toward the elevator.

Nick held the door open. Once Gaby was inside, he stayed put, blocking the hallway so that she either had to stay in place or get around him—an impossibility in the narrow space.

"Now," he said coldly, "why did Jackie lock you out? And don't hand me any fairy tales."

She looked up at him, cocking her head. "Are you sure? Because I know a great politically correct version of 'Goldilocks and the Three Bears.'" She smiled.

FIVE

"**I**'m waiting," Nick Chandler said icily, not responding to her pale attempt at humor.

She didn't want to rat out Jackie. On the other hand, it was a potentially serious situation. It could land Jackie in great danger, and God only knew what her mother would think if something happened and Gaby hadn't spoken up.

"I'll tell you, but not here," she said.

"Stay put."

He went down the hall, knocked on Jackie's door. There was a brief conversation. He grabbed a jacket from his office, closed the door and went back to Gaby. "Come with me," he said.

There was a nice coffee shop just half a block from the apartment. He sat Gaby down and asked what she'd like. His eyebrow arched when she said cappuccino. He chuckled. It was what he always ordered.

He got cups for both of them and escorted her out of the shop to one of the small tables with chairs that lined the sidewalk.

"We're out of the apartment. Spill it."

She stared into her cappuccino. "I hate telling tales."

"So do I. Start talking."

She grimaced, but she told him what she'd seen Jackie doing.

"What the hell! In public? And she's fifteen! How old was the boy she was with?"

"Probably about twenty-two going on forty," she muttered. "Purple mohawk, pierced everything, tattoos from the neck up and probably the neck down. And a colorful vocabulary, both verbal and physical."

"Damn!"

"A lot of sheltered girls get crushes on the wrong sort," she pointed out.

"Did you?"

She smiled sadly. "I got crushes on TV heroes," she replied. "*Grand-mère* was very strict when I was growing up."

"Where were your parents?"

She swallowed hard and sipped coffee.

"I'm sorry," he said curtly, reading between the lines.

"They died together, overseas on an archaeological dig," she said. "One would have died without the other, even then," she replied. "They were crazy about each other. *Grand-mère* took me in and raised me. I was thirteen."

"Do you have family other than your grandmother?"

"I have some cousins and a great-aunt in Texas. And some in France. I wouldn't know them if I met them on the street."

"France."

She nodded. "That's where my grandmother is from, originally."

"We have a lot of Europeans who immigrate here."

"Did your people…?"

"One of my great-great-grandfathers was from Friesland. It's close to North Holland. He was a sea captain. Another was from the Isle of Skye, in Scotland, and he was a sailor, as well. I suppose it's in my blood."

She was noticing his hands. He had calluses on his fingers. "You have calluses." She studied him. "Do you sail?"

"Observant, Miss Dupont," he mused. "Yes, I sail. I keep a yacht at the marina, and I take her out in the spring."

"One of my great-grandfathers sailed," she said. She didn't add that he also had owned a yacht. She smiled. "Another was a Texas Ranger, back in the days of the Mexican Revolution."

He chuckled. "An odd mix, sailors and lawmen."

"Well," she said, "most of us have mixed ancestries."

"My father was Italian." His face went hard. "He started out as a longshoreman in New York Harbor, but he moved here with my mother when I was four."

She winced. "That's a hard job."

"Hard. Yes. He worked on freighters on the Great Lakes. I signed on as a deckhand on one of them when I was just out of high school." He studied his coffee. "I loved sailing. I hated the work. I joined the Navy a couple of years later and ended up in the SEALs."

She was hanging on every word, without realizing it. She'd known nothing about him. He was complex. But it didn't surprise her that he'd been in the SEALSs. He was that sort of man, straightforward and afraid of nothing.

He glanced at her. He smiled quizzically. "You just listen, don't you? No chatter, no interrupting to bring the conversation to clothes or jewels or the best contestant on one of the talent shows."

"I'm not big on any of those."

His eyes went to her hands, long fingered, elegant, but no jewelry at all. He frowned. "Don't you like jewelry?"

"Not very much. It hangs on things."

He laughed. "What an image."

"You can laugh," she mused. "I'll bet you've never laddered your hose with a bad setting in a gemstone ring."

He did laugh then, his dark eyes bright with humor. "Not yet," he agreed.

"What did your mother do?"

"She endured," he said after a minute.

She grimaced.

"Exactly." He sipped coffee, wondering why he opened up to this quiet young woman when he'd never shared his past, or his sister's, with anyone.

"How did you end up in law?" she asked.

"I went to college while I was in the service, got my undergraduate degree. When I got out, I went to law school at night, working in the shipyards in the winter, crewing in spring and summer and fall."

"That must have been hard work," she said.

He gave her a kind smile. "Didn't you work your way through college?"

"Partially," she lied. "I got scholarships, too."

"Did you really minor in library science, Miss Dupont?" he said suddenly.

She ground her teeth. She'd been taught never to lie. She looked up at him with troubled blue eyes.

"What was your minor?" he persisted.

"Archaeology, and my major was anthropology," she confessed. "Well, honestly, trying to find things in your office really comes under that heading, Mr. Chandler," she added. "I do a lot of digging."

He chuckled. "I suppose so."

They finished the coffee.

"What are you going to do about Jackie?" she asked.

"I don't know. We have an excellent private investigator who works for the firm. I'll set him on her friend."

"Mr. Everett is going to investigate him, as well."

He stared at her. "What exactly is Mr. Everett's position with your grandmother? He doesn't strike me as a chauffeur."

She sighed. "He's a bodyguard. My grandmother is old and very frail, and well-to-do," she added, making it sound as if the older woman was less than the millionaire she truly was. "He was a mercenary. Before that, he did some top secret assignments with the SAS."

Both eyebrows went up.

"He's very nice," she added.

Nice. He was picking up a lot from his employee that wasn't verbal. She couldn't lie. She wasn't attracted to Everett, although he was a good-looking man. At her age, most young women had been through at least one love affair, but Miss Dupont there seemed absolutely untouched. It was curious. There was another thing. Her name. He couldn't understand why it sounded so familiar. Of course, it wasn't exactly rare. He'd known at least two or three people with that surname since he'd practiced law in Chicago.

He glanced at the thin gold watch on his muscular wrist. "We'd better get back before Jackie ties two sheets together and goes out the window."

"Why not out her bedroom door?" she wondered.

"I locked it," he said simply, and his eyes twinkled. "I'm not stupid."

"No, sir, you're far from that," she agreed promptly.

He got up and pulled out her chair.

"Nice manners," she mused. "Well, when you're not cursing cheesecake."

"You'd curse, too, if you had some of my clients," he muttered as he went to pay the check.

He came back and walked her down the street. He looked elegant even in casual clothes, she thought, and he was so big that he probably had to have his clothes tailor-made. They did fit nicely, emphasizing how fit he was. Mr. Everett had nothing on Nick, although Nick was certainly a few years older than the bodyguard. There were silver threads in the thick black wavy hair on Nick Chandler's head.

He glanced down at her. "Did you say something to Jackie when you found her with the boy?" he asked curiously.

"Not really. I just asked her 'friend' if he knew that she was fifteen and I might have mentioned something about statutory rape." Her face was harder than marble.

He stopped her, scowling down at her. "Statutory rape?" he asked.

She shifted uncomfortably. "He was leaning against her on a wall, just off the main street, in plain view of the public, and it looked very much to me as if he was tugging at her jeans," she added with a flush. "She's crazy over him. Mr. Everett said he probably had a rap sheet as long as his arm."

Mr. Everett was probably right, but he wasn't giving the man credit.

"What did Jackie tell you?" Gaby asked.

He let out a rough breath. "That she was talking to a boy she knew from school when you butted in—her words—and started a rumpus."

"She didn't know him from school, I can assure you. He looked to be in his twenties, and he was wearing designer clothes. She's naive and unsettled and insecure because of her mother's neglect— Sorry," she added when she saw his expression; she was speaking of his sister, after all. "And she's at that age when rebellion is almost mandatory."

"So she goes out and finds the roughest boy in the neighborhood to hang out with," he mused. He cocked his head and smiled. "Is that what you did when you were almost sixteen?"

Her reaction was immediate and disturbing. She wrapped both arms over her chest and made an odd gesture with her head. She kept walking. The question brought back nightmarish memories.

"What did I say?" he asked, keeping pace.

"I had a traumatic experience at sixteen," she said shortly. "I don't like remembering it."

Now he was curious, but she'd closed up like a water lily for the night. He strode along beside her. She was an odd mix of the mature and the juvenile, and an odd fit as his administrative assistant. But he genuinely liked her. It was a shame that Jackie didn't.

"She'll give you hell from now on," he thought aloud.

"She'll get it back, in spades," she said lightly. "I don't take guff from anyone, especially not a pierced girl with black nails."

He burst out laughing. "That was unfair."

She chuckled. "But accurate."

"Possibly."

They got to the apartment and he walked to the elevator just ahead of her, pushing the button. Then he leaned against the wall, hands in his pockets, and studied her. He liked the way she looked. She was pretty, in her way, and he liked that long chestnut hair with its red highlights and her perky attitude. She made him laugh, something his lovers, especially high-tempered Mara Crane, his current lover, had never managed. He remembered with pain the woman who had captured his heart, many years ago, and how tragically it had ended. The memory alone was enough to keep him single. Besides, why should he marry again? Women were as free as men to sleep with whom they pleased. Nobody, it seemed, was eager to rush to the altar with rings these days. Least of all him. He recalled with faint curiosity that he hadn't invited Mara to the apartment since Gaby had been in residence. Mara had remarked about it once. He'd just said that he was having issues with Jackie. Odd, he thought, that he didn't want Mara around Gaby. She was such a conventional girl, and Mara was sophisticated and blatant with her sexuality. It would make him uncomfortable, he decided, to put the two women together. He didn't consider why.

The elevator stopped and he and Gaby got on, crowding in between a family of five. One of the children, a little girl, grinned up at Gaby, who grinned back.

The sight was painful to Nick, who had memories he'd never shared with anyone. The little girl was sweet and pretty. She had blond hair, like another little girl…

The girl grinned at him and showed him one of her toys. He turned his eyes away from her deliberately, and without a word or a smile. Gaby saw that, out of the corner of her eye, and she was shocked at the way Nick had shut out the child. The little girl moved closer to her mother and looked straight ahead until the family got out at the floor below Nick's.

The elevator doors closed again. Gaby turned to Nick, her pale eyes curious and intent on him. "Don't you like children?" she asked abruptly.

Pain shot through him like a bullet. He gave her a glare that would have stopped traffic as the elevator ground to a halt. He walked away from her, to the apartment, unlocked the door and walked on in, leaving it open for her to follow. By the time she reached it, he'd gone into his study and slammed the door.

Gaby was stunned by his actions. She'd never seen a man who seemed to despise children. Even the icy Mr. Everett was tender with children, always responding to them when he and Gaby were together in crowds.

She went to her room without stopping to talk to her boss. The CD player in the Goth Girl's room was so loud that the walls were throbbing.

As Gaby closed her door, she heard a bellow. "Turn that damned thing down or I'll throw it through the window!"

The music stopped abruptly.

Gaby took a deep breath. It had been a day to remember, but not with happiness. She sorted her clothes so that she could do laundry later in the laundry room that she was permitted to use. The Goth Girl hated her, and now her boss was full of icy resentment because she'd asked a simple question. Perhaps this job had been her very worst idea to date.

She had an unexpected phone call later that evening. It was her grandmother.

"Our Mr. Everett," the older woman said, "has found out something about the man for whom your employer's niece has such an affection."

"Has he?" Gaby asked. "What?"

"An arrest and conviction for sexual assault," her grandmother said flatly. She added the particulars of the arrest, which had Gaby fuming inside. "The boy has been in and out of trouble with the law since he was barely a teenager, as well. Mr. Everett says that your employer should be told."

Gaby drew in a troubled breath.

"*Chérie*, what is wrong?" came the soft query, because the older woman knew so well the sound and what emotion joined it.

"The boss and I had a, well, a sort of tiff." Gaby tried to explain, and it was hard, because he'd looked at her as if she'd crawled out from under a stone. She still didn't know why.

"Have you argued with him?"

"No. Nothing like that," Gaby said at once. "I irritated him and he walked off and slammed a door between us."

"Pourquoi?" came the soft question.

"I don't know," Gaby replied. She hesitated. "There was a little girl on the elevator, coming up. He was cold as ice with her, and when I asked him why..."

"Ah," her grandmother replied. "There is something in his past, something very painful, yes?"

"I imagine so. He's kind to his niece," she added, puzzled. "Even when she's being more of a pain in the neck than usual."

"His niece is a teenager, however."

"Yes."

"So the memory must be of a young child."

Gaby smiled, recalling how intuitive the older woman was. "I suppose it must be."

"Still, you must tell him what Mr. Everett has discovered, while there is still time."

"I'll need a whip and a chair," came the resigned reply.

"Just patience, my child," her grandmother laughed. "That is all that is needed with most impatient, unpleasant people."

"I suppose so."

"He has not mentioned your grandfather?"

"No. And he's very standoffish, even though I work for him. I've been too intimidated to ask him anything."

"Perhaps when you have been there longer?"

Gaby couldn't see how time was going to change much in her turbulent relationship with her boss. But one didn't argue with her grandmother. "Perhaps," she conceded.

"Bonsoir, ma chérie," the older woman said softly. "Next month, you will come to celebrate my birthday. You must

have a grand gown, for it is to be a ball. I have hired a hall and an orchestra. There will be dancing."

Gaby recalled parties, grand parties, when she was much younger. Her grandmother could still dance, even at her age. She was like a fairy on the dance floor, lighter than air.

"I'll dance if you will," Gaby promised.

There was soft, almost girlish laughter. "Of course. Gold, *chérie*," she added. "It is your best color, with that incredible complexion."

"Gold it is," Gaby said. "I'll go shopping on my day off."

"You know where to go," came the reply. "I maintain an account there, and they are expecting you."

There went Gaby's hope of getting something pretty but inexpensive. Her grandmother would insist on couture, especially at such a party.

"Who's coming?" Gaby asked.

"Everyone, of course," her grandmother said smugly. "The mayor, the governor, the vice president, a few movie stars, that soccer star I adore and, of course, Mr. Everett, who dances divinely, as I recall."

She felt blatant relief that her grandmother hadn't mentioned Nick or the Goth Girl. It would blow her cover if Nick showed up and realized that the very well-known and wealthy Madame Dupont was her grandmother.

"I wouldn't miss your party for the world," Gaby told her honestly. "I'll get a gown that will do it justice."

"See that you do. *Bonne nuit, ma chérie.*"

"*Bonne nuit.*"

Gaby had planned to deliver Mr. Everett's verbal report to her boss the next day, but he left before she was up, and didn't come home until she was in bed. The second day, he was also gone before she got up.

The Goth Girl, of course, didn't speak to her at all. She pretended that Gaby was invisible and acted accordingly. And when Gaby tried to tell her about her boyfriend, before breakfast, she walked out of the apartment and slammed the door.

So much for a pleasant working environment, she thought. She went to Nick's office and started sorting out material.

An hour later, there were sirens down below. Surprised, Gaby put on a coat and went downstairs to see what the commotion was all about, because she had a premonition. Sadly, the premonition was correct.

Jackie was struggling in the grasp of a huge police officer. Her boyfriend was nowhere in sight.

"Let go of me, you idiot!" Jackie raged at the policeman and added a few choice unprintable words to the request. "I told you, my boyfriend wasn't robbing that lady, he was just trying to help her!"

"That's not what the victim said," the policeman muttered.

She spotted Gaby on the sidewalk and started yelling at her, as well.

"You sold me out, you," Jackie yelled at her, and the foul language flowed like wine. "You called the police, I know you did!"

Gaby, smiling vacantly, came forward. "I've only just come downstairs," she pointed out.

"Tell this big dope who I am!" Jackie demanded of her uncle's assistant.

"Do you know this young lady?" the policeman asked Gaby, struggling with the teenager.

Gaby glanced at Jackie, who was turning purple and still muttering insults. She pursed her full lips and smiled. "Sir," she told the policeman, "I have never seen this young woman in my life." Gaby put her hand over her heart.

"You stupid, ugly, piece of...!" Jackie raged. "I'll get you! I'll get you, if it's the last thing I ever do!"

Gaby sighed. "Isn't that terroristic threats and acts?" she asked the policeman with all innocence.

"We've got a laundry list already, and she just got out of three other charges thanks to her uncle," the policeman muttered. "Harry, give me a hand, will you?" he called to a fellow officer.

They wrestled Jackie toward a police car.

"Stop them!" Jackie raged at Gaby.

Gaby started dancing. And smiling. And waving.

Jackie used many more unprintable words.

As the police car drove off with Jackie in the back seat, one of the arresting officers was laughing his head off. Gaby was still on the sidewalk, dancing and waving.

Nick had to bail her out. Again. All the way home she raged about Gaby's behavior. Nick was still trying to cope with feelings his assistant had provoked when she asked him if he didn't like children. He'd behaved badly and he couldn't even tell her why. It made him more ill-tempered.

"Getting arrested for attempted mugging, thanks to your criminal friend," Nick ground out when they were in the elevator, thankfully deserted. "Yelling insults! Resisting arrest! I just got you out of trouble after the protest march, and here you are back in the slammer again! Do you have any idea how much trouble you're in?"

"Well, you're a lawyer, aren't you?" Jackie muttered. "You got me out of those other charges. Get me out of these!"

He made a rough sound in his throat.

Gaby was just coming out of Nick's office when they walked in the door. She smiled vacantly in their direction.

"Home so soon?" she asked. "I hope you both had a lovely time."

"Lovely…" His face hardened.

"You turncoat! You traitor! You wouldn't tell them who I was! You let them take me away in a police car!" Jackie yelled.

"Yes, and I did the happy dance while they were loading you into the car, too," she reminded her. She smiled at Nick. "Did you teach her all those words? My goodness, she does have a vocabulary, doesn't she?"

"I wish I could…!" Jackie began, almost choking on indignation.

"Go to your room," Nick told the girl. "We'll talk later."

"I don't want to!"

"I said, go to your room." He never raised his voice. He didn't have to. He was formidable in a bad temper. Even Jackie wasn't brave enough to cut through that cold formality.

The girl glared at him and Gaby and stalked off into her room and slammed the door.

"My, she does have a temper, doesn't she?" Gaby asked blithely.

He glared at her. "Why didn't you tell the police who she was?"

"Because she needs to understand that actions have consequences," Gaby said simply. "And even more, because of who her boyfriend is."

He scowled. "Explain."

"Mr. Everett has sources in law enforcement. Jackie's would-be boyfriend has a prior for sexual assault," she said quietly. She couldn't bring herself to tell him the rest of it. It brought back horrible memories of her own traumatic experience. "Arrest and conviction, by the way. He served two years."

His caught breath was actually audible. "I'll need facts, not gossip."

"I'll ask my grandmother to have Mr. Everett provide them." She studied his hard face. "She's looking for something or someone to fill the empty places inside her, Mr. Chandler," she said in an uncommonly soft tone. "Her mother doesn't seem to notice her. You're always at work. There isn't anybody else. Well, except the boyfriend."

"I work for a living," he said shortly.

"Of course you do."

"Her mother has issues," he continued. "Which are none of your business."

"Consider my lips sealed," she replied.

He drew in an angry breath. "She's too old to take to the movies."

"I haven't said a word."

The glare was getting worse. Before he could say anything else, his cell phone rang. He took it out, checked the number and answered it. "Hi." His voice was like deep velvet. "Sure. I'll expect you about seven. We'll have dinner first. Of course. See you then, honey." He hung up.

Well, obviously, he wasn't going to have time to address Jackie's issues tonight. Not that it bothered Gaby. She was still trying to recover from his icy attitude toward the pretty little girl in the elevator. He was a cold man. Perhaps he was different with a woman.

"Don't let Jackie leave the apartment," he told Gaby.

"Do you have a length of rope and a sturdy chair?" she asked blandly.

The scowl got worse. "All right, I'll tell her she can't leave."

"Good idea. She doesn't listen to me."

He hesitated. "Why was she arrested?"

"What did she tell you?" she asked.

"That she and her boyfriend—who took off and couldn't be caught, of course—were just trying to help an old lady with her purchases, when they swooped down and handcuffed her."

"I'm sure that's what happened," Gaby replied. "After all,

the police do that all the time to teenagers who aren't doing anything." She smiled.

He knew better, and so did she. The woman irritated him beyond bearing. If it hadn't been for Mara going out with him tonight, he'd have had more to say.

"They're charging her with attempted robbery, resisting arrest and terroristic threats," he added.

"Well, the resisting arrest part was the gospel truth," she replied. "The policeman had to ask for help or be thrown to the pavement, and he was a big guy. And I haven't heard language like that since a carpenter at my grandmother's house hit his thumb with a hammer."

"Terroristic threats?" he persisted.

"She threatened to attack me," Gaby told him. "Repeatedly."

"Why?"

"I have my reputation to consider," she said with mock haughtiness. "I wouldn't want it to be known that I even associated with someone who could use language like that! I mean, really!"

He wouldn't laugh, he wouldn't laugh... He turned away with a choking sound and went straight back to Jackie's room.

There was loud conversation, followed by a slamming door, followed by another slamming door, followed by the CD player going up to full volume. That was followed by a bellow that would have done a bull elephant proud.

After that, peace.

Gaby went into her own room and closed the door. But gently.

SIX

Jackie had to come out of her room to eat an early supper, but it was a silent meal. The housekeeper, Tilly, put the food on the table, mumbled something about an evening engagement and got out of the line of fire.

Gaby ate her way through poached salmon, herbed potatoes and green beans without a word and progressed to cherry pie for dessert.

"I'm not speaking to you," Jackie spat.

Gaby just smiled. "I noticed."

Jackie shifted in her chair, picking at her food.

"Your boyfriend has a prior for sexual assault. He served two years," Gaby said in a conversational tone.

"You're lying!" Jackie said, red-faced and furious.

"I don't have any reason to lie." She searched the younger woman's eyes. "I know about sexual assault," she said through clenched teeth. "Even if you think you love the boy, it's not something you want to have to live with for the rest of your life."

Jackie was suddenly less hostile. She blinked. "He says he loves me," she said.

"And you want him to, because you think nobody else does," she replied.

Jackie glowered at her.

Gaby studied her quietly, sipping coffee. "I lost my parents when I was thirteen," she said. "Both at once. I went to live with my grandparents. When I was sixteen, just a little older than you, in fact," she continued quietly, "there was an...incident. If my grandmother hadn't come into the room when she did, I would have been raped, while three grown men stood by and watched it." She put down the coffee cup, very carefully. "I can't forget how I felt, how afraid I was, how dirty I felt afterward. There were police and questions and..." She stopped.

Jackie hadn't said anything. But she was listening. "But he wouldn't do that to me," she faltered, not as sure of herself as she'd sounded earlier.

Gaby forced her mind out of the past and into the present. "Your boyfriend's victim," she said very softly, "said that he told her he loved her, too, before he raped her. There were witnesses." Her face tautened, because she remembered her own horror as she related what Mr. Everett had told her. "He wanted an audience, you see." She met Jackie's eyes. "She was a virgin. He told the police he liked having his friends watch. Except that two of them were sickened by what he did, and they went to the police. And it probably wasn't the first time he'd done it. Mr. Everett discovered two other arrests where the charges were dropped and the complainants suddenly had new luxury cars and fat bank accounts. His parents are quite wealthy."

Jackie's face was pale. She knew her boyfriend loved her. Keith would never do any such thing to her. Of course he wouldn't. But he had tried to pull her pants off with her standing against a wall, with people walking by, and he'd said things to her... Gaby had interrupted him. If she hadn't, there was no telling what might have happened. Jackie had no willpower when Keith started touching her. She wouldn't have been able to stop; she wanted him too badly.

But what Gaby said made her uneasy. She was uncertain, now. Nervous.

Gaby saw that. She didn't want to push the subject too hard. Let the girl think about it for a while, think about what could happen.

Jackie drew in a breath and finished her meal. "But he didn't serve much time," she said.

"No," Gaby replied. "His parents, as I mentioned, are well-to-do. They managed to get the charges dropped." She hesitated. "The two witnesses who'd testified suddenly developed memory problems and withdrew their accusations. There was a retrial and he was acquitted." Gaby hated knowing that, because she was facing the same thing with her grandfather's conviction. He had access to money because of his underworld contacts. He might be acquitted, as well. Gaby might end up being arrested for placing false charges, if the old man could get an attorney good enough to convince a jury of that—a lawyer as good as Nick Chandler.

Gaby came back to the present, a little rattled, but quiet. Jackie didn't say anything. She just stared into space. "What happened to the man who attacked you?" she asked suddenly.

"He was from another country," Gaby said, hating the memories the words provoked. "He had diplomatic immunity. He just went home." She didn't add that there were four men in the room, including her assailant and her grandfather. Gaby didn't tell Jackie, either, that Grandfather had engineered the incident for profit, or that he'd been convicted, or that

Jackie's uncle's firm had defended him. She was in over her head already. She wished she'd kept her mouth shut. But she had to reach the girl before something terrible happened to her. First love was heady and sweet and dangerous.

"My mother never wanted me," Jackie said in a quiet, wounded voice. "She told me once that she'd had too much to drink at a party and never even realized she was pregnant until I started moving."

"Parents sometimes say things they don't mean," Gaby said softly.

Jackie's eyes met hers. "She meant it. Uncle Nick doesn't know. She wants him to think she's the best mother on earth, but she's not. She likes excitement. She said my father was just a friend—she didn't even love him. She was getting even with her boyfriend for going out with somebody else."

"Whatever she felt, she should never have told you that," Gaby said quietly and winced.

Jackie saw that. "Uncle Nick doesn't really want me, either," she continued, stiffening a little. "Mama's new boyfriend was all touchy-feely with me, so I called Uncle Nick and asked if I could come stay with him while Mama was in Europe. Mama brought me here and left me, just like she did the other times. I'd wanted to stay with her at first," she added, indicating that this wasn't the first time her mother had dumped her on her uncle. "I get in Uncle Nick's way a lot. He has this girlfriend..." She stopped.

Gaby felt something like a jolt to her ribs when Jackie said that. She hadn't seen much evidence of a love life in Mr. Chandler since she'd been here. He did go out at night from time to time. And then there was the phone call she'd overheard, when Nick's deep voice had gone from irritation to soft, deep velvet...

"You don't like her?" Gaby asked, trying not to sound overly curious.

"Nobody likes her," she muttered. "Tilly finds reasons to leave the apartment when she's here. Not that she's been around as much since you came to live with us," she added, glancing at Gaby. "Maybe he thinks she'll get upset if she sees another woman staying in the same apartment. She's got a horrible temper."

Gaby laughed softly. "She wouldn't see me as a threat. I don't really like men."

"I guess not," Jackie said, and for once she didn't sound belligerent. "That bodyguard, though, he's a hunk."

"Mr. Everett is very attractive," she agreed. "But even though he's employed by my grandmother, he still goes away and doesn't tell anybody where or why. *Grand-mère* thinks he still goes on covert missions with a group of mercenaries he used to belong to. He wouldn't admit it, of course."

Jackie was frowning. "You call your grandmother a French name. I'm taking French in high school," she added.

Gaby smiled. "My grandmother is very French," she replied. "She had ancestors who were beheaded in the French Revolution."

"Wow! That's so cool!"

Gaby laughed. "It isn't really something to brag about, you know."

"I don't know. They had to be subversives. I like rebels." She glanced at Gaby. "I like to go to The Snap, that retro coffeehouse. They wear black and play bongo drums and recite poetry..."

"The Snap. You never said that, when I mentioned it before," Gaby said, recalling an earlier conversation. "It's one of my favorite places in the city."

"Mine, too," Jackie laughed.

"My favorite *Star Wars* character was Darth Vader," she confided. "Don't tell your uncle, though. He'd probably fire me. I like rebels, too."

Jackie smiled, and not sarcastically. "Darth Vader was awesome. I'm kind of hung up on Kylo Ren, though."

"Same story, different generations," Gaby replied.

Jackie finished her dessert and her soft drink with a sigh and stood up. "You're not bad," she said, and then turned away and went quickly to her room, as if she regretted the soft words.

Gaby sat finishing her own lunch. She hoped she'd helped the girl escape a possibly traumatic experience. She was going to have to ask Mr. Everett to keep an eye on her, though. She'd ask her grandmother's permission first, of course, but *Grand-mère* didn't often leave the apartment and it was Gaby who was under threat. So Mr. Everett kept Gaby under surveillance most of the time. She hoped he wouldn't mind looking out for Nick Chandler's niece, as well. The minute Jackie saw her boyfriend, she was probably going to forget everything Gaby had told her and rationalize that it was all lies. The boyfriend would help her believe that.

She would have liked to talk to Jackie's uncle a little more about the boy, but she hadn't felt comfortable with him since he'd glared at the child in the elevator and stormed off when she'd asked if he didn't like children.

It was an odd reaction from a man who had his niece living with him and seemed to tolerate even her worst behavior. Why would a small child that he didn't even know cause him to go ballistic?

She could, of course, discreetly, ask Mr. Everett to look into Nick's background, but that felt sneaky. It wasn't in Gaby's nature to go behind people's backs. Well, she'd gone behind the back of Jackie's awful boyfriend, but that was for a good cause. She had no reason to probe into Nick's past. And no desire to know more about him, she told herself firmly.

A little later, there was a small commotion in the apartment. Gaby, curled up in bed with a romance novel after a calming shower, got up, put on her thick pink bathrobe over her lacy pink negligee and peered out into the hall.

"...make her leave!" a gorgeous blonde woman was demanding, stamping her foot in an expensive high-heeled shoe that exactly matched the scarlet silk dress that clung to every inch of her tall, exquisite figure.

"I'm not making her leave," Nick said calmly. "She works for me."

"Well, you can get somebody else," the woman raged.

"You think I can just walk out to the sidewalk and find someone with the credentials to do the job she's doing?" he asked darkly. He moved into view, in black tie, wearing a dinner jacket with perfectly creased slacks and a spotless white shirt with a black tie. He looked devastating.

"There are employment agencies!" the woman almost shouted at him.

"I told you..." He glanced down the hall and saw Gaby standing there in a thick bathrobe with her long, chestnut hair waving around her shoulders. The lacy pink negligee was just visible in the opening of the robe at her throat. He just stared. She was beautiful.

"Now what?" the blonde demanded, her eyes following his. She gaped at Gaby. "She's sleeping with you!" she yelled at Nick. "I knew it, I knew it! No wonder you wouldn't let me come here anymore...!"

Gaby came out of her room and into the living room, her expression calm and serene. "I'm Gaby Dupont," she said softly. "I work for Mr. Chandler, but I have to live in because I don't work a nine-to-five job here. I can assure you that I have nothing to do with him on a personal basis." She smiled. "I don't like men. Not in the way you're thinking of."

The blonde had the wind taken out of her sails. She just stood there, her face still showing red traces of temper, her blue eyes wide as she stared at Gaby.

"I tried to tell you that, Mara," Nick told the blonde woman. "You wouldn't listen."

"He's rich and handsome." Mara faltered. "Every woman wants him."

Gaby just looked at her. "Not every woman."

"Well," Mara said. She calmed down. After all, the other woman was wearing a very concealing garment and she didn't act guilty or smitten. In fact, she hadn't looked at Nick once.

"I'll get back to my novel," Gaby said, smiling. "I hope you both have a lovely evening."

"Thanks," Nick said gruffly.

She didn't even look at him. She nodded to Mara and went back down the hall to her room. She closed the door behind her.

"I told you," Nick said to Mara, and his black eyes flashed angrily at her.

"Well, I didn't know, did I?" Mara muttered. She shifted her evening bag. "Are we ready to go?"

"Of course. Just a minute."

He walked down the hall past Gaby's door to Jackie's. "I'll be out until about one," he called through the door.

"Okay," Jackie replied.

He walked back to Mara, not even hesitating at Gaby's door. He was remembering the conversation they'd had at the coffee shop. Gaby was afraid of men. He wondered why. Well, it was not his problem. Gaby only worked for him.

★ ★ ★

But later that night, when he dropped Mara off at her apartment, his plans for the evening were suddenly and blatantly nipped in the bud. He kissed Mara and felt absolutely nothing. She realized it at the same time he did and pulled away.

"It's that woman!" she accused, red-faced and shouting. "You lied!"

"I didn't lie," he said, trying to be reasonable but quickly losing his temper. He'd never had an issue, not in years, and here he was with a beautiful woman and his body wouldn't cooperate. "I'm just tired," he lied, his voice heavy. "I'm having fits with Jackie."

"Oh." She calmed down. "Send her back to her mother. You give your sister far too much consideration, Nick."

He shrugged. "She's the only living relative I have," he pointed out. "I can't turn my back on her, or her child."

"Some child. Fifteen going on forty."

"Sometimes it seems that way," he confessed. "She's got this boyfriend..."

"Is that it?" She laughed. "Get her on the pill or the shot and let her do what she wants to. It's the twenty-first century, you know. Women can do what they like."

As Mara did, certainly, and not only with him. He knew that she wasn't particularly faithful. It wasn't in her passionate nature. She liked variety.

"You look like a Victorian father," Mara chided.

Father. The word went through him like hot lead. He turned away. "I've got a long day ahead tomorrow. I'll call you."

"You could stay," she said. "We could try again later."

He looked back at her from the door. "I'm tired." He forced a smile. "Have a good night."

She glared at the closed door. "Oh, sure," she drawled sarcastically. A minute later, she pulled out her cell phone and dialed the number of a cute financier she liked to spend time with.

Nick pulled off his jacket and his tie. He felt betrayed. He glared around at the apartment, hating the whole world. He wasn't capable with a woman. That was a first. He glared down the hall toward Gaby's closed door. It was her fault. He didn't understand why, but he knew it. She'd made him uncomfortable, by coming out and confronting Mara. She'd been quiet and calm and honest with the older woman. She didn't like men. So what? It wasn't his problem.

He remembered the glimpse of her he'd had, of the pale pink negligee under that enveloping garment that disguised her exquisite figure. Surely he wasn't attracted to her! She was old-fashioned, out of touch with the modern world. She'd had a traumatic experience, and it showed from time to time. He wondered what had happened to her. An overbearing date, probably.

She'd mentioned that Mr. Everett was her grandmother's bodyguard, but he was always around when Gaby had to go anywhere. That was curious.

He unbuttoned the top buttons of his dress shirt and sat down on the couch with a heavy sigh. It had been a long week and it wasn't over yet. He was still working on the case of the wife trying to kill her idiot husband, who still believed in her in spite of what she'd tried to do to him. Couples never ceased to amaze him. He'd come across total psychopaths a time or two over the years, people who were nice enough alone, but who turned into monsters when they were in a room together.

He wasn't certain how he was going to handle the case.

It wore on him. Then he thought about Jackie and became morose. He'd been landed with an overstimulated midteen who thought the sun rose and set on a career criminal. The boy had landed her with three new felony counts and if she didn't buck up and stay away from Keith, she was going to end badly, perhaps in prison. He might not be able to save her. This time there were eyewitnesses to the mugging her boyfriend had involved her in, and they were respectable people. It was going to take some work to keep her on the outside. He'd saved her bacon on earlier charges. This time, he might not be able to. How would he explain it to her mother. He glowered at the floor. *Her mother wouldn't care*, he admitted to himself. To her, Jackie was nothing more than a burden. She'd told him once, in confidence, that if she'd known she was pregnant sooner, she'd have had the pregnancy terminated. She didn't want children. She was having too much fun being a rounder.

But there were reasons for her attitude. His sister had gone through hell as a young woman. Their father hadn't spared her because she was female. She got the same brutal whippings that Nick got. After their father's death, she'd run wild, finally freed from the restrictive and frightening environment in which she'd grown up. She was still wild, still rebelling. But her child was paying the price. Miranda was running away from her problems with the lover of the month. Eventually, the love affair would wear thin and she'd come home. But that wasn't going to happen immediately and meanwhile Nick was landed with the unruly teenager.

He recalled what Gaby had said about Jackie, that she needed to know that actions had consequences. He hadn't paid much attention to the girl, who was always breaking rules, hanging out with unsavory people, being a royal pain in the butt. Her mother paid her even less attention. Jackie had nobody to love her, Gaby had told him, and so she went looking for love in a bad place and found Keith.

It had made Nick feel guilty. He hadn't given Jackie much structure, now or the other times Miranda had dumped the child on him. At least she hadn't been around as a very young child. He'd have gone mad.

He kept remembering Gaby's expression when he'd turned away from the pretty little toddler in the elevator. She didn't understand the anguish that drove him, the horror of what had happened to his child. He couldn't tell anyone. He never had, not even his sister. Of course, by that time, Miranda was well and truly off with the jet set to whatever romantic adventure she could find, with whatever wealthy man she could seduce. A dead distant relative had left a legacy that he and Miranda split between them. But Miranda didn't really need it. She had plenty of the world's luxuries from whatever millionaire she was seducing at the time. She'd been gone during the turbulent period of Nick's life. But then, she never bothered asking about Nick's private life, anyway, which was just as well.

The past haunted him. He'd tried therapy once or twice, but it hadn't helped. The guilt ate at him like an acid. It stood between him and everything he tried to do. The police sergeant had tried to explain to him that the woman he'd married had mental issues. It was even documented. He hadn't known. But he should have suspected something. She'd never been quite normal. She started fights for no reason. From time to time, she'd assaulted him with everything from lamps to vases.

He'd been much younger then, unaware of the struggles mentally ill people faced on a daily basis. He'd been in love, too much in love to admit that there were problems with the relationship.

When the baby had been born, he'd managed to get Glenna

to marry him. But she'd hated it. She refused to wear the wedding ring he'd given her, even to use her married name. She wanted to be free. It had been her mantra since the day they'd started dating. She liked men. Lots of men. Singly or in sets. He hadn't known. He'd been living in a daydream of the perfect marriage. He and Glenna had a baby girl, Samantha, and they were going to live happily ever after. He was in law school, going at night while working the docks in the daytime. His home life was such a change from the misery and fear of his childhood. He was going to make sure that Samantha had everything she ever needed, that she'd never be afraid in her own home. He was going to spoil her rotten.

The problem with his love for his child was that Glenna was violently jealous of anyone or anything that stood between herself and Nick. He hadn't realized that, either, at first. Only as time went by did he notice that she'd managed to separate him from his sister and all of his friends, wearing away at the connections until she broke them loose.

Why did he need friends when he had Glenna and the baby? she wondered aloud. And didn't he notice that his friends had their eyes on Glenna? She even told him that a couple of them had made blatant passes at her and encouraged her to leave Nick.

Young, idealistic, certain that he was living the romance of all time, Nick had given in to her every wish.

He sat down heavily and cursed himself for his lack of foresight. He hadn't realized what sort of problems he was creating. When she was lucid, Glenna was the perfect woman, attentive and caring and loving, even passionate. He couldn't get enough of her. He lived to get home from work and lose himself in her arms.

When Samantha came along, he had the gold at the end of the rainbow. Life was perfect. He and Glenna and the baby would live happily ever after. He'd get his law degree, get into practice, make a lot of money and give Glenna all the things she wanted.

Then had come the argument. He was spending too much time at his books, she complained. He had no time for her. When he wasn't studying, he was holding the baby, rocking her, talking to her. Glenna was pushed to the background, left alone while Nick indulged his own pleasures.

It had seemed like just a mild complaint. Glenna was frequently snippy and critical of him. One day he noticed that she'd alienated every person who came to the house where they lived. Even the friends from law school had been evicted because she said all the talking while they studied together was disturbing the baby's rest.

They'd gone to another student's apartment to study, and then she complained that Nick was neglecting his family for his stupid college classes.

He didn't know that she was using drugs. She was careful not to do them around him. But her mental issues were amplified by the drugs and her personality began to disintegrate before his very eyes.

One day, when he was just home from a hard day at work, getting ready to go to law school that evening, Glenna told him that she'd had enough of being ignored. If he didn't stop it, she was going to do something drastic.

He'd assumed it was just another threat. He'd smiled and tried to kiss her, but she'd pulled away and stormed out of the room.

A little later, he stopped by Samantha's room to kiss her goodbye before he left for class, but she wasn't in her little bed. Curious, he went looking. Perhaps she'd gone to find her mother.

The front door was open. That was odd. He walked out,

checking his watch worriedly because he was due in class very soon. Across the street was a huge high-rise under construction. He'd taken Samantha over there one day, just to the sidewalk, and told her all about buildings and how much work it took to put one up. She'd laughed, her blond hair blowing in the wind, her blue eyes shining. She'd patted his cheek with her little chubby hand and chanted his name. "Da Da."

He looked up and, with horror, saw that Glenna had started one of the elevators that the workers used to get to the top. She had Samantha in her arms.

Nick broke into a dead run. He'd been thinner in those days, very quick on his feet. He could move very fast when he had to. He didn't know why Glenna was taking their child up to the top floor of an unfinished building. His blood ran cold as he remembered the threat Glenna had made.

He pushed the button three times before the elevator finally started moving. It took forever to get to the top. He could hear Glenna. She was laughing. The sound chilled him.

He got off the elevator at the top floor and moved cautiously along one small edge of flooring that had been laid to give the workers a platform. Glenna, with a laughing Samantha in her arms, was standing on the very edge, looking at him.

"It's chilly out here," he said in a calming voice. "Sam will catch cold."

"She won't ever be cold again," Glenna said in a perfectly calm voice. She smiled at him. "And you'll never forget this moment as long as you live. I told you I'd do something drastic if you kept ignoring me."

"Da Da," Samantha chanted, laughing as she looked at him.

"Yes. Da Da," Glenna drawled sarcastically. "She can't even say Mama. Ever notice? I get no attention at all! I got rid of all your stupid friends, and nothing changed. You're never here! I'm tired of being shoved aside for this child and your job and your very important education!"

"Glenna," he began, because she looked wild. "Let's go down and talk."

"Go down." She laughed. "That's a good idea, Nick. Yes. Let's go down."

She turned, with Samantha still in her arms, and jumped.

Nick groaned out loud. He sat forward, with his face in his hands, reliving the agony, over and over and over again. He could hear Samantha scream as she realized what her mother had done. He could hear Glenna scream...

He drew in a ragged breath. His eyes were terrible to look into. The horror of that day would live with him forever, just as Glenna had predicted. There was a police report. A kindly police sergeant who spoke softly to him. There was the coroner's report, citing all the drugs that had been in Glenna's system when she killed herself and her child. It wasn't his fault. Everybody said so, even Glenna's poor mother, who'd come to the funeral and tried to comfort Nick. But he couldn't be comforted. He couldn't stand to be touched. He was encased in ice then, and for a long time afterward. His baby. His beautiful little Samantha, gone forever.

He'd loved Glenna, but Samantha had been his very heart. To lose both of them in such a way had been the worst single tragedy of his life. Later, with Glenna's mother's prompting, he'd been sent to visit with the psychologist who'd been treating Glenna since childhood. He explained to Nick that the woman had been suicidal from a very young age. She'd made several attempts to end her life. After one of them, her poor tormented father had taken his own life, unable to stand the stress any longer. Glenna hadn't even gone to the funeral. She had no real feelings, as normal people had them. She was concerned only with her own, something her mother had tried to tell Nick at the beginning of his relationship with Glenna.

The psychologist added that Glenna had stopped coming to see him several years earlier, assuring him that she'd found a chemical means of sustaining her bouts of deep depression. He hadn't realized that she was talking about illegal drugs. It had led to the bad behavior that had culminated in a murder-suicide on the top of that unfinished building.

So Nick had listened, smiled, thanked the man and gone home. And he'd stayed drunk for two weeks.

It had been Glenna's mother who'd come to find him, straightened him up, made him go on. He'd gone back to work, a job he hadn't lost because people understood why he'd stayed out of touch. He'd also gone back to law school, although the absence had caused him to repeat a course. He'd toughed his way through it.

From the time of Glenna's and Sam's deaths, getting his law degree and building a practice had been his only focus in life. There had been occasional women, but nobody serious. Even now, Mara wasn't a serious relationship. She was a body in bed when he needed one. No woman was ever again going to get the hold on him that Glenna had.

He remembered Glenna's mother with love and sadness. It hadn't been long after Nick's return from drunken oblivion that the woman had died of a heart attack, sudden and catastrophic. Nick had seen to the burial, because there was no family left to do it. He still put flowers on her grave from time to time; and on the graves of Glenna and Sam, who were buried near her in the same cemetery.

The experience, as terrible as it was, turned his focus to success, because he had nothing left in his empty life except the law. He worked hard, graduated, got a job as a public defender that rapidly turned into bigger and better cases until he was able to start his own law firm and become one of the best, and wealthiest, criminal attorneys in the country. But his life was still empty. He was the same tormented man who'd watched Glenna and Samantha fall from that top floor; he was just richer.

He heard a door open. He didn't even look up. If it was Jackie, he was going to bed. He'd had enough turmoil for one evening. Remembering the past hadn't helped.

"Mr. Chandler, are you all right?"

He looked up. Gaby was standing there, barefoot, in her thick, concealing robe, looking concerned.

He glared at her. She was a reminder of all the things he hadn't had in his life since the death of Glenna's mother, years and years ago. Comfort. Concern. Sympathy. Compassion. None of his brief affairs had given him anything other than temporary relief.

"No," he said after a minute. "I'm not all right."

He looked angry. His dark eyes were flashing. His face was set in hard lines. She tried not to look down, where his white shirt was unbuttoned and thick, curling black hair peeked out. He was a handsome, sensuous man, and Gaby didn't want to dwell on that. She wanted nothing to do with men. Not physically.

She pulled the robe tighter around herself, feeling self-conscious and stupid. She hesitated, her toes digging into the thick carpet. "Want some coffee?" she asked after a minute of being scowled at.

He drew in a harsh breath. "No, I don't want any damned coffee!"

She swallowed, hard. Her face colored. She looked hunted, like a deer in the headlights of a speeding car.

That made him feel guilty, too. He sighed. "Yes," he

amended, and softened his tone. "Yes, I'd like coffee. I'm sorry."

She knew that he was a man who rarely apologized for anything. It made her feel better. "Okay. I'll make some."

"Make it strong," he said shortly. "I have work to do in the study."

She walked into the kitchen and started the coffee maker.

He sat down at the kitchen table, worn-out, feeling every year of his age. He could imagine that he probably looked it, too. Nightclubbing with Mara wasn't doing his health any good. He drove himself. He'd never lost the habit of work. It had defined him for far too long.

He watched Gaby move around the kitchen. She was graceful. She was beautiful, in her way, and not from just a physical standpoint. She had empathy of a sort he'd rarely encountered.

Nick thought about the client he was defending from a brutal, murderous wife, and he laughed. "You'd never try to run your husband down with a car," he murmured dryly.

SEVEN

Gaby turned with the sugar bowl in her hands, her eyebrows arched over twinkling pale blue eyes. "Excuse me?"

He leaned back in the chair, sensuous with his shirt unbuttoned and his sleeves rolled up, smiling faintly as he studied her. "The man I'm defending from his homicidal wife," he reminded her. "She's still looking for ways to kill him and he can't wait to get out of the hospital and get back home to give her another shot at it."

She laughed. "Talk about things you can't fix," she murmured as she put the sugar bowl on the table.

"Things you can't fix?" He wasn't getting it.

"Stupid," she explained. "You can't fix stupid. It's something I heard a comedian say on TV."

He chuckled. His voice was deep and soft like velvet. His dark eyes twinkled as he studied her. He looked down. She had pretty feet. "No slippers?" he asked.

She made a face. "This is how I am in my own apartment,"

she said. "I hate shoes. I always go barefoot. I used to do it when I went on digs with my parents…" She stopped dead, the memory painful. She turned back to get the cream she'd poured into its container. She put that on the table, as well.

He winced. "That would have been hard, losing both parents at once."

She nodded. "I loved my parents very much. Almost as much as they loved each other." She smiled sadly. "Neither of them could have lived without the other. My grandmother said she'd never seen two people as much in love, even after years of marriage and a child."

"Your grandmother is elderly?"

"Oh, yes, but you'd never know it," she laughed. "She's taking tango classes." Her eyes twinkled. "She's seventy-two."

He burst out laughing. "She must be a character."

"Oh, she is," she agreed.

The coffee was ready. She poured it into two mugs—Nick hated formal china—and set them on the table, along with napkins and spoons. She had to be careful about what she told him. It was much too late to confess why she'd taken the job he had open, instead of asking him point-blank if his firm was going to represent her vile grandfather. She'd just have to live with the consequences. But she wasn't ready to have it come out. Not yet. She liked Nick. She could like him too much, another reason she'd have to be careful.

She sat down at the table, a little uncomfortable about being in the kitchen in her nightgown and robe with a man. It was a new experience.

He put cream in his coffee and studied her surreptitiously. She was antsy. He recalled what she'd told him, and later his date, Mara, about not liking men. She was nervous because she wasn't dressed. It touched him, when very few things about women did touch him these days.

"That was nice, what you said to Mara earlier tonight," he said after a minute.

She drew in a breath. "I hate arguments," she said simply. "My grandfather was always yelling at my grandmother about something."

His eyes narrowed. "You love your grandmother. It shows in the way you speak of her."

She nodded. "I love her very much. I owe her more than I can ever repay."

"And your grandfather?"

"She divorced him. I don't know where he is now." Not quite the truth, but she didn't know exactly where in Chicago he lived. "I don't care, either," she added shortly.

He leaned back in the chair with his coffee in one big hand. "You don't like men. Why?"

The question surprised her. She flushed and stared down into her cup. "I don't talk about it."

He'd prosecuted rape cases in his younger days at the bar, when he gave up being a public defender to work as an assistant district attorney. He knew the signs. He wasn't going to come out and say it, but he had a good idea of why Gaby was afraid of men.

"It wasn't a wise decision, you know," he said after a minute. She looked up, curious. "Coming to work for a man you didn't know," he explained, "where you had to live in. I could have been anybody. Just because a man works in a respectable profession doesn't necessarily mean he's trustworthy. I could give you examples of that from a dozen news stories in recent months."

She smiled faintly. "I know." She cocked her head and stared at him. "But I knew you were trustworthy."

His dark eyebrows arched. "How?"

"The Goth Girl," she said, and grinned. "If you were an

evil man, she'd never have gone on living here. She's got too much grit." She smiled. "I like her. She's honest and smart and sassy and she says exactly what she means." Her face softened. "If I ever had a child, there are worse role models."

His face closed up at once. He threw down the rest of his coffee and got to his feet, his face drawn into harsh lines. "I have work to do."

"It must have been something terrible," she said softly, and winced when he glared at her. "I'm so sorry, Mr. Chandler," she added quietly. "You're a good man."

"No, I'm not," he bit off.

"I don't believe that," she replied. "You've got your niece here. She's a handful, but you tolerate her and do everything you can to protect her. Actions truly speak louder than words."

"You don't know what the hell you're talking about," he said icily. "And my private life is none of your damned business."

She cocked her head and her eyes twinkled. "Ooh, curses and fire and brimstone. You should stand on street corners and direct all that fire and fury toward the lost souls of the business world."

He glared harder.

"You could get a megaphone, too," she added. "I mean, your voice does carry, but more people could hear you."

"Five."

Her eyebrows arched.

His eyes narrowed. "Four."

"I get it." She got up, put the dishes in the sink and went around the table the other way to the hall. "Don't think I'm running away!" she called as she got out of the range of fire. "My people fought off outlaws and hostile animals in Texas for five generations! I am not a coward…!"

"Three!"

Her door slammed. In fact, she locked it. Audibly.

He stood there, looking toward the hall. A big smile broke out on his face. He went into his office and closed the door, chuckling to himself.

The Goth Girl was hostile again by the weekend. She'd been with Keith, who'd convinced her that she was the love of his life, that he'd never let her be convicted of a felony, not even if he had to confess that the whole thing, robbing those people, was his idea.

Jackie had no idea that she was being played by an expert. At fifteen, she was still very naive, despite her street-smart attitudes. Keith loved her. Everything would be okay. And her uncle's nosy administrative assistant could just keep her nose out of Jackie's business!

Gaby noticed the attitude, of course, and she was wise enough not to complicate matters by trying to convince the younger woman that her boyfriend was playing her. She didn't try to talk to Jackie. She just smiled as the girl went past and concentrated on her job.

Nick was livid when he came home two days later, his chiseled mouth compressed into a thin line, his face hard with anger.

He slammed his briefcase down on his desk, making Gaby jump, because she was knee-deep in filing and hadn't heard him come in.

"If I have a heart attack, my grandmother will have you up in stocks on the town square and doused with recycled grass!" she burst out.

He didn't smile. He glared at her. He was having trouble

concentrating, for the first time in ages, and it was because of her. He didn't like it.

She noted his lack of conversation, shook her head and just went back to work. She was wearing a white V-necked sweater with dark slacks, her hair tied behind her back with a white ribbon. She looked young and pretty and very neat. Not at all sexy. But Nick reacted to her in ways that made him furious. He couldn't understand why. She was an innocent, but she could tie him in knots. While his lover, a truly sophisticated and gifted lover, couldn't even get him interested lately.

"Don't tell me," Gaby murmured as she noted the title of a book she was placing on the shelf. "The man had another close call."

He drew in a sharp, angry breath. "She sent him roses."

"Well, that sounds nice," she remarked, turning toward him.

"He has asthma and he's allergic to flowers," he bit off. "He thinks she's just trying to make up."

She rolled her eyes.

"If she offs him, I'll have her up for murder one if I have to get the local DA drunk in order to have her prosecuted."

Her eyes widened. "Of all the unethical remarks...!"

"It constantly amazes me," he muttered, throwing off his suit coat. "The utter stupidity of men when it comes to women."

"Not you, of course," she murmured dryly.

"No, not me," he said shortly. "I know too much about women to fall into the trap ever again."

She looked at the title of another book and marked it on the chart she was sketching. "No surprise there," she murmured absently.

"Where's Jackie?"

She looked up blankly, her mind still on the cataloging. "She went out a few minutes ago. She said she had to check with a schoolmate about some homework."

"She's got a cell phone," he said curtly. "So have most of her friends."

She sighed. "Mr. Chandler, I'm cataloging books. I didn't hire on as a nanny."

"I wish I had one," he shot back. "A retired Marine Corps drill instructor would do nicely."

She smothered a chuckle. "Yes, well, I'm not so sure that a lion tamer wouldn't be a better choice."

"Shhh!" he hushed her. "If anybody hears you, we'll be mobbed by animal protection societies."

She just shook her head. "Honestly, you can't say anything these days without offending someone. You mark my words, all this smothering of different attitudes will lead to even worse violence than we've already had. It's like covering up an infected finger with a bandage and no antibiotic. After a while, it will fester and burst."

He made a face. "Not a pretty analogy, but concise," he had to admit.

"People won't stop being what they are. They'll just hold it inside and hide it. Eventually, there will be a backlash of biblical proportions."

"I hope I'll be in a nursing home by then," he muttered.

"Now you really sound like a man in his fifties," she said, just to annoy him.

He glared at her.

She sat back on her heels and studied him. "It's all work with you, isn't it?" she asked somberly. "Well, work and your girlfriend, but you don't go out much and you spend all hours shut up in your office when you're even home."

His face hardened. "You're here to catalog books, not me."

She held out both hands. "Pardon me for breathing." She cocked her head, and her pale blue eyes were somber. "You're a heart attack looking for an emergency room," she said quietly.

The glare got worse.

"Fine," she sighed. "Pretend that your life is wonderful. You don't have a care in the world. You're not haunted by the past. Your niece is a perfect role model." She glanced at him. "Your latest client is beloved by his wife, who only wants the best for him."

He let out a curse of some heat.

"Mr. Chandler!" she gasped, standing up, enraged.

"I will not be psychoanalyzed by the hired help!" he said arrogantly.

"I don't have a license," she pointed out. "And it isn't psychoanalyzing just to comment that a man is working himself into an early grave."

He didn't reply, but his expression was worth a thousand angry words.

"Okay," she said, conceding defeat. "I'll quit. But you should talk to somebody. Your girlfriend. A colleague you trust. A doctor. Somebody."

"About what?" he asked, almost purring. "Do give me the benefit of your extensive life experience."

She knew when to quit. She pushed back a tendril of escaped chestnut hair. "No, thanks," she replied. "I don't have the medical insurance. Speaking of which, does your client have life insurance? If I were him, I'd name another beneficiary and make sure she knew it."

He let out a breath. "Yes, he does, and he blew up like a balloon when I gave him the same advice. Horrors! How could he leave his poor wife penniless if he died suddenly?"

She cocked her head and stared up at him. Her eyes twinkled. "Oh, for the old days of rubber hoses and hot lamps and gifted investigators in smoky rooms..."

He didn't laugh, but his eyes did. "Were you always this incorrigible, or is it a by-product of the work you're doing here?"

"A by-product, certainly," she agreed. "I've been corrupted by people with piercings and black nail polish."

His eyebrows arched.

"You could do with a nice earring," she said, noting his big ears. "It might make you look more approachable to your clients."

"Hell will freeze over first."

"I imagine it would." She shook her head. "Mr. Chandler, you're a lost cause. I'll bet you already have ulcers."

His eyes narrowed and he glared at her.

She sighed. "I quit. If you don't mind, I'm going to the park for my lunch hour."

"The park?"

"The pigeons look forward to my weekly visits," she pointed out. "Often they bring relatives from out of town, as well."

"Relatives." He was nodding.

"I only feed them rare imported European breadcrumbs from the best stale bread."

He turned away before he burst out laughing. "Go away."

"I was planning to..." She hesitated as the hall clock struck one o'clock. She frowned. "It's one o'clock. Why are you home?"

"I live here."

She gave him a glowering look.

He sighed. "Apparently it's a holiday," he muttered. "Nobody except me was in the office."

She pulled out her cell phone and glanced at it. "Well, yes, it is a holiday," she said.

"Which one?"

She shrugged. "Who cares?" she asked, and grinned at him. "But actually, it's Memorial Day, twenty-fifth of May."

He made a rough sound in his throat. "I'm going sailing. I'll leave a note for Jackie. You'll be back in an hour, right?"

"Oh, yes. I only have so many breadcrumbs."

"I hate pigeons," he muttered.

"That's because they don't bring their relatives to see you," she said haughtily. "Pigeon envy, that's what it is," she added, and went to get her coat.

She didn't hear Nick's reluctant chuckle as he went to his bedroom to change clothes. She left the apartment before he did.

"I can actually see you, you know," Gaby said out loud as she sat on a park bench under some trees, tossing breadcrumbs to the pigeons gathered nearby.

"Impossible," came the dry reply. "I'm disguised as a tree."

"Anyway, I'm on public display. What could happen in broad daylight?"

"Want to know?" Tanner Everett asked, hands in his slacks pockets, his one blue eye twinkling as he came around in front of her. He proceeded to list things that had been done to people in recent months due to civil unrest in cities.

"Okay, I give up," she said. "But there's no unrest here. Except for the pigeons, of course," she added. "Any minute now, they're going to start battling it out for the last few crumbs."

"Birds have more sense than most people do."

"Cynic."

"Count on it."

She glanced at him. He seemed more preoccupied than he usually was. "Problems with my grandmother?" she asked.

He sighed. "Personal ones. My mother wants to see me. I've been trying to think of ways to manage that. I can't go home."

She frowned. He never spoke of personal issues, but this one seemed to be disturbing him. "Should I ask why?"

"My father wanted me to stay home and run the family ranch, back in Texas. My younger brother has the cattle smarts in the family, not me, but I'm the eldest. Family tradition, you know."

"You should do what you want to do in life. It's hard enough managing that, without having to live up to someone else's pattern for your future."

He raised an eyebrow. "You have a degree in anthropology, I believe?" He was insinuating that she was following in her parents' footsteps.

"Well, yes, my parents did want me to grow up to be an anthropologist. I just never was able to see myself brushing off potsherds with a toothbrush for the rest of my life," she confessed. "When I went to college, it was like a link to them, what I studied. I miss them still."

"I imagine you never quite get over losing parents."

She glanced at Mr. Everett. "Is your father very opinionated?"

"More than me, even. He gets an idea in his head and it never gets out."

"Is there more than a brother?"

He nodded. "A baby sister. She sings like an angel. She's studying under an Italian voice instructor. She hopes to sing at the Met one day." He shook his head. "She was a hard case. She did some bad things when she was younger. Then she ran over a girl she'd persecuted and had to help get her back on her feet. It changed her. She's very different now, and she and the girl are best friends."

"Funny, how life works out problems we think are insurmountable."

"Sometimes."

She drew in a breath. "I'm trying to work up enough nerve to ask Mr. Chandler about my grandfather's hopes for a retrial. But he'll fire me if I confess who I am and why I took the job."

"A hard man," he pointed out.

"Yes. I'm sure there's a reason."

There was total silence from her companion.

She looked up, her pale blue eyes narrow. "You know why, don't you?"

He shrugged.

"Can you tell me?"

He smiled and shook his head. "Privileged information. I can't reveal it."

"You're not a priest," she pointed out.

"Still privileged," he returned. "I don't reveal things I hear about, not unless it's in the line of duty."

"Ah, well."

"You have a relative in Jacobsville, Texas, who has ties, although loose ones, to a notorious mob boss from New Jersey," he said abruptly.

"Yes. I have a cousin who married a Texas Ranger, and my great-aunt Rose, who doesn't mix with relations. They both live there. It's my great-aunt who has the mob ties. I don't know her, though. *Grand-mère* does."

"It might be worth asking her if she could find out anything about your cousin's affiliations in the city," he continued. "I have sources, but not here."

"My grandfather is far more problematic than my cousin

Robert," she pointed out. "And my cousin is never getting that property. It was left to me. I have the will and the deeds in my safe-deposit box."

"And as long as you don't keep hostages to fate, you'll be all right."

She frowned, looking up. "Hostages to fate?"

"An animal you love. A friend. A loved one. Those sorts."

"I had a cat but he died. I don't have friends," she added quietly. There had been one, but she'd married and moved to Holland. "The only person I love in the world is *Grand-mère*, and you're watching out for her." She cocked her head to one side. "So why should I be worried about Cousin Robert?"

"He's got a stepbrother who runs with the Outfit, and his father was a minor crime boss, so he has legitimate ties to organized crime. I don't know who the stepbrother is. I've tried all my sources, but none of them have any idea, and you don't just walk up to a member of the local bad-boy set and start asking questions. Even today."

She sighed. "I guess I could ask my grandmother to get in touch with my great-aunt in Jacobsville, Texas. They don't get along, but they're at least speaking." She frowned. "Why can't you ask my grandmother?" she added abruptly.

He let out a long breath. "I made an unwise comment on her tango practice."

"You did?"

"Well, she was walking around the room like a penguin. The tango is fluid, easy, sensual."

"She's seventy-two, Mr. Everett," she pointed out. "Hardly a sensual age."

"Well, of course. But if she teaches herself, and she does it wrong, there will be comments made by people who do see the mistakes, and she won't like them. She has a friend from Argentina. I assume he's the cause of the lessons."

Her heart jumped and she grinned. "She's got a crush on him?" she asked.

"I would not venture a guess."

"She has!" She laughed. "Then why don't you suggest a competent teacher?"

"She's taking lessons from an exiled South American who doesn't know a samba from a foxtrot," he said with real disgust. "He's playing her. And she won't hear a word against him."

She pursed her lips. "I can dance the tango. I'll make a point of visiting when her instructor is there and I'll point out every single mistake he's teaching her."

He burst out laughing. "Your grandmother is right. You really are incorrigible."

"It's in my blood," she said, smiling. "My mother had a smart mouth, too, and she said exactly what she thought."

"Did she look like you?"

"Oh, no. She was beautiful," she said with a sad sigh. "She had reddish-brown hair like mine and dark eyes. She was always laughing. My father adored her."

"Do you favor him?"

"Oh, yes. He had pale blue eyes like mine and chestnut-brown hair, also like mine. I guess there was a recessive gene for blue eyes on Mama's side of the family, because brown eyes are usually dominant."

"They are in my family, except for Odalie and me," he added with a laugh. "She's blonde and blue-eyed, like my mother. I got my father's dark hair and my mother's blue eyes."

"Odalie. Your sister?"

He nodded.

"Does your brother look like you?"

He shook his head. "He has dark eyes and blond-streaked brown hair. And he's as big as a house."

Mr. Everett was tall and slender, very muscular, but without it being obvious. "Do you get along with him?"

He nodded, smiling. "Very well," he said. "We text each other back and forth, and when he's in town, he comes to see me."

"Is it a big ranch?"

"One of the biggest in Texas. My father runs purebred Santa Gertrudis cattle."

"We had a relative who ranched, near Jacobsville," she recalled.

"Do you know what time it is?" came a deep, angry voice from behind them.

Nick Chandler was walking their way. He was wearing a sweater and khakis with deck shoes, and a frown that could have stopped traffic.

"It's my lunch hour," she began.

He flipped his wrist up and looked at his watch. "It was," he said. "It's two thirty."

"Oh, my gosh," she burst out, gathering up her trash. "I was feeding the pigeons," she said in her own defense.

Nick glared at Tanner Everett, who just smiled at him.

"He doesn't look as if he needs much feeding," Nick said sarcastically.

Gaby glared at him. "The pigeons, not Mr. Everett," she pointed out. "And why are you walking around spying on your employees?" she added.

"I'm on my way home, then to the hospital," he said curtly. "I had a call in the middle of Lake Michigan and I had to head back to the marina."

"Oh, dear. More flowers?" she asked, while Tanner's eyebrows arched.

"Two vases full," he said shortly. "I had them removed."

"Didn't your client object?"

"He might have, if he hadn't been having an asthma attack at the time," he said. "They were giving him adrenaline when I phoned. He'd gone into anaphylactic shock."

"I hope he doesn't have a hidden heart condition," Tanner commented. "We had a guy with us on a mission who was allergic to bee venom. He was stung and the doctor put adrenaline straight into his heart. Killed him. He had an arrhythmia that nobody knew about."

"Great," Nick muttered. "Something else to plague me. I'll go find out." He glanced at Gaby. "Jackie's in the apartment. You can unlock her door when you get there, if she hasn't picked the lock already."

Two pair of eyebrows arched.

"I caught her in the hallway with her boyfriend, just before I left the apartment to go sailing," Nick said with utter disgust. "I sent him packing and I locked her in her room. Kids!"

"I'll try to talk to her," she said.

"Wear body armor," he advised, and kept walking.

"Flowers?" Tanner asked when they were walking back toward Nick's apartment.

"He has a client whose wife is trying to kill him without obvious involvement," she said. "He's allergic to flowers."

"Why doesn't he divorce her?"

"He loves her too much," she said dryly. "It's not her fault, of course. She hasn't done a thing wrong. Nobody understands that she really loves him. She's just trying to show it."

"He has life insurance, I gather?"

"Lots, apparently."

"Some women are more mercenary than others."

"I've never understood why people don't just get jobs and save their money instead of trying to take it from other people."

He was amused by that. "Greed springs from laziness."

"I wouldn't know how to be lazy," she pointed out.

He laughed. "That makes two of us. I've got the car. I'll drop you by your boss's apartment and save you a few steps."

"I hope Jackie can't pick a lock," she said. "On the other hand, it might not be a bad idea to wait until her uncle comes home and let him unlock the door."

"She's a handful, I imagine."

"Trust me. You have no idea." And she meant it.

EIGHT

There were loud curses coming from Jackie's room, followed by violent rattling of the doorknob.

Poor Tilly was wringing her hands in the kitchen.

"How long has that been going on?" Gaby asked in a near whisper.

Tilly grimaced. "Ever since I got back from shopping, ten minutes ago," she sighed.

The rattling and the curses got louder.

"You aren't planning to let her out, are you?" Tilly asked worriedly.

"Not without armed backup," Gaby assured her. "I thought Mr. Chandler was on his way home? I saw him in the park while I was feeding the pigeons. He said he'd locked Jackie in her room."

She grimaced. "He probably stopped by Mara's apartment," she said. "When he's in a really bad mood, sometimes he…" She stopped and cleared her throat. "Well, more often than not, he comes home in an even worse mood…!"

That stung and Gaby didn't understand why. "Maybe he's at the hospital," she said.

She stopped as a key was inserted in the door outside and they both turned as it flew open to admit a furious Nick Chandler.

He relocked the door, put his hands on his hips and glared at both of them.

"I have to put away the groceries!" Tilly said at once, seeking shelter.

"Coward," Gaby whispered under her breath.

Tilly just grinned.

With a long sigh, Gaby put both hands over her head and walked toward him. "Please keep in mind that I'm unarmed," she said.

He'd been furious. But the sight of her like that warmed a cold place inside him. He didn't smile, but there was a pronounced twinkle in his dark eyes.

"Come on into the office. We'll clear away some work," he said. "Tell Tilly to bring coffee."

Gaby's eyes widened. "It's a holiday. You said so yourself."

"It's only a holiday if I say it's a holiday," he said shortly. "In this apartment, right now, it's Monday morning." His expression dared her to argue.

"Do you like roses, Mr. Chandler?" she asked sweetly.

He glared at her.

"Any allergies…?" she added with a wicked smile.

He burst out laughing.

There was a sudden rattling of a door down the hall, followed by more extremely vulgar and obscene language.

"You watch your damned mouth!" Nick shouted down the hall.

The rattling stopped.

"Pot," Gaby said under her breath.

NOTORIOUS   131

He stared at her.

"Calling the kettle black," she finished the old adage. "You're cussing."

"I don't use obscene language. And she wouldn't, if she wasn't trying to hang out with a street-smart jailbird who should be put away!" He'd raised his voice.

A belligerent grumble penetrated the door down the hall.

She moved a little closer. "Bad choice of words," she said. "You're encouraging her."

He scowled. "What?"

She motioned him toward his office.

"Tilly, bring coffee!" he called before he followed her into the room and perched on the edge of his big oak desk. "Okay, explain that."

"The more you denounce the boy, the more she'll want him," she said. "It's human nature."

"Don't tell me," he said sarcastically. "You took sociology and psychology courses in college."

"I had a friend my freshman year," she replied. "She was a minister's daughter. Sang in the choir at church, belonged to all the good youth organizations, lived her faith. Then she got mixed up with a boy who'd been in prison. She was very naive. He told her how beautiful she was, how her family was holding her back, making a laughingstock of her. Her parents tried to tell her that the boy was ice-cold, that he had no faith, that he didn't know how to love anyone. The more they talked about him, the more she listened to him. He said she needed to grow up and act her age. So she did." She shook her head. The memory was sad. "Long story short, she got pregnant. Her parents would have taken her back, even so, but the boy told her that if she didn't get rid of the child, he'd do something to make sure she couldn't have it. She didn't believe him." Her eyes closed, missing the tormented look on Nick's face. "He pushed her down a flight of stairs. She lost the baby. A week later, she jumped in the river and drowned herself."

He'd turned away. She was walking on broken bones and she didn't even know it. He knew what it was to lose a child. She had no idea about the dark secrets in his past.

"So sometimes you can push too hard and it backfires," she finished, curious about his sudden withdrawal.

He rammed his hands into his pockets and stared out the window, unseeing.

Before she could question his odd behavior, Tilly came in the door with a tray. "Here you go. I made cookies, so I put some of those on here, too. Chocolate chip," she added. She glanced at Nick, taciturn and unresponsive, and looked a question at Gaby, who just shrugged.

"Thanks, Tilly," Gaby said.

"You're welcome."

Tilly left. Gaby sat down on the couch and poured coffee into two mugs. "The cookies look good," she said, her eyes wary on her boss's broad back.

He drew in a long breath. It was hard, wrestling with the dark past. He couldn't get Samantha's face out of his mind, the last time he'd seen it. He was in hell.

"Boss?" Gaby repeated.

"What?" He turned blindly, his mind still in limbo.

"Chocolate chip cookies," she repeated. "Hot coffee?"

He grimaced. "Oh."

He sat down in his easy chair on the other side of the coffee table and took a cookie from the platter, along with the coffee Gaby had poured for him. He didn't speak.

Gaby sipped coffee. He looked hunted. She didn't think his client was responsible, either. There was something terrible in his past, so terrible that he couldn't even speak of it, and it involved a child. She'd worked that out for herself. But she could see that it wasn't worth her job to do any more probing.

His expression was acutely painful to her. She liked him far too much. She was keeping secrets of her own, that she didn't dare share with him after concealing her identity for so long. He was going to be furious when he found out who her grandfather was. In fact, it might push him into defending her grandfather, because he'd be so outraged at her behavior. She hadn't considered that before, and she could feel the blood draining out of her face.

"And what the hell's your problem?" he asked abruptly. "You look like you've seen a ghost."

"Oh, yes, it's just over there," she said, with mock horror. "It's the ghost of obsolete typewriters haunting the place!"

He glared at her. "The typewriter is not obsolete. It's electronic."

"It was obsolete twenty years ago," she said sweetly. "It's been replaced by computers."

"Show me a computer that I can slide a form into and type on," he retorted.

"Gladly. All I need is a spreadsheet program and a computer."

He got up, indicated that she was to precede him to the desk and opened a drawer. "Keyboard," he pointed out, closing the drawer. He indicated a tower on the carpeted floor under the desk. "Computer," he added. "Printer." He pointed to it. "Scanner." He indicated that. "And base phone with answering machine. All very modern."

She gave him a glowering look. "I haven't been asked to type anything so obviously I haven't been searching for the computer. Which is a good thing, because I'd have gone goofy looking for the keyboard. Who keeps a keyboard in a drawer?"

"An attorney who needs desk space to look over briefs," he returned blandly.

"I give up."

"Can you type?" he added.

"Only a hundred words a minute," she said absently as she sipped coffee. "I used to be faster, but *Grand-mère* likes her messages handwritten. She says typed ones are too impersonal."

"Your grandmother sounds like a fascinating person."

She laughed. "She is."

"Does she have other grandchildren?"

She shook her head with a sad smile. "My father was her only child." She looked into her coffee cup. "She said that life was unfair when a parent had to outlive its child. But she had me. She said I was the only thing that kept her sane after the accident."

She was interrupted by the hard slam of the coffee mug on the coffee table. Nick got up, not looking at her. "I'll get my briefcase. If you can type, you can work up a brief for me. My administrative assistant at the office apparently believes in holidays, too."

He walked out without another word. She stared after him, curious and unsettled.

"I don't know how to type a legal brief," she said when he walked back in.

"That book," he pointed to one of the law books that contained forms.

She pulled it off the shelf. "Yes?" she said, holding it up. "There are a few hundred pages of forms?"

He stared at her.

"I'm not a lawyer!"

"I noticed. You've filed the criminal code and civil code

books intermittently instead of separately." There were several volumes of each.

"I was actually hired to organize your library," she pointed out.

"The criminal and civil codes are part of my library."

"And why do you have civil codes anyway?" she asked. "You're a criminal attorney."

He let out a rough sigh and glared at her. "It would take too long to explain it to you."

"In that case, don't expect me to waste my valuable time explaining how to date projectile points to you," she said with mock hauteur.

"Projectile points?"

"Arrowheads, to the uninitiated."

"I think that word would apply to you more than it would to me," he said unexpectedly and with suddenly twinkling dark eyes as he studied her.

She wouldn't blush, she wouldn't blush...!

He only smiled. "I have a program on the computer that contains all the forms you might need. I'll show you."

"As soon as I get back. I'll ask Tilly for some more hot coffee while you find the form you want typed," she said curtly, and handed him the book on her way out. It wasn't sporting to make her think she'd have to find a form in a book and copy it on the typewriter. But it seemed to amuse the boss, and it drew him out of whatever memory was tormenting him. All good.

Eventually, he had to let Jackie out of her room. She was fuming. She'd been crying, so black mascara ran down her face like tears. Her spiky hair was disheveled, and her nose was red.

"How dare you lock me in my room!" she raged at her uncle.

"It was that or call the law," he pointed out. He cocked his head. "How did you like the holding cell, by the way?" he added.

She flushed. Her lips made a thin line as she worked furiously to contain the words she wanted to say.

He just nodded. "I didn't think so."

"Have you talked to the prosecutor about my case?" she asked.

"Actually, I haven't," Nick said surprisingly. His eyes narrowed. "You haven't learned yet that actions have consequences. I've bailed you out of trouble every time. But this time, I'm not doing it. You helped commit a crime. You can live with the penalty."

Jackie's face went white. "You're not serious!"

Gaby, listening, was remembering having said that to Nick before, that Jackie didn't expect consequences because she didn't have to face them. Nick certainly wasn't going to let the girl go to jail without a fight, but he was showing her the possibilities that might arise if she kept on the path she was walking.

"I'll call my mother!" Jackie raged.

"Good luck finding her," Nick said shortly. "She left Madrid with her new boyfriend and didn't leave a forwarding address. And her cell phone number has been changed."

Jackie swallowed. Hard. She just stared at her uncle with faint anguish, trying to conceal the fear and the pain of it.

Gaby winced.

Jackie saw that and fought tears. The older woman had been an adversary, a sometimes ally, a quiet listener. She cared. It was painful to realize that a total stranger had more feeling for her than her own mother did. And certainly more than her cold-eyed uncle was showing her at the moment.

She didn't say a word. She went back into her room and closed the door. She didn't even slam it.

Gaby moved closer to him, but not too close. He was affecting her. She didn't like it or understand it, and she certainly didn't know how to handle the emotions he was kindling in her. "You're not going to really let her go to jail, are you?"

He cocked an eyebrow. "She's a juvenile."

She blinked. "Yes."

"And it's her first real offense. She won't do time. Maybe a short probation, probably not even that. But I'm not telling her so. And neither are you." His dark eyes narrowed. "You were right about that. She's never had to learn that actions have consequences. As many criminal cases as I've tried, you'd think I'd have known the dangers of bailing anyone out of trouble so quickly."

"Mr. Everett said a kindly police officer had a talk with his father, when he was a teenager and got caught using drugs. The officer advised him not to go rushing down to bail his son out, but to let him see the trouble he could be in for breaking the law. So he got left in jail for several days before his family attorneys got on the case." She smiled. "He said it was what saved him. He was running with a rougher crowd than his father knew."

"He still runs with a rough crowd, unless I'm badly mistaken," he returned, and he didn't like the idea of Everett. He didn't know why, either, which irritated him.

"He was a mercenary for a lot of years. He still dabbles in it, but he had some sort of injury that he said imperiled comrades if he went on missions with them. So he's logistics, now. He helps plan assaults." She sighed. "His father disowned him over it. He says he can't even go home to see his mother. He has to meet her off the family ranch."

"His father sounds hard."

"From what I've heard about him, very hard. Ranching is a rough business."

"And you'd know?" he asked.

She laughed. "From relatives only," she said. "My mother was raised on a ranch outside Jacobsville, Texas. She could ride anything with hooves. *Grand-mère* still owns the family ranch, but she has a manager oversee it. Not that she couldn't do that herself, if she wanted to."

"Was your mother an only child?"

She nodded. "So was my dad. Except for cousins and a couple of great-aunts and my grandmother, I have no family living."

"No hostages to fate."

"Well, I'd do anything to save my grandmother," she said, and worried about what her grandfather might do in his efforts to get his case overturned. Also, in the background, was her greedy cousin, Robert Matthews, trying to swipe the property she'd been left. None of which Mr. Chandler knew anything about. And, she hoped fervently that she could keep it that way.

Jackie was subdued at the supper table. Nick had gone out, dressed in black tie, to take Mara to a concert downtown. Gaby had to concede, he was a striking man, despite his taciturn demeanor. She wondered what he was like with a woman, if he was always so reserved and untouched. And then she flushed and chided herself for even allowing the question into her mind.

Gaby finished the delicious chicken dish Tilly had prepared

and pushed her plate aside to dig into the wonderful cherry pie that accompanied the meal. Tilly could cook!

"Tilly, this is delicious," she told the older woman when she came in to bring more coffee. "You're an excellent cook!"

Tilly flushed and grinned. "Thanks, miss. I love cooking. I can do most anything. Well, except quiche," she added. "You cook very well yourself."

"*Grand-mère* thought I needed to learn the skill, so she sent me to a Cordon Bleu chef here in the city and had me taught." She studied her coffee cup, concealing a smile, because the chef was her grandmother's. In fact, he still cooked for her in her apartment. "She said I might marry a man who didn't employ cooks, so I needed to know how to prepare food." She made a face, not looking at her companions. "I'll never marry."

"That would be a waste, ma'am," Tilly said softly.

Gaby just smiled sadly. "We do what we can in life. There will always be things we can't do, but there are compensations."

"Oh, yeah?" Jackie muttered. "Name one!"

Tilly made a face and rushed back to the kitchen.

"Sunsets," Gaby said softly. "When the sky turns all red and pink and white. The sound of thunder in a storm. Sitting on a park bench and feeding pigeons while they flock around your feet. Petting a kitten."

Jackie was giving her the oddest look. "Not parties and dancing and shopping?" she asked abruptly.

"I don't go to parties."

"Can you dance?"

"Oh, yes. I was taught in my teens." She smiled. "I can even do a tango." Her face tautened. "That reminds me, I have to find out when *Grand-mère*'s tango teacher pays her a visit so I can be there. Mr. Everett said that the man can't even do a samba properly, much less a tango. He's playing my grandmother, and he's not getting away with it." Gaby's soft voice had a steeliness to it that surprised her companion. Jackie wouldn't know, but Gaby had grown up with great wealth and power and she knew how to use it when it became necessary.

"You can dance a tango?" Jackie exclaimed. "I've always wanted to learn." She made a face. "Keith can't dance and he doesn't want to."

Gaby sipped coffee and chose her words very carefully. "Why were you locked in your room today?" she asked with apparent innocence.

Jackie sighed angrily. "My uncle saw me kissing Keith in the hallway and just lost it. I guess he'd had a bad day already."

"Oh, yes," Gaby agreed, not mentioning anything about Keith seemed wise. "He didn't know it was a holiday. I pointed it out to him, but he said that it wasn't a holiday in this apartment." She sighed as she finished her coffee and got to her feet. "So I guess I'll get back to cataloging."

Jackie looked up at her. "Aren't you going to lecture me about Keith?" she asked, a little belligerently.

Gaby just smiled. "People in love don't respond well to lectures. The fever has to burn itself out first."

"Have you ever been in love?"

"Certainly! I went crazy over Batman in the *Justice League* movie. Totally gorgeous!"

"Not a film star. An actual man."

Gaby went away without leaving the room. Her face was carefully blank of emotion. "No."

There was an uncomfortable little silence.

"I'd really like to learn the tango," Jackie said after a minute. "I have a friend at school—just a friend, not a boyfriend—who's from South America. He says he can do it."

Gaby forced herself to sound nonchalant. "Couldn't you invite him to the apartment and get him to teach you?"

Jackie sighed. "I don't think so. It would make Keith go ballistic."

"If you truly love someone, you want them to have anything that makes them happy," Gaby said softly. "Even dance lessons from a friend. What does he look like, this boy from South America?"

The question stalled a crisp comment from Jackie about the true love bit.

"Antonio?" she asked. "He's tall and olive-skinned. Jet-black eyes and a flawless complexion that I wish I had." She even smiled. "He's nice. Always polite and respectful to the teachers."

"Does he live with his parents?"

"His parents are dead," she said quietly. "They were killed by insurgents before he came to this country. He can't even talk about it. He said it hurts too much."

"Who does he live with?"

"A great-aunt, and his great-uncle is staying with them," she said. "I went to his house one day to ask Antonio about some homework in English class. His great-uncle is nice, too."

"Then you might be able to go to his house if Antonio was willing to teach you how to do the tango." She smiled. "It's very complicated and absolutely beautiful to watch. I have a black-and-white film that shows actual people teaching it. It's nothing like the tangos you see in movies." She scowled. "I take that back. There's an excellent example of it in an old, very old, Rudolph Valentino movie called *The Four Horsemen of the Apocalypse*, which dates from 1921. You can find the dance on YouTube. It inspired a tango craze. If you watch it, you can see why. Valentino was awesome."

"I'll have to look that one up." Jackie got up, too.

"Your uncle loves you, Jackie," she said, her eyes soft and affectionate on the young girl's face. "He just shows it with a loud voice and curses and orders."

Jackie fought a grin. "I noticed." She grimaced. "He caught Keith kissing me in a, well, in a sort of lewd way. That's why I got locked in my room."

"I know you love the boy," Gaby said. "But I have to tell you that a boy who respects you won't subject you to public demonstrations of affection, especially vulgar ones."

"How do you know?" Jackie shot back. "Do you date men?"

Gaby repressed a shudder. "No. I don't. But I know other women who do. And I was raised in a household where virtue and respectability had value. My grandmother was very, very strict. She still tries to protect me from life."

Jackie frowned. "You're really pretty," she said surprisingly. "I guess men would want to date you."

"A few have." She sighed. "I'm locked up inside myself," she added absently, voicing her thoughts. "I can't get out, and nobody else can get in." She noted her companion's solemn expression. "I guess I spend too much time alone."

"Me, too. Being locked in my room." She drew in a breath. "Well, I guess I'll go try to find that Valentino movie. I can't get out of the apartment for a week, except to school, thanks to Uncle Nick, so maybe I can get a few tango pointers from the film." She hesitated. "Do you know the name of that black-and-white tango film that teaches how to do it?"

"No, but you can google it. The film was made by a woman and she went to South America to be taught how to do the tango, although some of it takes place in other countries. The dancing is pretty awesome."

"Okay." She hesitated. "Thanks. For listening, I mean, and

for not going off on a tangent about, well, about Keith. Uncle
Nick had a lot to say."

"He's responsible for you, and you're a minor," Gaby said
gently.

Jackie sighed. "And he's stuck with me and I get in the way
of his love life, I guess. He didn't like me spending time with
Mara, even before you came. I guess he'd see it as a bad influence on me." She laughed bitterly. "As if my mother was any
better than that. She never spared me. She had men all over
the house." She made a face. "Maybe that's why it seems so...
well, so normal for Keith to kiss me in public like he does. My
mother's just like him." Her face clouded. "Some role model!"

"I expect there are things in your mother's past that made
her the way she is," Gaby replied.

"Yeah," Jackie drawled sarcastically. "She and Uncle Nick
got beaten by their father, even when he was sober. They
were terrorized by him. So was their mother. It was a long
time ago, but neither of them ever got over it. If Uncle Nick
ever had kids, I can almost guarantee he wouldn't take a belt
to them. Mama never hit me. Not ever." She drew in a long
breath. "Of course, she had boyfriends who did."

Gaby's face contorted. "You poor kid," she said softly, and
meant it. "What a life you've had!"

Jackie felt warm all over. This woman, who'd started out
as her worst nightmare, cared about her. Nobody else seemed
to, not even her uncle.

"It's not so bad here," Jackie said after a minute. "Uncle
Nick's not so bad..."

The door opened and slammed, hard. Nick came into the
dining room, scowling and cursing under his breath.

"A cup of coffee, Mr. Chandler?" Tilly asked quickly. "I'm
about to leave, but I can get it before I go."

It was a good half hour before Tilly was due to leave, but

she knew Mr. Chandler in this mood and all she wanted was to get out of the line of fire while there was still time.

"Yes, bring me a cup," he said. He glared at Jackie. "If I ever catch you…!" he began.

"Never again. Honest. I promise," Jackie said quickly. "I'll just go to my room and look for that Valentino movie!"

She was gone and her bedroom door closed before Nick had time to ask a question.

He looked at Gaby, whose face was showing traces of discomfort. "Why in hell is she going to watch silent films?"

"Rudolph Valentino, 1921, *Four Horsemen of the Apocalypse,*" she began. "He did a dance…"

"Yes, the tango. It's been called the most famous tango ever filmed, and he danced it magnificently. So why does my niece want to see that?"

"She wants to learn to tango," Gaby said, sitting back down.

There was a brief pause while Tilly said her good-nights and left. Nick picked up his coffee cup. "You were saying?"

Gaby grinned. "Jackie wants to learn to tango. There's this handsome, well-mannered South American boy in one of her classes, who dances the tango. I suggested that she might want to ask him over here for a lesson."

His eyebrows arched. "What an amazing talent for manipulation you have, Miss Dupont."

"I'd curtsy, but it's too much work," she said with a soft laugh.

"So what did she say when you suggested it?"

"She's going to think about it." She pursed her lips. "I also mentioned that someone who loved her wouldn't subject her to public demonstrations of affection with lewd overtones."

"Nice."

"I have hidden talents," she pointed out.

"And you said you didn't sign on as a nanny," he said in a faintly mocking tone.

"I like her," came the quiet reply. "She's been through the mill in her young life." She studied his hard face. "She said that you had, too."

The look in his eyes as she said that had her jumping to her feet. "Sorry. Work to do. Got to go right now."

She put down her cup and took off to the office like a bird fleeing a cat.

Nick watched her go with blazing eyes. How did Jackie know about his past, and what had she told Gaby? He was outraged. Gaby was an employee and he wasn't about to share personal information with her. Neither was Jackie. He'd have to have a talk with the girl, but not today. He was tired and irritable and worn-out. Sailing usually blew away his problems, but it hadn't worked today. His client in the hospital was under immediate threat of death from his beloved wife, and Nick had had enough. He was going to get a good private detective on the case to document the homicidal wife's behavior, documentation that would stand in any court of law. He was going to save his idiot client, no matter what it took.

NINE

Gaby was asleep when she heard a sudden sound from nearby. She got up, tugging on her bathrobe, and opened her door stealthily.

There it was again, that sound, a groaning sound full of anguish, pain. It was coming from Mr. Chandler's room.

She stood in the hall, uncertain of what to do. She didn't know if the man slept nude. Anyway, she wasn't walking into a man's bedroom in the middle of the night, no matter if he was fully dressed.

But that sound, that anguish, touched something deep inside her. She'd had nightmares years ago from her bad experience. And Mr. Chandler had something probably equally bad in his life. She felt sorry for him. He was closed up like a clamshell, safe from the world, safe from people who could hurt him. Except that the clamshell wasn't doing a lot of protecting, from the sounds she heard.

All at once, there was one last groan. Then the sound of feet hitting the floor. His bedroom door was jerked open and he came out into the hall, stopping suddenly at the sight of a barefoot, gowned and robed Gaby biting her lower lip.

"What the hell are you doing out here?" he asked, lowering his voice because they could both hear soft snoring coming from Jackie's room.

"Wondering what to do," she said simply. Heavens, he was beautiful like that, wearing nothing but navy blue silk pajama bottoms, his broad, muscular chest brown and thick with black, curling hair that ran down to the low-slung pajama waistband and probably even lower. She wondered at her reaction to him, because it was blatantly sensual. She swallowed, hard, and bit her lip again.

He ran his fingers through his disheveled, wavy black hair. There was just a touch of silver at both temples, just enough to make him very sexy. He drew in a sharp breath. "Come have coffee with me."

In other words, come make it, because she didn't imagine her boss had ever seen the inside of a coffee canister.

"Okay."

She padded to the kitchen ahead of him and made a pot of coffee. He still hadn't said a word when she carried it into the living room. He was sitting on the sofa with his head in his hands.

"Probably whiskey would make more sense," he muttered, thanking her for the hot mug of steaming black coffee she'd put on the coffee table in front of him.

"Nightmare?" she asked.

He nodded. His broad, leonine face was taut with pain.

"I used to have them," she said as she curled up in an easy chair with her cup.

"How did you stop them?"

"I didn't," she said. "I just…found ways to sleep."

Both thick eyebrows arched.

She grimaced. "I went to therapists. Two of them. The only thing they did for me was teach me how to avert the nightmares. It doesn't always work, though." Her pale blue eyes were sad. "I think we carry the past around in our minds like extra luggage, and there's no way to get it out."

He nodded. It made sense. He sipped his coffee.

"You can't talk about it, can you?" she asked softly.

He needed to. It wasn't something he was eager to share with this virtual stranger, but she had a depth of compassion that made him hungry for intangible things, for emotions that he'd shut out of his life long ago.

"I was married," he said after a minute, "and we had a little girl." He didn't look at her, so he missed the faint shock in her face. He sipped more coffee, grimacing as the memory of Sam claimed his mind. "My wife was jealous of any attention I gave to anyone, including our little girl, who was just a little over a year old. She was using drugs. I didn't find that out until...after. I was working as a longshoreman, going to law school at night. Glenna said I was neglecting her. She'd already chased most of my friends and fellow students out of the apartment, but when I went to their homes to study, that ticked her off, as well. One day, she said she'd had enough, I was paying too much attention to Samantha, much more than I was to her. She was going to make sure I didn't do it again."

He sighed. "She made threats all the time. I didn't pay them much attention. I was getting ready to leave for law school. I stopped by my daughter's room to kiss her good-night, like I always did. She wasn't there."

Gaby's face tautened as she watched him relive it. She had a terrible feeling about his child.

"So I went to look for Sam. I was just in time to see Glenna, with Sam in her arms, getting on the elevator they rigged to get workers to the top floors of the high-rise they were constructing across the street from our small apartment." He put his coffee cup down and lowered his eyes to the floor. "I ran after them. The elevator took so long to come back down." He swallowed. He'd never shared this with another living soul after Glenna's mother died. "Glenna had Sam in her arms. She was standing on a girder that jutted out over the building site. I felt so damned helpless. I tried to reason with her, but she was high as a kite. I'd never seen her like that, but I knew it was drugs. I knew the signs. I couldn't make her listen. She told me that Sam would never come between us again and that she'd make me sorry." He looked up, his dark eyes black with torment. "She jumped," he said, and had to stop, because the pain was choking him.

Gaby got up from her seat, pushed him back on the sofa, crawled into his lap and just held him tight.

He hesitated, but only for a few seconds before his arms enveloped her and held her. He rocked her in his arms, his face buried in the soft, clean, thick hair at her neck. She felt wetness and said nothing. She just held him.

Now she understood his reaction to the child in the elevator. It was this tragedy that kept him single, that made him hostile to children who would have reminded him of it. She couldn't imagine the pain he must have felt, still felt all these years later. She was surprised at herself for comforting him. She didn't like men close, physically, but it felt right to be held against Nick. It felt good. She shouldn't have done it, of course. He'd hate his own weakness that made him tell her about the past, and he'd blame her for that weakness. But in the meanwhile, she offered what small comfort she could. Perhaps just the retelling of it had helped him a little. Obviously, he didn't share things with his niece or his lover, but everybody shared secrets with Gaby. She had that kind of effect on people.

After a minute, he took a deep breath and sat up, with Gaby still in his arms, watching him quietly. He dashed at his eyes, but he didn't try to move up, or let her go.

He looked down into compassionate light blue eyes and wondered how a face could show so much compassion. Because it was there, along with faint apprehension and unconcealed attraction.

He shifted her so that her head fell back against his shoulder. "I've never spoken of it," he said, his deep voice faintly husky with emotion. "Not even to my sister."

"I'm a clam," Gaby said softly. "I never gossip."

"I knew that," he replied. He drew in a deep breath. "I see them, you know, when I have nightmares. I see their faces just before Glenna jumped. I hear the screams as they fell." His eyes closed and he shuddered. "I'll never get the memory out of my mind."

"One of my therapists said that there's a sort of passive coping skill. Essentially, you picture a tragedy in your mind but you go back and stop it from happening. I know, it sounds very strange, but it worked for me. After a fashion."

He was watching her face. She was pretty, but not in a conventional way at all. And with her chestnut hair bright and reddish brown, thick and long trailing around the neck of her robe, she looked young and fragile.

"What are you coping with?" he asked.

Her heart jumped. She didn't dare tell him, not after the masquerade she'd put on to get this job. She compromised. There was just the bare bones. She could talk about it that way.

"I was...assaulted when I was in my midteens," she said after a minute, and she didn't look at him as she spoke. Her body stiffened in his arms. "Just one man, but there were, well, spectators who didn't help me."

"Dear God," he said heavily. He drew her closer, so that

her face was now in his throat. She could smell soap and expensive aftershave on his face. "No wonder you don't date."

"I'm afraid of men, mostly," she said. "But not of you. It's odd..."

"You can think of me as just a big teddy bear," he said with a faint laugh.

"A teddy bear with big teeth and claws, boss," she murmured dryly. "And the bite of a crocodile."

"Now, now, I'm being nice. Don't spoil it. I'm almost never nice."

She sighed and relaxed against him. "Well, that's true enough," she teased.

"Glenna's mother pulled me back from the brink," he said. "I stayed drunk for two weeks after it happened. She made me go on."

"Does she live near you now?" Gaby asked.

"She died, not too many years after Glenna did, of a massive heart attack. I still put flowers on her grave, hers and my family's." He sank back against the sofa with a long breath. "I never wanted to get involved with a woman after the tragedy. But life goes on. Just the same, it's never serious. Women come and go in my life."

"Jackie says Mara's been around for a while."

He laughed. It had a hollow sound. "She's possessive as hell of me, but she has other lovers."

Gaby frowned. "Don't you mind?" she wondered aloud.

He lifted his head and looked down into her surprised pale eyes. "Why would I mind?" he asked. He was serious.

"When you're involved with someone, aren't you supposed to be faithful to them?"

"But we're not involved." He shrugged. "Not emotionally, at least," he clarified.

"You don't want emotional involvement," she said softly. "I understand why now."

His big hand smoothed over her long, thick chestnut hair. "Have you ever been involved with a man since the bad experience?"

She shook her head. "I'm like you, except that I don't have lovers. I'm afraid..."

His thumb rubbed softly over her bow-shaped mouth, and he wondered at the tenderness she drew out of him. It had been a very long time since he'd felt it. "Afraid of being assaulted again?"

"Men are very strong," she said quietly. "And it's a modern world. Men have expectations of women that couldn't apply in my case. There are still men who think women who say no really mean yes."

"A few."

"So I keep to myself." She smiled. "One of my girlfriends asked me, years ago, didn't I miss being with someone intimately. I told her that I'd never been intimate with anyone, so how could I miss it? She was ready to call men with nets. She thought I was unnatural. Of course, she didn't know what happened to me." She sighed softly. "It made me feel dirty. So dirty that I'd never be clean again." She looked up at him. "I'm broken. And there's no way to fix me."

His strong, warm hand pressed against her cheek. "I'm broken, too," he confessed. "It's why I react the way I do to children. I see Sam..."

She lifted a soft hand to his face and drew it down his cheek. "Every life has a purpose," she told him. "There are reasons why things happen the way they do, even if we don't understand those reasons."

"Don't tell me," he mused, his tone mocking. "This is something you learned at church."

She smiled. "It is. Faith was what kept me going when my parents were killed, when I was assaulted. It was all I had. Faith, and my sweet grandmother."

"You've had a lot of tragedy in your young life."

She shrugged. "A lot of people have more. I just put one foot in front of the other, pretend there's no tomorrow, and I keep going."

His fingers were tangling in her hair. "I love long hair," he said absently. "Yours is thick and silky."

She laughed softly. "Yours is wavy."

"And going gray," he pointed out.

"Oh, you'll never be old," she said. "You're too fiery. You radiate that energy that keeps you going."

"You see deep," he said. "How? Why?"

"My great-great-grandmother was a witch."

"What!"

She grinned. "Not that sort. She could dowse for water and find it. That skill was very handy when there were droughts. She never charged for it, either. She said it was a gift and she'd lose it if she started selling it."

"Where did she live?"

"On our ranch in Texas. It's been home for five generations. Jacobsville is between Victoria and San Antonio. Most everybody who lives there works on a ranch or owns one. It's very agricultural."

"It sounds like it. I was in Texas once. I had to try a case in Dallas. I remember the thunderstorm more than I remember the case, however. I was on the top floor when the storm came. We have storms here, of course, but Texas storms are much stronger. The whole top floor of the hotel shook with the thunder. There was one elevator and everybody crowded into it." He chuckled. "I remember wishing I weighed less, and hoping that the elevator cables wouldn't break. Then there was this woman." He rolled his eyes. "She was looking around at us and mentioned how sad it would be if the elevator stopped and we were trapped together. She said, 'Remember the Donner party? Chomp, chomp.' Everybody broke up."

She laughed, the sound soft and husky in the quiet room. "You must have had some adventures."

"More than I like to remember, some of them."

The hall clock sounded. It was two o'clock in the morning.

"Tomorrow's Tuesday and you have to go to work," Gaby reminded him.

He sighed. "I guess so." He bent and, before she realized what he was going to do, his chiseled mouth came down very slowly on hers.

She felt the very texture of him as he nibbled at her top lip and then her lower one, coaxing her lips apart. Then his mouth hardened, just a little, and he drew her up close as his mouth fed tenderly on her own.

She clutched at his arm. It was warm and muscular. Involuntarily, her fingers moved into the thick, soft mass of hair over his broad chest and settled there lightly. His own hand came up and moved her hand hard against him, holding it there while the kiss awakened something in her that was disturbing.

She drew away, breath by breath, flushed and breathing unsteadily and a little frightened of the sensual sensations he'd provoked in her body.

But he only smiled. "You should have been a doctor," he said softly. "You have a depth of compassion I've rarely seen in any of my friends."

"I just care about people," she said simply. "I learned that at home, that wealth means nothing, social position means nothing. Caring and compassion are worth worlds more."

"Who taught you that?"

"My mother and father. And then, my grandmother."

"My father taught me to duck. My mother taught me that years of abuse can cripple the hardiest spirit. She died first. A pity. And my father followed her just six months later. I always thought he put my mother in her grave. He was the most abusive man I've ever known. I didn't even mourn him."

"I'm sorry about that." She studied his taut face. "You're like me. You don't have much family, either. Well, I have my grandmother. But she's all I have in the world. Do you have anyone in your family besides your sister and Jackie?"

He shook his head. "Just them. And I could never tell them what I've told you."

"It's sad that you and your sister aren't closer," she said.

"It's even sadder that she isn't close to her daughter." He sighed. "I think abuse damages you more than just physically. It destroys lives. Not mine. Not yet, at least."

He cocked his head and smiled at her. "Not yours, either, I see."

"Oh, I'm a rubber ball. I just bounce back."

"You need to bounce back to bed. So do I. It's going to be a long day tomorrow."

He stood up, with Gaby still in his arms, and started for her bedroom.

"I can walk," she protested weakly.

"I know." He kept walking. He carried her to her bed and put her down on it, very gently. "Thanks," he said gruffly.

She smiled up at him. "You're a tough guy," she said softly. "Eventually, you'll come to terms with it. And I don't gossip," she added, in case he thought she might tell anyone what she knew about him.

"I know you don't gossip. That's why I told you." He stood over her with his hands on his hips, studying her quietly. Then he smiled. "Good night."

"Good night, boss. Thanks for the lift," she added with twinkling pale blue eyes.

He chuckled as he went out and pulled the door shut.

He was his old self at breakfast, complaining about the way Tilly had cooked the eggs and remarking darkly to his two female companions at table that they should finish their meals promptly.

"You'll be late for school, and you—" he indicated Gaby "—will be late for work."

"I would never point out that you're the one not eating and if anybody's late, it will be you."

"Oooh, feeling brave, are we?" he taunted, but his eyes were twinkling.

"I told you," she replied, "I can type. Anybody who can type will never grace the unemployment line, even in these hard times."

"Rubber ball," he murmured, and laughed.

Gaby just grinned at him.

Jackie was getting her jacket on. "What did he mean about the rubber ball?" she asked Gaby.

"I told him I bounced back from things like a rubber ball," she replied with a smile.

Jackie picked up her book bag that contained her small computer and a couple of textbooks. She stopped beside Gaby. She looked worried. "Listen, Uncle Nick is really nice. I mean, even when he yells, it doesn't mean he's mad or anything. Something that happened to him keeps him away from people. Well, except for women like Mara." Her face was full of empathy, something that touched Gaby. "Don't let him hurt you," she added with faint embarrassment. "He doesn't get involved with people. Not emotionally. Not ever. And you're...well, you're nice."

Gaby smiled at her. "You're a sweet girl," she said softly. "Thanks for caring. But your uncle is just my boss. I don't get emotionally involved with men. Well, I don't get physically involved, either. I should have a dodo bird tattoo on my arm. I belong to an extinct species," she added in a whisper.

Jackie burst out laughing. The girl almost never smiled. It changed her. "You're very pretty when you smile," Gaby told her.

Jackie flushed. "Uh, thanks," she said, obviously unsettled by the compliment. "Gotta go."

She went out the door as if demons were pursuing her.

Tilly was still busy in the kitchen. "It's amazing, how well you handle her," she told Gaby. "She's changed since you've been here. So has the boss. He doesn't yell as much."

Gaby laughed. "At least I'm doing something good. Cataloging that library is more challenging than I expected it to be. I love the work. I'm just slow."

"Nobody minds. It was all together, nicely waiting on the bookshelves to be moved over to this apartment from the other one. Then something the boss said set Jackie off, and she and her boyfriend knocked over all the bookcases and scattered books everywhere. The boss grounded Jackie for a month." She rolled her eyes. "Talk about having an uncomfortable working life! She raged and cussed and made threats. Just rolled off the boss's back like water off a duck's. She stayed grounded. Didn't do much good. She was right back with that evil boy in no time. He's going to get her put in prison for life if she's not careful. I only met him once, but I could see exactly what he was like. Poor Jackie. No matter what happens, she's going to be hurt. Such a shame that her mother is so remote."

"Jackie's a sweet girl. She blusters and complains to keep people from seeing what she really is, inside."

Tilly stared at her. "Do you really think she's sweet?"

"I do. If we could get her away from Keith, she'd change. It's how to make that happen that keeps me worried."

"You like her."

Gaby smiled. "I really do. She's got such promise. She's got a quick mind and she's sensible. Well, not about that boy, but about most things. She hides her real self away, so that she won't be hurt by other people."

"Her mom told her she was an accident," Tilly said shortly. "I'd never say such a thing to a child of mine, even if it was true."

"Neither would I," Gaby replied. She finished her coffee, thanked Tilly for it and went back to work in the office.

She started on the next shelf, carefully noting the names and titles of the books as she went along. It would have been just as well to have used the Dewey decimal system, but her boss was impatient. He'd be looking for title or author, not numbers.

Her heart jumped as she remembered their closeness the night before. He'd been uncommonly open with her. It was flattering that he'd told nobody else, not even his sister, of the tragedy that had shattered his life. But he'd told Gaby.

She smiled, remembering. He'd kissed her. She sighed. It had felt nice. She hadn't been kissed, not really, in her adult life. Oh, there had been parties in college and the inevitable mistletoe at Christmas. But she'd dodged any sort of intimate contact and presented her cheek to any of the boys who came close. She'd never dated. There had been plenty of specula-tion as to why, and some people had asked if she preferred another lifestyle. She just smiled.

It was lonely in her shell. She knew now that Nick had

one of his own. Neither of them could get out. They were trapped in the past, incapable of moving forward.

She wondered as she worked why he'd been willing to confide in her. He wasn't the sort of man who ever talked about himself or his accomplishments, much less about his private life. Everybody knew about Mara, but nobody knew about the ghosts that haunted him. Nobody, except Gaby.

Nick was a handsome, sensuous, intelligent man. If she'd been whole, he was the sort of man she'd have wanted in her life. But she was not comfortable with a carefree, no-strings lifestyle. Mara had other lovers and he didn't care. If she'd meant something to him, he'd have been livid if she went out with someone else. It was an indication of how little he felt for the beautiful woman in his life.

Gaby wasn't sure if she should be pleased about that. She had to get a grip on herself. The last thing in the world she could afford was getting too close to Nick Chandler. If he ever found out exactly who she was, there would be fireworks. If nothing else, he would consider that she'd lied to him, and he'd be furious. At the very least, she'd be out of work.

That wasn't a worry, because she was quite comfortable financially. Well, there was the will that left her great-aunt's property to her, the one her cousin was trying to get his hands on. Robert would never be able to prove that her will was a fake, or that her great-aunt was not in her right mind when she made the bequeathal. So at least her fortune was safe.

Her heart was another matter. And she wasn't listening to it.

A few days later, her grandmother called and asked her to come over. It was Saturday, her free day that she was spending in her room, reading. But she got up and got dressed. It was unusual for her grandmother to ask for company. She hoped there was nothing wrong.

When she opened the apartment door to leave, she found Mr. Everett lounging against a wall, waiting.

"I was on my way down," she began.

"It's more complicated than that," he said quietly. "Things have happened. Let's go."

Her pulse went wild. "Not my grandfather?" she began worriedly.

"No. Your cousin."

"What is he doing?"

He shook his head. "Wait until we get to your grandmother's apartment. I have things to share with both of you."

"Okay."

He opened the back door of the sedan for her and got behind the wheel. "Your boss isn't home today?" he asked.

She laughed softly. "He's out on the water somewhere. He has a yacht and he loves sailing. Mostly he's out of the apartment on Saturdays. Sundays, too, occasionally."

"How about the Goth Girl?"

"When I left, she was in her room playing some sort of god-awful music," she replied. She shook her head. "How she's not deaf is a miracle. Tilly actually had on earplugs in the kitchen. Heaven knows what the neighbors are thinking."

"You could ask her to turn it down."

She gave him a blithe look. "I don't have the medical insurance," she said. "And her uncle wasn't home to back me up. She's a handful when she loses her temper. But at least I don't have to worry about that boy today. He told her that he had to go somewhere with his father this weekend."

"Maybe they've cased a bank and they're out to get rich."

"If I knew they were, and where, I'd have the police sitting there waiting for them," Gaby said with some heat. "Jackie's a nice girl. But not when she's mixed up with that boy. And she's still facing felony charges. At least I convinced her uncle not to rush down and bail her out this time. She spent several days in lockup. She was very thoughtful when he brought her home."

"Good for him. Good for you, too," he said. "Actions have consequences. It's a crime not to let children learn that. The prisons are full of people who never learned it."

"Amen."

When they got up to her penthouse apartment, Madame Dupont was pacing. She had on a neat beige dress and no shoes. She turned when Gaby walked in and opened her arms.

Gaby hugged the little woman close, loving the scent of Nina Ricci's *L'Air du Temps* that clung to her. "It's good to see you," Gaby said softly. "What's the matter?"

Her grandmother sighed. "My darling," she said softly, "your cousin phoned me. He says that he has a will that supercedes yours and he's going to challenge your ownership of the property in court."

"He can't have a later will. My great-aunt—your sister—died not a day after she made the change in her will, and we were with her constantly!"

"Yes, I know." She drew in a steadying breath. "He will produce witnesses that will swear that your will was forged."

Gaby sat down on the sofa, hard. "How?" she exclaimed.

Grand-mère nodded toward Mr. Everett.

Gaby looked at him, too.

"Your cousin had blood ties with the Outfit. We all knew that to begin with. They have a master forger, and they're very good at producing witnesses who are, to anyone's mind, the cream of society. Paid, of course."

"Then what do we do?" Gaby asked, seeing her inheritance going down the drain.

He looked at her grandmother. "You need to talk to your

daughter-in-law's aunt in Jacobsville," he told her. "You're the only one in the family she'll speak to. Nobody else has a hope of getting to her." He sighed. "She has ties to a New Jersey crime boss. He, in turn, has ties to a major crime boss. They might be willing to help."

"The Outfit?" Gaby exclaimed. "They kill people!"

"Only bad people. Honest." Mr. Everett grinned. "And right now, we need all the help we can get."

"So we do," her grandmother said solemnly. She grimaced. "Rose and I rarely get along. But I will phone her and ask for her help."

Gaby picked up *Grand-mère*'s cell phone and helpfully handed it to her.

TEN

There was a very brief conversation, during which Madame Dupont made her late daughter-in-law's aunt understand the gravity of the situation. Gaby stood to lose everything if the hated cousin had his way. And that wasn't their only problem. Gaby's grandfather was all set to have his conviction overturned, and if he was successful, he could convince a jury that Gaby had lied under oath. She could actually go to jail.

Gaby's maternal great-aunt, Mrs. Rose Bartwell, finally gave in. She knew Gaby and she was fond of her. Perhaps, she thought, she was wrong to isolate herself from her relatives. She said this to Madame. She agreed to get in touch with the crime boss she knew, the New Jersey mobster who was, fortuitously, in town visiting in-laws in Jacobsville, Texas. She would ask him for a contact in Chicago that Mr. Everett could speak with.

Before she hung up, she passed along a tidbit of gossip. Gaby's cousin Clancey, who was married to Texas Ranger

Colter Banks, was pregnant. Gaby already knew this, and so did Madame, but it wasn't mentioned. Rose said that everyone was delighted for them. Clancey was a character, and she had many friends in Jacobsville since she'd married Colter. She was the guardian of a little brother, Tad, whom both Clancey and Colter loved very much. Clancey was still working for the Texas Department of Public Safety that also employed Colter.

"Rose will get in touch with her contact," Madame said after she ended the conversation.

"Bless her heart," Gaby said with some relief.

"Family is family," her grandmother replied quietly. "We may disagree, even fight, but when the chips are down, we take care of each other. And she was your mother's favorite aunt, as I recall."

"Will she call you back when she's spoken to the man she knows?" Mr. Everett wanted to know.

"I'm certain of it. And I will tell you immediately." She hugged Gaby one more time. She looked at the younger woman's outfit with disdain. Gaby was wearing black leggings and black loafers with a bulky white knit sweater that reached to her hips. Her long chestnut hair was in a braid, and she looked very young and very ordinary.

"You have a closet full of couture," *Grand-mère* began sadly.

"Yes, well, we don't want Mr. Chandler to uncover the grisly truth about me, now, do we?" she asked gently.

Her grandmother sighed and smiled. "Of course we don't. But will it take much longer, this job you're doing for him?"

Gaby's heart jumped and dropped at just the thought of leaving Nick's apartment for good. It was a surprise and not a nice one. Why should it bother her? He raged around for no reason, yelled, cursed, was generally unpleasant. Then she remembered him in her arms, the wetness at her throat as he poured out his tragic past. Deep inside that tormented man was someone she wished badly to know. She didn't want to leave.

And what a time to discover it, when she had less than two weeks' worth of sorting left. Unless Nick might want her to stay on as his personal administrative assistant. Yes, he might want her to stay. It lifted her spirits and she smiled.

"Not much longer, to catalog the books in his library," Gaby said, "but that isn't all I do. I take dictation, type up briefs, answer the phone, make appointments—things like that."

"Yes, but, my darling, there is always the risk that he might find out who you are," her grandmother said very softly, because she could read the other woman's expression very well. "You don't want to leave him," she added.

Gaby swallowed, hard, and ground her teeth together. "Of course I want to leave him," she said, forcing her voice to sound normal. "But the longer I wait, the easier it will be…"

"The easier it will be for him to discover your identity, my sweet," her grandmother interrupted. "And he will be furious."

Gaby drew in a long breath. "Yes, he will," she agreed. She searched her grandmother's pale blue eyes. "You think I should go when I finish cataloging the books."

Grand-mère nodded. "I am truly sorry."

Gaby blinked. "Sorry? Why?"

"Because you love him, do you not?"

Gaby's heart jumped up into her throat. "No," she bit off. "No, of course I don't! He's just my boss. I'm…fond of him."

But the older woman knew better. She hugged Gaby again. "We will contact you when we know something more. Do not worry. Promise me?"

"I promise," Gaby said.

"Now, back to your cinders and ashes, my girl," she said with a little laugh.

Gaby burst out laughing. "I'm not Cinderella," she pointed out.

The older woman laughed, too. "No, you are not poor. But maybe Snow White?"

Gaby glowered at her. "I don't know any little people in pointed hats," she replied.

Grand-mère smiled at her. "So much for fairy tales," she agreed. "But do be careful, my sweet."

"Have you heard any more from Grandfather?" she asked.

"No. Our Mr. Everett is trying to dig out information, but his sources here are limited, hence the call to your great-aunt in Jacobsville. If she can gain us a hearing with her acquaintance, perhaps he may know how to approach the gentlemen in the underworld here."

"Perhaps. We can only hope." Gaby kissed her. "Stay well."

"You, too, *ma chérie*," she said softly, and kissed Gaby back.

"You'll phone me, as soon as you know something?" Gaby asked Everett when they arrived at the door to Nick's apartment.

"Of course. And don't you forget the birthday party next week. She was too unsettled to remind you," he pointed out quietly.

"I know. I hate having her upset."

"It won't be for much longer," he said with a steely blue eye. "We'll get this sorted out very soon."

"I hope you're right."

"Don't go out alone," he said abruptly. "Not unless you let me know where and when. Things are in motion around us."

"I figured that out." She sighed. "Thanks," she said, and smiled at him.

He smiled back. Sort of. "No problem."

The door opened abruptly and Nick Chandler stood there, fuming. "I thought I heard voices."

"Mr. Everett is just leaving," Gaby said. "He took me to see my grandmother. She wasn't feeling well."

There wasn't a real answer to that, just a gruff grunt.

"I'll talk to you later," Everett told her. He nodded at the older man and sauntered back to the elevator.

Gaby went into the apartment. "Sorry," she said without meeting his eyes. "I should have told somebody I was going out."

"Yes, you should have. Jackie left soon after you did," he said hotly. "Tilly couldn't stop her."

Gaby ground her teeth together. She hadn't signed on as a nanny, but she still felt responsible for Jackie.

"She'll come home eventually," he said abruptly.

"Keith is out of town. She can't be meeting him," she said softly.

He drew in a long breath. "How do you know that?"

"I never share my sources," she said, aping Mr. Everett, who used that phrase far too often.

Nick's eyebrows went up. "You never told me that you were a journalist."

Gaby glowered at him. "I'm not, but I'm still not telling you how I know about Keith."

"Sure I know. He's about six feet tall and missing an eye." Nick glowered down at her.

"Mr. Everett never shares his sources, either," she said.

He cocked his head and looked down at her. Not a hair out of place, no evidence that she'd been on a date or with a man. Her pretty mouth still had a trace of lipstick and she smelled of spring flowers. He didn't want to notice that. She worked for him. He didn't want emotional ties.

But there she stood, apprehensive, uncertain of him, a little flushed. And not because of the elusive Mr. Everett, either. His chin lifted and he looked down at her with pure possession.

She saw that in his dark eyes and felt little jolts of lightning travel down her body. He made her uncomfortable. She felt things that she didn't want to feel when he was close to her. It was exciting. And frightening.

He saw the faint fear. It was the only reason that he didn't wrap her up in his arms and kiss her breathless. Besides all that, he had a lover. Sure, a lover he didn't even want to touch anymore. He'd thought he was impotent until he'd had Gaby in his arms that night he'd told her about his past. He'd been passionately aroused and keen to make sure Gaby didn't know it. It would embarrass her. Maybe it would frighten her, too. She'd never been with a man. That made his blood run hot. He'd never been the first man with any woman in his life. And he shouldn't be thinking such things about Gaby.

"I know it's Saturday, but I have a brief that needs typing," he began apologetically.

She let out a faint sigh of relief. He was very disturbing, especially when he fixed those dark, wise eyes on her face. "Sure thing, boss," she said at once.

"Fine. Let's get to it."

Several minutes into the brief he was dictating, Gaby's cell phone exploded with the soccer World Cup theme. She grimaced and dug in the pocket of her tight leggings to fetch it out.

She murmured an apology to her boss, but the screen read that the caller was Everett. "I have to take this. It's urgent," she said.

He drew an impatient breath, but he nodded, a curt jerk of his head.

"Hello?" Gaby said.

"I thought you might like to know where Jackie is," came the reply.

Her breath caught. "Where?" She expected the next words to be, *in jail again.*

He chuckled. "She's sitting in a church around the corner from her uncle's apartment, talking to a priest."

"Oh, my gosh!" Gaby exploded. "Are you kidding?"

"I never kid. Just thought you'd find it interesting. Talk to you later." And he hung up.

"Well, who was it?" Nick asked. "If I'm not invading your privacy?"

"It was Mr. Everett," she replied. She laughed. "He told me where Jackie is."

"Where?" he asked at once, concerned.

"You're not going to believe it," she continued.

"Tell me!" he growled.

"She's sitting in the church around the corner, talking to a priest."

Nick just stared at her. "She's what?" he exploded a few seconds later. "Jackie? My Jackie?"

Gaby nodded, smiling.

"It must be the apocalypse," he said heavily.

"That's exactly what I thought. But Mr. Everett never lies."

"You like him," he said, his voice baiting.

"He's really nice," Gaby protested. "And my grandmother wouldn't leave her apartment if she didn't have him to go with her."

He frowned. "Why does your grandmother need a body-guard?"

This required precise answers, so that she didn't give herself away. "*Grand-mère* is very well-to-do," she said finally. "She's had some issues in the past with a family member who wanted what she had."

He scowled even more. "But Everett keeps an eye on you, too, doesn't he?" he persisted.

She flushed. "I suppose so. My grandmother is concerned for me. You see," she said with sudden inspiration, "I could be kidnapped and held for ransom. She has quite a lot of money."

That made sense. Of course the old lady would need a bodyguard. So would Gaby. He studied her surreptitiously. She was very pretty like that, with her hair in a braid, dressed in clothes that Jackie might like. But he remembered her thick, reddish-brown hair loose around her shoulders, her slender body in a gown and robe, holding him in the early morning of the day, comforting him as he dealt with the past.

She was due to leave when she finished cataloging the books. That would be a week or so away. He wished she was already gone. She'd disturbed what little peace he'd been able to find in his life, made him hungry for her soft voice, her incredible empathy. How was he going to feel when she left?

He straightened in his chair. "You're almost done with the cataloging, yes?" he asked abruptly. "You'll be glad to get back to your own life."

She stared at him blankly. He wanted her to go. He wasn't going to ask her to continue as his assistant. "Well, yes," she lied, and she forced a smile to her lips. Inside, she was wilting away.

"Shall we say two weeks from now?" he asked.

She drew in a breath and hoped it didn't sound as shaky as she felt. "That would suit me very well."

"Okay. Let's get back to work."

He refused to think about his apartment with no Gaby. He dressed in black tie for a date with Mara. They were guests of the British Embassy for some gala affair or other, and he had business ties with one of the officials, who'd invited him and his date.

Mara, of course, was thrilled. She pulled a couture garment out of her closet. It had been a present from one of her admirers, and it suited her slender body nicely. It was gold lamé, sleeveless and backless, fantastic with her olive skin and snapping black eyes and long black hair. Nick had her meet him at his apartment, so that he could make sure that Gaby saw them together. He wasn't sure why.

Mara was supposed to come an hour before they were due at the party, but she showed up barely fifteen minutes before they had to leave.

"You look beautiful," Nick had to admit, admiring her gown and the soft wrap she had around her shoulders.

She smiled at him. "You look devastating," she had to admit.

Gaby was in the kitchen, helping Tilly tidy up. She stared at them as Nick brought Mara closer.

"How do I look?" Mara asked her, smiling with faint superiority. She knew the younger woman couldn't afford couture. She probably bought her dresses off-the-rack.

Gaby knew the designer of the dress Mara was wearing, and knew that it was last year's fashion. She just smiled. She had a closet full of couture gowns at home. "You look terrific!" she said, and she smiled.

"It's a Gordon Mays original," Mara cooed. "I love his styles."

"They're quite nice," Gaby said, and almost mentioned a rival designer, but caught herself in time. A poor college graduate, such as the one she pretended to be, couldn't admit that she had designer things, not with Nick listening to every word.

"You must read fashion magazines," Mara replied, insinuating that this was the only way poor Gaby would know about designer clothing.

"Well, yes, I do," Gaby confessed. She smiled. "I love pretty things."

"We'd better go," Nick said.

"Yes, we can't be late. It's a party at the British Embassy, you see," Mara added as an aside. "We were specially invited, because Nick does business with one of the officials. A high-up one," she emphasized.

No way would Gaby tell her that *Grand-mère* had been invited to the same party, but had refused politely to go. She'd had her fill of foreign diplomats. Gaby had, too. Her own past haunted her. The man who'd assaulted her had never been brought to justice because he had diplomatic immunity.

"I hope you both have a lovely time," Gaby said.

"I expect it will be a very long and sweet night," Mara replied, her eyes covertly on Nick. She sighed, just to make the point.

Nick wasn't comfortable with innuendos, not around Gaby, who was as innocent as a lamb. "Let's go," he told Mara.

"Of course. Good night," she called over her shoulder to Gaby.

Just as Nick turned to leave, he spotted Jackie standing inside the door. She was wearing leggings with a short patterned skirt and a blouse that was just barely decent. She'd colored her hair purple and she was wearing sandals.

"Nice dress," Jackie told Mara. "There must be a sale on somewhere."

"Jackie!" Nick snapped.

"Sorry. It was a gift, then?" she persisted with an innocent smile. She'd heard the way the brunette had been speaking to Gaby and it irritated her. Gaby was a kind person. Mara would throw anybody under a bus to enrich herself.

"Jackie, don't you have something to do?" Nick asked sharply.

"Oh, yes. I'm going to sit in my room and play hip-hop until the neighbors call the police."

Nick glowered at her.

She shrugged. "Okay. I'll wear earphones."

She dismissed them both with a languid wave of her hand, actually winked at Gaby when they weren't looking and went on to her room. Gaby worked hard to prevent a smile.

"Good night," Nick said curtly, escorting Mara out.

The door closed behind them. Gaby let out a sigh.

"That woman," Tilly said. She'd tried to look invisible while the turmoil was going on.

"Well, Mr. Chandler likes her," Gaby replied.

"Mr. Chandler is blind," Tilly retorted with a snort. "If he got sick, she'd be off hotfoot to spend time with one of her other lovers. She'd never take care of him. If he marries her, he'll regret it for the rest of his life."

Gaby felt her pulse run away. "Is he planning to marry her?" she asked, hoping she didn't sound as uneasy as she felt.

"Who knows? She's been around a lot longer than the other women he's dated," Tilly told her. "They were all like her. Brassy women who value money over people."

"Money's nice, if you have enough to pay the bills," Gaby said. "But people are far more valuable than diamonds."

Jackie's door opened and she came into the kitchen. "Imagine that skanky woman running you down," she said to Gaby. "That dress was last year's," she added, "and she probably got given it by one of her lovers!"

Gaby let out a breath. "How do you know about couture dresses?" she asked.

"My mother had a friend who designed for one of the more famous couture firms in Paris," she said simply. "I learned a lot from her. Now I read the fashion magazines and dream about how I'd look in one of those dresses." She grimaced and looked down at herself. "Well, not all of us can shop at Saks," she pointed out and grinned.

Gaby laughed. "That was sweet of you. What you said to her."

Jackie colored a little. "You've been kind to me," she said. "I didn't like her running you down. Why didn't you say something?"

"I work here," Gaby said, and smiled. "The boss wouldn't like it."

"Uncle Nick's just as bad as she is," she muttered. "He curses and growls and roars and shouts at people."

"Not so much, lately," Gaby defended him.

"Not since you've been here," Jackie replied, and smiled a little. "And especially lately. He's been really different."

"That could be because of Mara," she pointed out.

"Ha!"

And with that, Jackie smiled at Tilly, and at Gaby, and went back to her room.

It was early in the morning when Nick came back in the door, muttering to himself as he went into the kitchen and tried to figure out how to make coffee.

Gaby heard him banging things around. The sensible thing would be to ignore the growls and go to sleep. But, then, Gaby was rarely sensible lately. Especially when it came to Nick Chandler.

She got up and slid into her bathrobe, making sure it was fastened all the way up. On bare feet, she walked into the kitchen just as he raised the coffeepot with a fearful look on his face.

"If you break it, we won't have coffee for breakfast," she pointed out.

He turned, glaring at her. "What are you doing up?"

"Couldn't sleep for a lion roaring about in the kitchen," she replied, tongue in cheek.

He put the coffeepot down. "Do you know where the hell Tilly keeps the coffee?" he asked in a driven tone.

"Yes. Sit down and I'll fix you a cup."

He dragged out a chair and sat in it. He was still dressed in black tie, but as Gaby worked to make coffee, he took off his tie and dinner jacket and tossed them into an empty chair. He unbuttoned his shirt down to his collarbone. He was hot. And Gaby, even in that concealing bathrobe, was making him hotter.

"Bad night?" she asked.

He made a rough sound in his throat. "You might say that."

She put the coffee on to drip and turned to him. Her hair was down around her shoulders, thick and red-tinted and beautiful.

"I had a little tiff with Mara," he said after a minute. Gaby had put utensils on the table and he toyed with a silver tea-spoon.

"People argue," she said. "They get over it."

"Optimist," he muttered with a glare.

"Optimism is free," she pointed out. "And you can get more with a smile and a gun than you can with a smile." She grinned.

He laughed shortly. "Where did you get that from? Never mind. Your ever-present Mr. Everett, I assume?"

"Yes. He has a gift for odd phrases. I guess it comes from hanging out with mercs and pirates."

"Pirates?" His eyebrows arched.

"Actually, he was hired on with his group to protect a huge

yacht, one of those that cost over two hundred million dollars. It had to go through a place that was thick with pirates. Sadly for them, the pirates didn't expect the owner to shoot back. They planned to take the yacht and sell it on the black market. Probably kill the owner, as well."

"Was it the *Seaspray*?" he asked abruptly.

She blinked. "I don't know. Mr. Everett doesn't share information. Just tidbits of his past, now and then."

"Do you offer him the same comfort you gave to me the other night?" he asked in a purring deep tone, but his eyes were frankly hostile.

"Heavens, no!" she exclaimed, surprised by the question. "Mr. Everett isn't that sort of acquaintance. He doesn't really like women, you see. He protects me, but I'm more like a distant cousin than a single, available woman, if you get my meaning." She smiled. "Most women would run from a man like him, anyway. At least, the sensible ones would."

She paused to pour coffee into two cups and cut off the coffee maker. She put his mug of strong black coffee in front of him and sat down.

"Why?" he wanted to know.

"Mr. Everett makes his living with some pretty deadly skills," she said. "And even though he doesn't actively participate in missions with the other mercs in his group, he's very often in the line of fire." She smiled. "Imagine sitting at home with children while your husband was in the middle of a firefight in some foreign country, and you didn't know if he'd make it back home at all." She shook her head. "It takes a very special woman to marry a man in law enforcement, or a soldier stationed overseas in a combat zone, or a man who likes danger."

He'd frozen over when she mentioned children. His face was taut, his eyes blazing.

"Mr. Chandler," she said softly. "It isn't my business and I shouldn't say this. But living in the past robs you of the future. Bad things happen to people. Tragic things. You can't change them—you can't rewind your life. You just put one foot in front of the other and go on."

He sighed roughly. "In your twenties and you're already a philosopher."

She shrugged. "I've had bad things happen to me," she said simply. "I had to go ahead. I couldn't saddle my poor grandmother with a weepy child who spread gloom and doom everywhere she went."

He seemed to relax a little. He sipped the strong, black coffee. "I miss my daughter," he said after a minute, and there was torment in the words.

"I'm sure you do," she said. "I can't imagine how painful it is, especially considering the circumstances."

He sighed, staring into the black, hot coffee. "I'll never see her dressed up for school. I'll never watch her go out on her first date, learn to drive a car, graduate from high school, get married, have kids of her own." He swallowed the lump in his throat and chugged down two swallows of coffee to make it disappear.

Gaby didn't say a word. She just listened.

He stared at her. He stared hard at her. He was trying to put the past away, and the present was killing him. "I couldn't do anything with Mara," he said curtly. "She gave me both barrels and then she said she was going to call one of her other lovers who could actually perform and wasn't over-the-hill. I walked out and slammed the door."

Gaby's heart was racing. He didn't want the beautiful brunette he'd brought home to show off to Gaby? Why?

She still hadn't spoken. She just looked at him.

"You don't understand, do you?" he asked quietly.

She flushed a little, hating her own naivete. "Well, no. I've never indulged."

He finished his coffee. "A man's biggest sore spot is his prowess in bed," he remarked. "When he can't make it with a woman, it hurts his pride like hell. She's beautiful and sensual. And I don't want her."

He sounded tormented.

"You've had a lot of pressure at work," she began. "And problems with Jackie getting in trouble…" She cleared her throat. "I read that men have that problem from time to time, all men do. It's not just you."

"Yes, well, the problem is that I had it with Mara. And it isn't the first time." He drew in a long breath and sat back in his chair. "I don't know what the hell's wrong with me."

Gaby thought he was the handsomest man she'd ever seen. Lounging back like that, his big body relaxed, his hair-roughened chest on blatant display, he was like something out of a romance novel. She could control her tongue, but not her fascination. He…disturbed her. Very much. And it showed.

He smiled at her, very slowly. His hand went to the buttons of his shirt and he flicked the rest of them out of the buttonholes. "It's warm in here, isn't it?" he asked, and his deep voice was like velvet in the silence of the room.

Her breath caught in her throat and her heart ran wild. She should get up right now and run for her life, barricade the door to her room, nail it shut. He was a worldly man. He probably could see every thought in her mind.

"Come here, Gaby," he said, very softly.

Her mind said *run*. Her body got up and went to him, helplessly in thrall.

He reached up a big hand and pulled her down into his lap. He wrapped her up against him and bent to her soft mouth. He kissed her with a tenderness she'd never have expected from him. And all at once, he became very capable and in the position she was in, she felt it at her hip.

He lifted his lips from hers just enough to allow speech. "And now you know why I was impotent with Mara, don't you?" he whispered. His smile was worldly. "It's all right," he said when he saw the faint fear in her eyes. "I won't do anything that you don't want."

That was what she was afraid of. She was learning things about herself by the second, and the most surprising thing was that she wanted him, too. But she didn't dare let this go any further. It was dangerous to get involved with him. Sooner or later, he'd know who she really was, who her grandmother was, and he'd hate her for lying to him.

She buried her face in his chest, where the hair was thickest, where he smelled of soap and some exotic cologne. He was so beautiful, she thought while she could think. He made her boneless, helpless, when he held her like this.

His mouth nudged her lips apart and he groaned softly as he stood up with her in his arms and carried her to the sofa.

"This," he whispered as he laid her down on the plush couch and followed her down, "is a very bad idea. Are you sure this is what you want?"

She couldn't speak for the thunder of her heartbeat. She just nodded, clinging to his neck.

"What the hell," he murmured, and he slid over her and buried his mouth in her soft lips.

ELEVEN

Gaby had never dreamed she was capable of the sensations Nick drew out of her. She loved the feel of him so close, so warm and strong as he lay against her, his bare chest on her thin gown. Somewhere along the way, he'd removed her thick robe. His big warm hands were all over her, teasing, taunting, tender.

She arched as she felt them teasing at the edge of her firm breasts, moaning softly as the pleasure grew and grew.

He didn't speak. His mouth pressed against her throat, the soft flesh below her collarbone. She felt the fabric give as it was moved aside. Then she felt his mouth on her breast, sliding over it, taking it inside with a faint suction that arched her slender body and made her helpless to stop him.

"You taste like honey," he whispered. "Your breasts are perfect. Beautiful!"

She trembled, afraid and excited, all at once, as he found the other breast with his mouth and repeated the tender possession. All the while, his big hands were on her back, sliding down, lifting her against a hardness that told her more than words. He wanted her. His skin was damp. He was breathing heavily and his mouth grew quickly more insistent.

She had to stop him before it was too late. His big hands were already sliding up her thighs, under the gown. She couldn't afford to be more intimate with him, not with the secrets she was keeping.

"Nick," she whispered unsteadily, "I can't!"

The soft protest got through the fog of pleasure that had enveloped him. He lifted his head and looked down at her, drawing a long breath. "Sadly," he whispered, "I can." He managed a wan smile. "Do you have any old wives' tales that teach you how to calm a man down when he's this excited?" he teased.

He was so uninhibited. He didn't mind sharing intimate secrets with her, and it was puzzling, because he was a man who didn't want marriage. And Gaby was a woman who was afraid of most men. Not of this one. He was unique.

"Come here," she whispered, and drew his face down. She kissed him tenderly on his faintly bristly chin that needed a shave, on his cheeks, on his eyelids, his temples. Soft, slow kisses that had the most amazing effect on him.

Gaby felt him relax, felt the need go out of him. She smiled against his eyelids.

"Where did you learn that?" he asked, and felt jealousy bite into him.

"From one of my romance novels," she confessed.

He chuckled softly, lifting himself on one elbow so that he could see her pale blue eyes, fascination making them brighter. "I guess you're saving it up for marriage."

She smiled gently. "I am," she confessed. "I know I'm out of step with the world, but my grandmother was very strict. I had some of my first education in a convent school. I was—I still am—very religious."

"I used to be," he said. "Before Glenna."

He was closing up again. He looked what he was, a haunted man.

She reached up a small hand and put it against his cheek. "You have to let go," she said softly. "It was a terrible tragedy. You'll never forget it, not really, but you can push the bad memory away and remember the good things." Her hand moved gently into his thick, wavy hair. It felt cool and wonderful under her fingers. "Your little girl isn't gone, Nick. She's sitting up there somewhere watching you, loving you."

He fought down a wave of anguish. He closed his eyes. "Do you really believe that?"

She nodded. "I miss my parents. But I've always thought they were watching over me," she added.

He hugged her close for a minute before he pulled her up and fastened her robe again. She sat there watching him with soft, pale blue eyes that adored him. He saw that and ignored it. He didn't want the sort of involvement she'd want. She wasn't a good-time girl, and he was too honorable to take advantage of her attraction to him. He didn't understand why it felt so damned good to know that she wanted him, trusted him, when he knew how afraid of men she'd been.

He got up and pulled her up, as well. "We have to stop meeting like this," he pointed out. "Jackie and Tilly will start talking about us."

She grinned. "We can swear them both to secrecy," she returned.

He chuckled. He sighed as he looked at the clock. "It's four in the morning," he mused.

"How time flies when we're having fun," she murmured, her eyes twinkling.

"Fun, huh?" he replied, and his own dark eyes glittered as he looked down at her, her hair disheveled by his hands, her mouth softly swollen, her cheeks a deep pink with excitement. "It was fun, all right. But I don't want to get married, and you don't want to have an affair. Does that about cover it?" he added, forcing levity into his tone.

She recovered swiftly. The smile remained, but now it was a disguise. "Well, I'm heartbroken," she said flatly. "I mean, the way you have with women is just devastating to a woman who's never indulged. Where will I learn what to do with a man now?"

He burst out laughing. She had the gift of lightening his black moods, digging him out of them with sassy remarks, teasing. He smiled, and it was genuine. "You can read some more romance novels," he suggested. "Vicarious tutoring."

She made a face. "Nothing half as much fun as the real thing," she commented, and her eyes ate him from head to bare chest to handsome face. "Wow," she added with an audible sigh.

He rolled his eyes. "I'm going to bed. And don't follow me," he said abruptly, with dancing eyes. "I have every intention of locking my bedroom door. I know all about you sex-crazed innocents. Given any incentive at all, you'd be trying to pick the lock."

"Well, I never!" she exclaimed.

He grinned. "I know."

She turned back to the cups, shaking her head. "I give up. And just for the record, you're perfectly safe. I forgot to bring my lock picking tools with me," she added with a wicked grin.

He chuckled all the way down the hall.

At breakfast, he was back to normal, muttering about the overcooked bacon and the undercooked eggs, glaring at poor

Tilly. Jackie and Gaby exchanged amused glances, but they didn't let Nick see.

"You're in Mara's bad books," Nick told Jackie. "You don't make snide remarks to people about their clothes. Especially couture dresses."

"It was last year's model," Jackie said easily. "And she was picking on Gaby. I didn't like it."

Nick was vaguely surprised. He didn't pursue the subject. Imagine Jackie, the little hellion, actually caring about his administrative assistant's feelings. It was a new thing, a delicate thing. He wasn't going to say anything to discourage her. Jackie was calming down.

Gaby noticed it, too. Jackie had surprised her as well with the comment about Mara's dress. It made her feel warm inside. She was fond of the girl.

Gaby smiled at her. "Want to go pub crawling with me tonight?"

"Hell, no!" Nick said at once, glaring at her.

"Not that sort of crawling," she replied. "I want to go to The Snap downtown."

"Anarchists!" he ground out.

"People who long for the old days of coffeehouses with white linen on the tables and silver services, eating dainty pastries and listening to Strauss waltzes," Gaby said, her eyes faraway, seeing the coffeehouse her parents had taken her to, just before they left for overseas.

The sadness countered the memory. She drew a breath. It was a long time ago.

"You won't find any dainty pastries or Strauss waltzes at The Snap," Nick assured her.

"Bongo drums! Bad poetry! People dressed all in black!" Gaby said. "Oh, the excitement!"

"Oh, the Molotov cocktails," he muttered.

"I promise you that we won't try to overthrow a country," Gaby said. Her eyes went to Jackie, who was actually enthusiastic. "Want to go?" she asked.

"Does water freeze?" Jackie returned. "Yes!"

Gaby laughed. "They do serve sandwiches and coffee. We can eat dinner there."

"Great," Nick muttered. "You get sandwiches and I get fish stew." He said the last two words in a bare, angry whisper, and both women laughed helplessly.

"You could come with us, Uncle Nick," Jackie said.

He made a face. "I'm too old."

Gaby stared at him, curious. "You aren't," she replied, her voice soft with emotion. "Age is a thing of the mind. You can be old at twenty and young at ninety. It's all up here." She touched her forehead.

His dark eyes twinkled. He thought about it. But then he remembered Mara and his determination never to marry, never to have another child, never to suffer that horrible loss again. He shrugged and forced his voice to reflect disinterest.

"You two kids go and have fun," he said. "I'm taking Mara to a blues concert." He turned and went into his bedroom.

"Let's meet here at six. And we should get dressed up," Gaby told Jackie.

"I have this radical black outfit," Jackie said as they walked down the hall. "Got anything black?" she asked Gaby.

The older woman just chuckled. "Wait and see."

Later that day, Gaby came out of her bedroom in a slender black dress that came almost to her ankles, with a high rounded neckline and a tight waist, and black slingbacks with an ankle strap. She looked very sexy with her long reddish-brown hair swirling around her shoulders and the pert black beret that completed the outfit.

Jackie was wearing a short skirt with leggings, both black, and a black blouse with bangles. She had a beret, too.

They laughed, taking in each other's new look.

"We're leaving," Jackie called through her uncle's door.

The door opened. He was almost dressed to go out. He was buttoning his shirt as he studied Gaby in a silence thick with emotion. She was exquisite. Most of her clothes were bulky and didn't show her figure. That dress made her look like something out of a fantasy, and he was hard-pressed not to wrap her up in his arms and never let her go. The thought irritated him, and it showed on his hard face.

"Have fun," he said. "Don't overthrow any countries. And don't spread bad poetry around the block," he added to Jackie.

"That's right, spoil our fun." Gaby pouted.

He sighed. He was angry because he wanted Gaby and he couldn't have her. The anger lingered on his features. Gaby saw it and couldn't understand it.

"We'll be back before midnight," Gaby promised.

"Take a cab," Nick said firmly. "There and back."

"We could pick up a nice anarchist who drives a Ferrari..." Gaby teased.

"Out!" he barked.

They left the apartment, laughing.

But inside, Gaby was hurting. Why was he so changeable? He seemed to care about her from time to time, and then he'd come out with something unpleasant, meant to make her back away. She knew too much about him. He was a very private person.

Gaby's conscience was hurting, as well. Nick didn't know why she'd taken the job. And when he found out, there would go any chance of happily ever after with him. Well, there would be no future in loving him, no matter what happened. He'd never marry again. He lived in torment with his ghosts, all alone.

They got to the curb and Everett was standing by the sedan, holding the back door open.

"Nice timing," Gaby laughed.

He shrugged. "Your grandmother is concerned about you. So where you go, I go."

"We're going to an anarchist hideout," Jackie told him with a bland face. "Where we'll learn to overthrow countries."

Everett chuckled. "My kind of place."

He put the women in the back seat, got into the front seat and drove them to the back alley where The Snap was located.

There was another sedan parked nearby when he pulled into a parking space. It contained two men. It was parked with the license tag in view.

"Just a minute, before you get out," Everett said, and there was authority in his deep voice. He pulled out his cell phone and punched in a number. He waited. A muffled voice came on the line.

"License check. Here's the number." He gave it. There was a long pause. Everett was nodding while the women watched, curious. "Okay. Thanks. I owe you one. No, they won't try anything while I'm here. Yes, I am positive." He glanced in the back seat. "She's fine. She and Mr. Chandler's niece are going to learn how to overthrow countries." He laughed. "Yeah. Me, too. Thanks."

He hung up. "Okay, we'll go in."

"You're staying?" Gaby asked, and now she was worried. She'd seen enough movies to suspect who might be in that plain black sedan.

"You bet I am," Everett said quietly.

"Mr. Everett," she began.

"Later."

He escorted them in, past the bouncer, who was employed because liquor was served here, along with coffee.

Everett escorted them to a table against a wall, in a corner. Someone was on the stage, shaking a little with nerves as he got up enough courage to read his poetry to just the sound of bongo drums.

The waitress came around and gave them a menu. Gaby ordered chicken soup and chicken salad sandwiches.

Mr. Everett made a face. "How can you eat chicken?" he asked.

"Well, since the chicken is already deceased and there's no immediate family that wants to bury it…" Gaby began with twinkling eyes.

Everett chuckled.

"I want beef," Jackie said. "They have enchiladas here, and they're almost as good as the ones at El Mercado."

"A girl after my own heart," Everett murmured. "Beef is good eating. But chicken…" He wrinkled his nose and made a rough sound in his throat.

"Okay," Gaby teased. "You've convinced me. I'm having the grilled fish and a nice salad."

"Fish."

"Fish is good for you," she said.

"This fish is covered in a sauce made of God knows what," Mr. Everett said flatly. "And one man who ate it ended up in the emergency room. I'd order something else if I were you."

"Well, you're not me, and I love fish." She smiled at the waitress and gave her order.

The poetry wasn't bad. All three of them watched as shy, introverted people took the stage and became different as they poured their hearts out in verse, or at least something resembling it.

Jackie was taking it in and obviously enjoying what she saw. Gaby smiled at her. She smiled back. It was nice, having company that was congenial. Mr. Everett had gone to the back of the room and he was talking to a man who looked like one of the bouncers. Gaby wondered what they were saying. Surely she wasn't in danger here!

Everett came back a few minutes later. "Some new developments. Nice ones," he told Gaby.

"I can't wait to hear them," Gaby said with a grin.

"What developments are you two into?" Jackie asked.

"Not really us," Gaby prevaricated. "Some that my grandmother found interesting and wanted to know more about."

"Oh." Jackie quickly lost interest and her eyes went back to the stage. After a minute, she caught her breath. "There he is! That's the boy I was telling you about, the one who can do the tango. Excuse me. I'll be right back!"

"A boy who can do the tango?" Everett asked, puzzled.

"He's from South America. He and Jackie are friends at school. He's the exact opposite of Keith, and she wants to learn how to dance the tango." Gaby chuckled softly. "A match made in heaven," she added, nodding toward the back of the room, where Jackie and her tall, handsome friend were talking together.

It was getting late. Jackie was reluctant to go. She invited her friend to the apartment the next weekend and she was going to watch YouTube videos and also buy a tango DVD so that she could practice after he taught her the rudiments of the dance. The boy, whose name was Antonio, was extremely polite and courteous. Gaby approved of him.

When they were back at the apartment, Jackie unlocked the door and went inside. "You coming?" she asked Gaby.

"Just a sec," she said. "I want to know what Mr. Everett found out about grandmother's investment."

"Okay. Door's unlocked," she added with a grin. She closed it.

"Spill it," Gaby told Everett.

"Those guys in the sedan?" he said. He smiled. "You've got more protection than you know."

"Goodness. Are they…?"

"Yes, they are. But they don't break people's knees with bats anymore. What they do has more to do with making money than hurting people. Although they will act if someone jeopardizes the families."

"My cousin Robert," she said. "Is he mixed up with them?"

"Not with this bunch," Everett said. "He's got contacts in another family, a rival one to the one that's protecting you."

"Maybe I need a gun," she joked.

"If you shoot the way you ride a bike, I'm leaving town when you get on the gun range."

She made a face at him.

"So anyway, with a little help from the men watching you, I found a master forger. I sent a couple of guys I know over, after I was tipped off. And guess who was with him? None other than your cousin Robert. I phoned the police and he was taken into custody with the forged papers in his pocket. And the forger was happy to tell what he'd wanted, in return for a lighter sentence. Everybody was happy."

"Thank God," she whispered, her eyes closed. "I was so afraid of losing my whole inheritance. Not that I couldn't get a job and support myself. Well, I have a job, but it was only temporary. Nick…Mr. Chandler that is…says all I'll need is two more weeks here and I can go back to my apartment."

He noticed the faint torment on her face but he was too discreet to mention it. Poor kid. Nick Chandler was a rounder. Since Glenna, he hadn't dated anyone for more than a couple of weeks before his current interest, Mara, and he had a reputation in wealthy circles for his ability to draw beautiful women. None of them lasted long. The minute they started to cling or get possessive or mention marriage, they were out the door.

Gaby knew that, too. She was in no doubt that she'd never fit into Nick's world. She had plenty of money, but she was no party girl. She kept to herself, often staying overnight with her grandmother. She liked a quiet life, relaxed, peaceful. At heart, she was a country girl. Her childhood had been full of visits to her mother's parents, who'd lived on a ranch outside Jacobsville, Texas.

"Is Robert likely to want to come after me if he gets out on bail?" she asked Everett.

"It's a possibility. That's why you have so much protection. Just between us, I don't think he'd dare go against the big boss."

She relaxed a little. "Okay. Thanks, Mr. Everett."

He smiled, said good-night and headed for the elevator.

"Want to watch a movie with me?" Jackie asked from the living room. She'd turned on the television and she was switching channels. "There's this old adventure movie…"

Jackie pulled it up and Gaby let out a little shriek. *"Romancing the Stone!"* she exclaimed. "I love that movie!"

"Me, too," Jackie agreed. "Let me see if Tilly can do us some popcorn." She headed for the kitchen. Before the movie began, she was back with a big bowl of buttered popcorn, and Tilly.

"Tilly never gets to do anything fun around here, so I invited her to the movie," Jackie said.

Gaby grinned at Tilly, who sat down beside her on the sofa. "This is a terrific film. Have you ever seen it?"

"No, but I've always wanted to," came the reply. "I love adventure."

"Me, too, but I'd never want to find myself at the mercy of snakes in a jungle," Gaby said, laughing.

The movie was great fun. Afterward, Tilly left for home and Jackie went into her room to listen to records.

There was a tap at the front door. Nobody was left to answer it except Gaby and, expecting that Nick had lost his key or Mr. Everett had another piece of information to impart, she opened the door with a pleasant smile.

It wasn't either of the men she expected. She realized, after a shocked minute when she was being dragged out into the hall and the door shut, that it was Jackie's boyfriend, Keith.

"So you're trying to take her away from me, are you?" he asked coldly. "Well, she isn't getting mixed up with anybody else. My father just threw me out the door, so Jackie's more valuable than she used to be. I've got plans for her!"

"Disgusting plans, and let me go!" Gaby struggled.

He was strong for a wiry boy. At least he was alone, not accompanied by his usual two cohorts. Or so she thought.

Two other boys, a little younger than Keith, came from around the corner.

"Just in time," Keith said, and he smiled. It was a vicious smile. "Hold her."

Gaby was terrified. She was back in time, in her grandfather's study, with an amorous man and spectators, and she was helpless to free herself. She struggled, but the boys were too strong.

She fought, but she knew it would do no good. Her pale eyes were round with fear and nausea. What would they do to her? Keith liked virgins, and she was one. But he didn't know. So what was he thinking?

"Just so you know better than to interfere again," Keith said, and drew back his fist.

They left her on the carpet, crying and cursing, with bruises all over her chest and arms and stomach, and pain everywhere.

She doubled up on the carpet. She heard footsteps. The voices were deep and strange, and the highly polished black shoes were unfamiliar.

"Call 911," one of the men said. "Hurry!"

"What if they send the cops?"

"It's not a precinct near ours—they won't recognize us. Now do it!" the deep voice growled.

Gaby managed to open her eyes and she looked up, through layers of pain. They were wearing nice suits, all three of them. One had thick wavy black hair with a lot of silver in it. He looked much older than Nick, but just as formidable. The other two weren't as good-looking, and she noticed bulges under the suit coats.

The oldest one went down on one knee next to Gaby. "You poor kid. That damned little punk. We'll have a few words with him," he added curtly. "You won't have any more trouble. Hell of a shame, after what you've already been through. We've got your back, honey. Don't worry."

She swallowed, hard. "Thanks," she whispered.

He touched her disheveled chestnut hair. "No problem. Just lie still until the EMTs get here. I'm so damned sorry. We saw the boy and his buddies, but we didn't realize he was going to be a threat to you."

"Neither did I," she whispered.

Sirens sounded outside. Not long afterward, there was a commotion in the hall as the EMTs came with a gurney.

Jackie, having heard the commotion, opened the door and gasped. "Gaby!" she exclaimed, going on one knee. "Are you okay? What happened?"

"Your boyfriend happened," the oldest man said harshly. "And he's going to be very sorry that he did."

She bit her lower lip. "Oh, Gaby," she said softly.

"I'm okay," Gaby managed.

"Hey, Antonio's going to teach you to tango," the older man told Jackie with a smile. "He's my great-nephew."

"You're Uncle Jacob!" she said. "I know you!"

He chuckled. "Yeah. I'm Jacob."

They were standing back away from Gaby. The EMTs were checking the damage. "We're taking her to the hospital," one of them said. He gave the location. "They'll probably keep her overnight at least, but she'll need someone to sign her in unless she's able to do it herself."

"I can do it," Gaby said, feeling sick.

"I'll come with you. Let me get my purse and lock up, and I'd better call Uncle Nick…"

"No," Gaby said firmly. "Leave him a note. He's at a concert. Don't bother him."

Jackie hesitated.

"Please," Gaby emphasized. She didn't want Nick to leave Mara and cause more trouble for him. "I'm not killed, you know, just bruised."

"He'll be mad," the younger girl said.

"I'll square it with him. Leave a note."

"You can ride in with us," Jacob told her. "We won't let anyone hurt you."

"Okay," Jackie replied. She grinned. "Can I have a gun?"

Jacob just laughed. "Get out of here."

"I'll just grab my purse," Jackie said.

Gaby was checked out by a tall man in a lab coat, and she was wheeled into the imaging department for tests, to make sure there was no internal damage. There wasn't. No broken bones either, thank goodness.

"You've got multiple bruises and you'll be sore for a few days," a nice resident told her. "We'll give you something for the pain tonight, but we won't need to keep you."

"Thanks," Gaby said with a sigh.

"You will need to speak to the police, however," the resident added. "They're waiting outside the emergency room, with some, ahem, rather rough-looking gentlemen."

"Not to worry, it's just the local branch of the Mafia," Gaby assured him with a grin.

He chuckled. "Sure."

She checked herself out. Jackie was in the waiting room, thumbing through a magazine. A police officer was standing apart from Jacob and his two cohorts. They were staring at each other.

"Miss Dupont?" the officer said politely. "Do you feel up to giving me a statement?"

"You bet I do," Gaby said gruffly. She glanced at Jackie and winced. "Sorry."

"No, I'm sorry," Jackie said surprisingly. "I didn't realize how dangerous Keith was until he did this." Her face tautened. "Nobody beats up my friend."

Gaby smiled warmly. "You sweetheart."

Jackie actually flushed.

Gaby gave the police officer a statement. He listened carefully and offered his support. After a quick smile of reassurance, he left. Jacob and his boys were ready to drive Jackie and Gaby home, and they were headed for the front door when a furious Nick Chandler came through it.

He had an equally furious Mara in tow. "What the hell happened?" he demanded. He looked at Gaby and the anger grew exponentially as she murmured that she'd been attacked outside his apartment. She could barely stand and her face was stark white. "Who did that to you?" he asked in a tone that could have stopped a charging tiger.

"My boyfriend. Keith," Jackie said quietly. "He was angry that Uncle Jacob's great-nephew, Antonio, was going to come and teach me the tango." She glanced at Gaby and winced. "I'm so sorry, Gaby. I thought he was just talking big. He said you were trying to get me away from him and he'd get even. I'm just so sorry. I'd have said something if I'd had any idea he was serious!"

"It's okay," Gaby said, her voice faltering. "I'll be fine. I'm just bruised."

Nick looked at her with pained dark eyes. He knew what it must have been like for her, after what she'd endured as a teenager. "God, I'm sorry I wasn't there," he said. "I'd have made mincemeat out of that boy!"

"Now, now," Jacob said in a soft tone, "you're an officer of the court. Let's have no such talk. Besides," he added with twinkling dark eyes, "that's our department. We'll take care of the little twerp."

Before Nick could open his mouth, Mr. Everett came in the door and looked around, spotting Gaby. He looked as furious as Nick did.

"We're going to look like a parade," Gaby said on a sigh.

"What happened?" Everett demanded. "Your grandmother had a call from your great-aunt, who had a call from a man in New Jersey, who called an acquaintance in New York who called...Jacob?" he asked, surprised. "This isn't your turf!"

Jacob shrugged. "Detroit's not that far from here. And we had an invite from the guys whose territory this is," he added with a smile. "How you doing, Everett? Long time no see."

"I'm in the protection business these days," Everett replied with a smile.

"Now, that's our racket," Jacob protested.

"Not that sort of protection. I don't use baseball bats," he added.

"Neither do we. Unless people hurt somebody we like." He glanced at Gaby. "Case in point," he said, indicating her.

"Who?" Everett asked curtly.

"My boyfriend," Jackie said with a sad little sigh.

"Your ex-boyfriend," Uncle Nick emphasized.

"The one night I thought it was safe to go out to eat," Everett said with faint sorrow.

"We'd better get Gaby home," Nick said.

"We can drive her," Jacob offered.

"I've got the limo outside," Everett seconded.

"She's going with me," Nick said, and dared anyone else to protest.

"But, Nick," Mara began.

He just looked at her and she was immediately silent.

"Thanks, guys," Gaby told the three men, and Everett.

They all shrugged.

It was a quick, silent ride home. Nick was fuming. Mara was fuming. Unseen, Jackie was holding Gaby's hand in the back seat. Gaby was grateful for it. She felt very uneasy.

TWELVE

It was a very tense few miles back to Nick's apartment. Mara was furious and not bothering to hide it. She said she'd wait in the car while Nick took Gaby and Jackie upstairs.

Nick didn't argue. He herded Jackie and Gaby into the elevator, which, fortunately, was empty.

"I didn't know he wasn't just making a threat. Honest," Jackie told her uncle. "I wouldn't do anything to hurt Gaby."

"I know that," Gaby said quietly. She smiled at Jackie.

"You aren't to see him ever again," Nick told the girl angrily. "And if you hear a word from him, I want to know."

"I'll tell you if I do," Jackie promised. "Uncle Jacob may find him before then, though."

"Uncle Jacob?" he asked.

"Well, he's Antonio's great-uncle, really. He's from Detroit, but he's been staying with his sister and Antonio." She grinned. "Antonio's late father was from Argentina and he won dance contests, so he taught his son lots of fancy foot-work. Antonio can dance the tango."

"So can I," two voices replied.

Nick and Gaby stared at each other.

"Wow! You never said, Uncle Nick," Jackie chided.

"I never had a reason to." He studied Gaby's poor face, drawn with pain. Some small bruises on her face were just beginning to come out. He winced. "You'll feel worse in the morning, I'm afraid," he told her. "I've been in fights a few times. The second and third days are always the worst. Don't do anything for a couple of days. I'll manage."

"It's only bruises," Gaby protested. "I can still type."

"If you go out, anybody who sees the way you look will assume that you didn't type fast enough, and I'll get a visit from our local police precinct," he said with returning humor.

She laughed softly and then winced when it hurt. "Okay."

"Antonio's coming over this weekend, okay?" Jackie asked her uncle.

He actually smiled at her. "Okay, honey," he said.

Jackie beamed. It was like a new start for her in the family.

Nick saw that. It made him feel better. Of course, he'd still like a shot at Jackie's boyfriend. He couldn't forget the pure rage he'd felt when he read the hurried note Jackie had left on the living room coffee table. He and Mara had planned to go on to a nightclub, but he wanted to check on Gaby first. A good thing he had. He could only imagine how horrible he would have felt if he'd been nightclubbing while Gaby was in the hospital emergency room.

"I won't keep you up, but tell me how it happened," Nick said to Gaby, who sat down on the sofa after Jackie called good-night and went to her room.

She explained about Keith and the two boys coming to the door. She'd opened it without thinking.

"Don't ever do that again," Nick said quietly. "The chain latch is there for a reason."

She nodded. "Okay. I'm sorry…"

"Don't apologize," he said shortly. "None of this was your fault. I'm going to look into a warrant for that young man."

"Good luck finding him," she said. "If Uncle Jacob finds him first, they'll have to put what's left over in a shoebox."

"Uncle Jacob?" he asked.

"Sorry, everybody was calling him that."

"And you know him, how?" he persisted.

"It's like this," she said. "My late maternal grandmother has a sister, Rose, who lives in Jacobsville, where my mother was from. She has a friend who's a boss in the New Jersey crime family. He, in turn, has a friend who's a boss in New York and the New York boss has ties to a crime boss in Detroit. So the boss in New Jersey called the boss in New York, who called the boss in Detroit, who's, apparently, Antonio's great-uncle Jacob."

"I'm getting a headache," Nick said as the connections whirled around his brain.

"Anyway, Uncle Jacob's three guys were very support-ive. They called 911 and got an ambulance and some EMTs here, and they stood watch to make sure Keith didn't come back. So, yes, it's sort of an uncle Jacob situation, if you see my meaning."

"I'm so damned sorry I wasn't here," he said through his teeth, and his eyes bored into her, ablaze with anger and some-thing else, something deep and unidentifiable.

"It's okay," she said. "I'm fine." Her phone in her jeans pocket exploded with the soccer World Cup theme. She an-swered it and grimaced. "*Oui, Grand-mère*, yes, *oui. Je suis bonne.* Yes, of course. They did come. Yes. Yes. I'm all right. A few bruises. They'll fade in time for your birthday party, yes, and I have plenty of concealing makeup. *Oui.* Don't worry. *Je t'aime aussi. Oui. Bonne nuit.*"

"You speak French beautifully," Nick said softly.

"I learned it as a child, during summers with my grandmother in France," she said, smiling. "She had a huge estate outside Paris."

She still had it, but she made it sound as if that was a thing in the past.

"You're sure you're all right?" he asked.

"I'm sure. Thanks for coming to get us."

"No problem. I'll drive Mara home. Go to bed."

"On my way," she promised. She got to her feet and forced a smile. Mara bothered her. She didn't understand why.

"Gaby."

She turned, a question in her pale eyes.

He moved a step closer, tilted her chin up and bent and kissed her so tenderly that she felt it all the way to her toes.

"We're not all animals," he whispered.

She felt shaken all over. She smiled and nodded, her eyes lost in his for a few long seconds before she forced herself to turn and walk down the hall to her bedroom. He was still standing there, watching her, as she went in and closed the door.

It took several days for the bruises to fade and the discomfort to ease. Meanwhile, she did Nick's typing, answered the phone and finished up the cataloging of the books in his library. Another week and Gaby would have to leave the apartment, and Nick and Jackie, behind. It depressed her just to think about it. She'd become fond of Jackie, and too fond of Nick. Since her attack, he'd been supportive and kind, but he'd removed himself emotionally. She understood, in a way. He wasn't going to let himself get too close to her. He was still stuck in the past, in his own tragedy, trapped and unable to let go. In a way, it made things easier for Gaby. She didn't want to leave; she was crazy about Nick. But she understood that he was never going to marry anyone, and Gaby was impossibly old-fashioned about falling into a casual physical relationship, even with a man she adored. It was impossible.

Grand-mère's birthday party was Saturday. Gaby both looked forward to it and dreaded it. She didn't like crowds, and parties were a painful reminder of what had happened to her in her teens. But she loved her grandmother; there was no question of missing the party.

So she concentrated on her work, except for a couple of hours on Friday that she took off to go to her own apartment and pick up the couture gown she'd purchased for this special event.

It was from a famous French design house, palest amber, pure silk, close-fitting with a plunging neckline and low back, ankle-length and extremely flattering. The diamonds *Grand-mère* had given her only a few days ago, a family legacy that her grandmother decided she should have now, would complete the outfit. She had a necklace with a thick gold chain and a huge tear-shaped diamond in the setting, surrounded by smaller diamonds. There were matching earrings and bracelet, the set in 18 karat yellow gold. The dress was plain, but the diamonds would complement it.

"I'll come for you about six tonight if that suits you," Everett said over the phone early Saturday morning.

"I'll be ready. Thanks."

"Oh, no need for that. You'll have another escort, not quite as visible as I am."

She burst out laughing at the thought of being watched over by guardian angels in black limousines. "But Keith's in jail."

"His buddies aren't," he replied drolly. "Nobody's taking any chances. There's still Cousin Robert, who's out on bail and mad as a wet hen."

Gaby sighed. "Well, it may be a memorable birthday party for my grandmother," she said.

"She'd love it if she got to meet any of your invisible protectors," he chuckled. "She's been shaking information out of me about Uncle Jacob."

"She finds bad boys fascinating."

"As I recall, you had a brief infatuation with the antagonist of the new *Star Wars* movies," he murmured. "A memorable 'bad boy.'"

"Yes, but fortunately, the type who isn't real and can't put me in the hospital," she said. "Good thing the bruises have faded enough to be concealed. I'd be the star attraction."

"No surprise there."

"Who's coming this year?" she asked.

"Everybody who's important in the city, and the state and the country. And a few scalawags."

"Oh, did she invite you, too?" she teased.

He chuckled. "Naturally. Somebody has to keep the peace."

"Who else?"

"Nobody you don't know."

She relaxed. She was fairly certain that her grandmother wouldn't invite Nick. "Okay. Thanks, Mr. Everett."

"It's my job to keep you all safe. But you're welcome. I'll see you later today."

"I'll be ready."

She'd worried about wearing the gown and the diamonds in front of Nick. He might not recognize a couture gown, but he would certainly know diamonds and real gold if he saw them. But Nick was out for the evening. He'd left before dinner on a date, wearing black tie. He looked so devastatingly handsome that Gaby had been hard-pressed to hide her admiration. But she had, only smiling when he wished her a curt good-night.

Jackie had gone over to Antonio's house to practice the tango. Uncle Jacob had sent one of his men to fetch her, and neither Nick nor Gaby had any reason to fear for her safety.

It was a relief, to walk out in her slinky gown, with a cashmere wrap around her shoulders, without worrying about someone seeing her in her true feathers.

When she arrived at the party, her grandmother was wearing a couture gown of her own, lavender, with sapphire jewelry twinkling in the lights of the chandelier in the drawing room and the sprawling living room. Even in her early seventies, her grandmother still had beauty in her face and she moved with the grace of a fairy.

Gaby paused to kiss her soft cheek. "You look marvelous," she said softly.

"Ah, and so do you, *ma chérie*," her grandmother replied. "There is champagne. The finest vintage, from our own estates outside Paris." She leaned closer. "Eat something before you drink much of it, yes?"

Gaby laughed. "Of course!"

Mr. Everett looked snazzy in a dinner jacket, she thought as he escorted her to the bar. She told him so.

He made a face. "I'm much more comfortable in another sort of black suit," he remarked.

She looked around, smiling. "At least you won't have to dodge bullets in here," she remarked.

He sighed. "Apparently so."

★ ★ ★

There was a small band, situated on a hastily erected stage. They were very good. The buffet table drew crowds, as did the bar, but soon there was dancing. The rugs had been moved to the sides of the huge room, along with the grand piano that Madame played and the exquisite furniture.

Gaby was standing on the edge of the dance floor with a flute of champagne when a friend of her grandmother's came to ask her to dance. He was tall and handsome still in his fifties. Guy Denton had been almost a father to her over the years. He'd taken her sailing in one of the yachts he built when she was much younger. He was the kindest man she knew.

"Am I too old a partner for you?" he teased.

"You certainly are not, Guy," she replied. He was a millionaire in his own right. He built yachts. He was one of her grandmother's best friends and certainly one of Gaby's. "You dance divinely."

"I try, Gaby," he chuckled, as he led her onto the dance floor.

They were playing an old-fashioned waltz. He danced Gaby around the area, laughing with her at the joy of the music. "Don't they play well?" he asked.

"They do. It's why they keep getting asked back. But I have it from the drummer that they'd much rather play heavy metal."

"No problem. I like that, too."

"So do I," Gaby agreed with a smile.

"I spent a year in Vienna, where they turn out magnificently for waltzes. I learned it there. I must have been twenty-two or so."

"*Grand-mère* had me taught," she replied, smiling up at him. "She thought that I should learn some classic dances, along with the more modern ones." She made a face. "She thinks people should dance together, but she's never found a dance she didn't like or couldn't do, with a little tutoring."

"Speaking of tutors," Mr. Denton replied, "she has a new tango instructor."

"I know," Gaby said, and tiny lights glittered in her pale eyes. "I have every intention of being here for her next lesson, too."

"Ah. I wondered if you knew about him."

"Mr. Everett ferreted out some information."

He grinned. "I expect he could ferret information out of a rock, Gaby."

The music had stopped and they were standing at the open balcony, which stretched from one end of the apartment to the other, overlooking Lake Michigan. They walked just to the doorway. "It's beautiful out here," Gaby remarked.

"Indeed it is." He slipped an arm around her waist and she leaned her head on his shoulder. He chuckled. "You used to lay your head on my shoulder when you were thirteen," he remarked.

"Yes, just after I lost my parents. You were like Dad. I never told you how much I appreciated having you in my life," she added, turning toward him.

"I loved having an adopted daughter," he said with a sigh. "I should have married and had kids."

"Yes, you should…" She stopped in midsentence and her face went white. Nick Chandler was standing across the room with Mara, in a fabulous burgundy gown. Also last year's, Gaby was thinking before the panic set in. But Nick was staring at Gaby with eyes that burned even at a distance. She moved a little closer to Guy instinctively.

She wasn't sure what to do. It would be impossible to hide. But she felt like it when Nick came striding across the room with Mara in his wake, oozing icy anger.

"Oh, dear," Gaby murmured with a sigh. "Here we haven't even had dinner and I appear to be the appetizer..."

Her partner turned and saw who was coming. "Nick!" he exclaimed, grinning as he extended a hand. "Nice to see you again. How's the yacht?"

"Purring like a kitten," Nick said, barely containing the anger he felt. "Your craftsmanship is without peer." He paused. "You know Madame Dupont, I gather?"

"A friend of many years. Oh, do you know Gaby...?" He indicated his partner.

Nick was breathing slowly so that he didn't lose his temper. "Yes. She works for me."

"She what?" Mr. Denton exclaimed, with a puzzled glance at Gaby, who was red in the face and obviously unsettled. "But she has no need to work!"

"Obviously." Nick was adding up the diamonds that Gaby was wearing, and obviously, he'd come to a dark conclusion about how and from whom she'd obtained them.

"If you'll pardon me?" Nick asked with a forced smile, and moved to catch Gaby's arm and tug her out onto the balcony, leaving behind a fuming Mara with a surprised Guy Denton.

"Nice diamonds," Nick said icily. "Denton's right, you sure as hell don't need to work. I gather he's your sugar daddy?"

Gaby stared up at him, wide-eyed. "I beg your pardon?"

"You mercenary little opportunist," he said through his teeth. "He's at least fifty-three, if not older. But I guess you don't notice the gray hairs, do you?"

Gaby's pale blue eyes began to flash warning signals. "I don't need a sugar daddy, thank you very much! And just where do you get the idea that anything I do is any of your business?"

He looked her up and down with eyes that condemned every inch of her. "Poor little innocent, afraid of men, working so hard for her living. It was all a lie. You had your cap set at me, didn't you? Except that Guy Denton's worth a little more than I am. Isn't that right?"

Gaby was almost shaking with righteous indignation, her small hands curling at her hips. But she forced a smile and cocked her head at him. "He's worth a lot more than you are," she said with pure venom. "And I don't have to wear last year's couture models because I can afford the new ones!" She'd raised her voice deliberately so that Mara, just inside the doorway, could hear her.

"Don't insult my date!" Nick raged at her. He was jealous and full of self-hatred because he was jealous. He'd been certain that Gaby was what she seemed to be, and she was the exact opposite of the woman she'd pretended to be. No way was he confessing how close he'd come to wanting her in his life forever.

"Why not?" she asked. "She's not shy about insulting me."

"She has impeccable bloodlines," he said furiously. "Her great-grandfather was a former mayor of the city!"

"Oh, gee-whiz, and here's little me with no illustrious ancestors to mention," she said on a mock sigh. "How sad."

He was ready to explode. "You lied to me! You fed me a load of bull about your bad experience and I fell for it. What a good thing I agreed to come with Mara tonight, so that I could see you for what you are."

"And what's that?" Gaby asked with a blithe smile.

"A prowling she-cat on the take. Damn, you'd think I'd be able to recognize one when I saw it, at my age."

"You should try not to get so upset over things," she advised. "I mean, a man of your age…" She let her voice trail off.

"I'm younger than your lover by a damned sight!"

"Oh, youth is in the mind, you know. Mr. Denton is very young-minded." She smiled even more broadly.

He looked as if he hated her. He did. She'd played him. His pride was smoldering, along with a piece of his heart. But she'd never know how badly she'd hurt him. "Pack your things and get out of my apartment tonight, is that clear? I never want to see you again. Jackie's out of your life, too, but I think you can assume that without any help from me."

He was condemning her, hating her—it was all there in his face. He'd jumped to conclusions and she had no hope of convincing him that he was wrong. It was just as well. He wasn't the sort of man to forgive and forget, and it was hopeless anyway. He'd never want her for anything other than a few hours in bed. She might as well let him enjoy his tarnished image of her. So she went back to Guy and slid her arm through his.

"Sorry to leave you high and dry, Guy. I had a few things to iron out with my former boss," she said. She even smiled at Nick.

Mara clutched at Nick's arm. "Darling, the buffet's being set up and I'm starved." She glanced at Gaby, as if she'd just noticed her. "Oh, hello. Robbed a bank, did you?" she added when she noted the very real diamonds the other woman was decked out in.

"Only Guy Denton," Nick said for her, his face hard as stone. He took her arm. "Let's get something to drink. See you around, Guy."

He tugged Mara away while she was trying to plant another insult on Gaby.

"Why didn't you tell him where the diamonds came from?" Guy asked curiously.

"He doesn't want to get married. Neither do I. And you know what my grandmother would say to anything else," she said, keeping her voice light although her heart was like a pincushion in her chest. "Sorry to put you on the spot, though."

"Oh, I loved it," he teased. "I'm quite happy to have people

think I can attract a woman as beautiful and young as you."
He chuckled. "Gaby—" he sobered "—are you sure you don't
want me to explain?"

"I'm sure. But thanks."

Nick had poured himself a full glass of whiskey at the bar.
He turned, while Mara was picking at food on the buffet, and
raised his glass to Gaby with a mocking smile. She turned
her back on him.

While Gaby was trying to restrain herself from picking up
one of her grandmother's revered pieces of pottery and going
over to slam it into Nick's thick head, the band stopped the
music and played a fanfare.

The birthday cake was wheeled in, a huge concoction with
multiple layers but few candles. Madame told nobody her
real age.

She came to meet the cake, smiling. "Thank you all for
coming. The cake looks quite delicious! And now, *ma chérie*, you come and help cut it. Most of you know my granddaughter, Gaby Dupont," she added as she beckoned to the
younger woman.

Nick's face went pale under its olive tan even as Gaby's
eyes spit lances at him. He was gaping at her. Gaby turned
on her heel, delighted at his shock, oblivious to the deer-in-
the-headlights look on Mara's face, and walked elegantly to
the older woman, smiling.

Madame Dupont slid an arm around her waist. "You are
trembling," she whispered in French. "A disagreement with
the handsome man there, yes?"

"He's Nick Chandler," Gaby choked out. "Didn't you know
when you invited him, *Grand-mère*?" she asked huskily.

"Mr. Chandler? That is he?" She actually gasped. "It was the
woman with him, Mara, who was invited. Her uncle owed her
a favor, he said, and asked that she could come. It is, of course,

one of the premier social events of the season." She kissed the other woman's cheek. "Oh, my poor lamb, I am so sorry!"

"Don't be. Obviously, he's leaving," Gaby replied, watching Nick escort a protesting Mara out of the room and, presumably, out of the apartment.

"It's your birthday," Gaby reminded her grandmother, with a forced smile. "So you enjoy it. Come. Let them light the candles. You can blow them out and we'll all have cake!"

There was a slight hesitation, but the older woman agreed. It was too late to do much about what had happened.

It was late when the party broke up. Gaby's grandmother stopped dancing long enough to tell her goodbye. She was dancing mostly with Uncle Jacob, which brought a tiny amused smile to the younger woman's face.

"Don't you worry, my guys will be right behind you all the way home," Jacob assured her. He gave her grandmother a thoughtful look. "I'm going to teach your grandmother how to tango. Some idiot's been teaching her the wrong way to do it."

Gaby felt utter delight, especially when she saw her grandmother flush like a young girl on a first date. After all, Jacob was pretty close to her age, according to Mr. Everett, who'd checked him out. "That will be nice."

"Well, yes," her grandmother stammered. She laughed suddenly. "It will be very nice." She winked at Gaby, unseen, before she hugged and kissed her and wished her a goodnight. Gaby wished her a happy birthday, once more, and went away with Mr. Everett. There was still an uncomfortable chore to perform.

Mr. Everett took her by Nick's apartment but refused to come inside.

"I only have one good eye left," he said by way of explanation. "Your boss was spoiling for a fight when he left your grandmother's apartment."

Gaby sighed. "I'll get my things and be right out," she promised.

She unlocked the apartment and went inside. She hesitated, dreading a confrontation. But nobody was home, she noted with a relieved sigh. Tilly would have left already. Jackie wasn't home yet, and Nick certainly wasn't. He was probably at Mara's apartment, Gaby thought miserably, raging about Gaby and her deception. Just as well, too. She could evacuate in peace.

She gathered up her things and put them in her case, careful to check all the drawers as she went. Before she left, she penned a note to Jackie and left it on her bed, along with her keys to the apartment. It was Gaby's address and phone number, in case Jackie ever needed someone to talk to. She'd grown fond of the girl. It was a wrench to leave her. A wrench to leave Nick, too, but now that he knew who Gaby's grandmother was, he'd be sure to remember the case that involved her grandfather and he'd figure out very quickly why Gaby had come to work for him. At least she was spared from that unpleasant confrontation.

As she paused at the door, she took one last look around and winced. So much of her life was being left behind here, so many wonderful things she'd experienced that would probably never come again for her. She let out a sigh and closed the door. It was actually painful.

Nick came home from Mara's apartment half-asleep and so morose that Jackie, who'd been home for just a few minutes, wasn't comfortable asking him why Gaby had left. Because it was obvious that Gaby was gone. Jackie had knocked and gone into the bedroom to tell her all about Antonio and found it empty. That explained the note and keys she'd found on her bed.

She had a sneaking suspicion that Gaby's sudden departure had something to do with her uncle Nick. Judging by his appearance, it had a lot to do with it. She'd never seen him look like that before.

She was going to miss Gaby. The other woman had brightened up the apartment with her laughing outlook on life. Now there was just Tilly, who was mostly glum, and her uncle, who was mercurial and unpredictable.

Still, she would have asked him about Gaby, but he went into his office and poured himself a drink. A very large one from the sound of it. She expected the door to close, but he came out, the drink in his hand, his jacket and tie off.

"Is Gaby asleep?" he asked.

She bit her lip.

His expression changed. He went down the hall and threw open Gaby's door after a quick knock. He stood there, devastated. Well, what had he expected after what he'd accused Gaby of doing? Loudly, and in public, and at her grandmother's birthday party, as well.

He leaned against the doorjamb and took a swallow of his drink. "So, she's gone."

"Yes. She didn't even leave a note." That wasn't quite true. She'd left Jackie contact information, but Gaby hadn't wanted him to know it and had spelled it out to Jackie with a brief note under her contact information. Obviously Nick hadn't expected Gaby to leave, after whatever had happened.

He sighed. "Just as well," he muttered to himself and shouldered away from the jamb. "Just as well." He stopped suddenly and turned. "You watch where you go," he said gently. "Keith may get out on bail."

"Not likely," she said. "His dad threw him out. He's out of

drug money. I expect that's why he was so mad at me, and at poor Gaby for encouraging me to hang around with Antonio."

"Gaby's grandmother could buy half the city if she wanted to," he remarked to no one in particular.

"Excuse me?" Jackie asked, having no idea what he was talking about.

"The party Mara was invited to was at the apartment of Madame Melissandra Dupont."

"Yeah, she's in the society pages all the time. They say she owns this huge wine-making estate outside Paris. She's super rich. So...?" Jackie prompted, because he wasn't making any sense.

He glanced at her. "She's Gaby's grandmother."

Jackie stared at him. Gaby's grandmother was rich. She had a bodyguard, Mr. Everett, who was looking out for Gaby. "Well, I knew her grandmother had money. I just didn't know who she was," Jackie said.

Nick took a deep breath and a huge swallow of whiskey. "Gaby was wearing a couture gown and a fortune in diamonds and dancing with a guy in his fifties." His lips made a thin line.

And suddenly Jackie knew what had happened. She just stared at him. "But Gaby's not like that," she began. "I mean, she could have dressed like an ingenue, but she never did. She kicked around in jeans and loafers and T-shirts. Even if she had a rich family, she never cared to act rich, Uncle Nick."

He cocked his head and smiled at her. "Fifteen, and you're smarter about people than I am, despite the fact that I've spent years in courtrooms seeing the absolute worst in human behavior."

"Gaby was kind to me," she said simply, and felt a terrible sense of loss.

His jaw tautened. "She was kind to me, as well. Which

makes what I said to her tonight even more unforgivable..."
He turned away, his heart leaden in his chest. "I've got some
work to do. Good night."

Before she could answer him, he was in his office behind
a closed door.

Gaby had blurted the whole miserable story out to Mr.
Everett as he escorted her back to her own luxury apartment
near her grandmother's, carrying her bags with him.

"He'll get over it," he said.

"Not once he realizes who I really am, and why I was
working for him, I'm afraid," she said heavily.

He put her bags down in the apartment. "Time heals," he
said.

"Sure it does," she returned cynically. "Thanks for the
ride."

He shrugged. "Keep your door locked."

"You can bet on that." Her phone rang. For a blissful instant, she thought it might be Nick. It was her grandmother.
She smiled sadly as she noted the caller ID. "*Grand-mère*,
checking on me. I'll say good-night," she told Everett.

"You have a good one."

"Thanks. You, too."

She closed the door, locked it and answered the phone.

Nick wasn't at the breakfast table. Jackie had told Tilly
briefly what was going on. Uncle Jacob had been vocal about
what happened, so Antonio heard all about it and told Jackie.

"But she's not like that," Tilly argued in a whisper. "Gaby
doesn't put on airs or even act rich."

"Men are blind," Jackie said with street smarts.

"Very." Tilly bit her lower lip. Breakfast was on the table.

"Shall we draw straws to see who calls your uncle to the table?"

"I'll go," Jackie said. "If you hear screams, just ignore them," she added with a twinkle in her eyes.

She knocked on her uncle's bedroom door. "Uncle Nick?" She knocked again. "Uncle Nick!"

Hesitantly she opened the door and peeked in. The bed was still made. It hadn't been slept in. She wondered if he'd gone to Mara's last night. Then, on an impulse, she went to his study door and knocked.

There was a mumbled groan.

She opened the door. Her eyes widened like saucers. Her uncle might take a social drink once in a while, and he had a highball when he was wired. But he was obviously extremely hungover. His hair was mussed, its thick waves disturbed. He needed a shave, badly. He was still sitting at his desk, and had obviously been sleeping at it.

"Uncle Nick?" Jackie asked, her voice rising involuntarily, because he was a shocking sight.

"Don't shout," he muttered, holding his head and wincing.

She whispered. "I wasn't. Tilly has breakfast."

"Breakfast." He blinked. "Breakfast."

He got up, a little unsteadily, and worked his way to the door. "What time is it?"

"Ten. I slept in."

He drew a steadying breath. He was feeling a little nauseous. Food might help. He sat down heavily at the table, oblivious to Tilly's shocked stare. "Coffee. Black," he muttered.

Tilly poured him a cup and put it beside his plate.

He fumbled it to his lips.

"You look awful," Jackie remarked.

"Thanks."

She and Tilly exchanged glances.

Nick ate a little of his breakfast and pushed his plate away. He'd hoped that his memories of last night were just a bad dream, but the coffee woke him up and he realized it wasn't a nightmare.

"Where did Gaby go?" he asked Jackie.

"No idea," she lied.

"Maybe to her grandmother's," he said on a heavy sigh. He sipped more coffee. "Some of her grandmother's people were executed during the French Revolution. Her family goes back a long way in France. In fact, her grandmother is a distant relation of the pirate Jean Lafitte..."

He stopped dead. French Revolution. Lafitte. Madame married a Chicago native of French ancestry named Dupont. Dupont. Madame had been involved in a very nasty divorce action a few years back, which resulted in her husband's arrest and prosecution. He remembered the case. His firm had represented Charles Dupont, for God's sake!

He jerked up out of his chair, startling the two women, and stalked back into his study. He turned on his computer and pulled up a file. Dupont. His firm had represented a man named Dupont, who was charged with selling his teenage granddaughter to a foreign diplomat to pay off gambling debts.

Gaby. That had been Gaby, and he'd never connected her name to the case. He sat back heavily in his seat and closed his eyes. And she'd been working for him. How? Why?

An answer presented itself. There were rumors that old man Dupont was eager to reopen the case, with the help of some new "witnesses" and get his name cleared and his license to practice law back. That was a standing joke in local legal circles. The man had been caught red-handed. No decent attorney in town would touch the case, not in these times when attacks against women drew more fire than ever before. The man must be insane if he thought he could get someone to represent him.

Then he thought about it. Was that why Gaby had asked for the job? He recalled that she hadn't inquired about the position until he'd remarked that she was late to her appointment applying for it. An opportunity and she took it.

Had she heard something about her grandfather's hope of a retrial, then? She and her grandmother both, perhaps? And, frightened, Gaby had taken the chance to see what Nick was like, if he and his firm would be willing to represent the old goat a second time.

It seemed unlike Gaby, to do something so underhanded. Perhaps she didn't see it that way. If she'd been desperate to find out if Nick, one of the most famous trial lawyers in Chicago, perhaps in the country, was willing to handle the case, it would make sense that she'd have wanted to know where he stood on the case.

Gaby had been afraid. She was still afraid, probably, if she didn't know how Charles Dupont was regarded in Chicago legal circles.

He sat down behind the desk. His head hurt. He felt sick. Gaby had gone away before she had the chance to ask Nick about her grandfather. And very probably she'd never speak to him again as long as he lived.

It was a bad time for the phone to ring and for Mara to demand his presence at a party one of her social-climbing friends was hosting.

THIRTEEN

Jackie was eavesdropping shamelessly as her uncle Nick raged over the telephone, using words that amused her. Her uncle had a wonderful vocabulary when he lost his temper, and he wasn't shy about sharing it with the world at large.

"It's Sunday," he concluded. "I'm not spending my evening with a bunch of pretentious social wannabes who have no ambition past buying couture clothes and name-dropping! Sure," he added angrily after a pause. "Why don't you do that?" He turned the phone off and threw it at the wall.

Jackie let out a whistle. What a good thing that he had a nice, padded case on that cell phone. It bore scars of many previous bouts of ill temper.

"My damned head hurts," Nick raged as he picked up the phone, checked to make sure it still worked and slid it into his pocket. "And I feel like hell!"

Jackie and Tilly, apparently with unplanned coordination, both raised their hands over their heads in mock surrender.

He glared at them. Then he choked down involuntary laughter. "I'm going sailing. If anybody calls the landline, tell them to go straight to—"

"I'm going over to Antonio's and Tilly's off this afternoon," Jackie interrupted him.

"Oh, what the hell, the answering machine's on," he said, and looked so miserable under the bad temper that Jackie felt sorry for him.

"Don't fall in the lake," Jackie admonished.

"I have never fallen in the lake," he huffed as he went toward his bedroom.

"Yet," Jackie murmured to herself as his bedroom door slammed.

"I have never seen him in such a state," Tilly remarked as she cleared away the kitchen and paused as she was leaving. "What in the world happened last night?"

"He saw Gaby in a couture gown, dripping diamonds and dancing with an older man at Madame Dupont's birthday party. He accused her of being a gold digger, right in front of God and all her very wealthy grandmother's guests," Jackie said, her eyes twinkling. "She gave him back as good as she got and he took Mara and left. I got that from Antonio on the phone this morning. He got it from his uncle Jacob, who was also at the party. So Gaby came home and packed and went away."

"Oh, what a shame," Tilly said sadly. "And just when I started to think that, well…that…" She faltered.

"That Uncle Nick was having some inconvenient flashes of feeling about her? Yeah, me, too. Well, she's not likely to want to see him again anytime soon."

"Do you think that's why he was drinking?" Tilly asked. "I've never seen him drink so much!"

"Me, neither," Jackie replied. "I wish…" She hesitated as

NOTORIOUS   221

her phone rang. She pulled it out and looked at the screen.
She bit her lower lip. Her anguished eyes met Tilly's.

"Who is it?" Tilly mouthed.

"Keith!" Jackie said. She glared at the phone. "How did
he get out of jail?" She bit her lower lip. "I guess maybe his
dad came up with bail money. Well, I'm not answering it.
He got me messed up with the law and hurt my friend. I'm
not speaking to him ever again."

"Don't you go out that door until you tell somebody,"
Tilly warned.

"I know just who to tell," Jackie said, and relaxed a little.
She waited until the phone was quiet, quickly blocked Keith's
number and phoned Antonio's home.

"Antonio, I'm coming over to see you," she began.

"Hi, *cara*," he said softly. "I know…"

"Keith just phoned me."

"Did he, the *pendejo*?" he muttered. "You stay in the apartment. Uncle Jacob will send two of his guys over to get you
and bring you here."

"Okay." Jackie sighed. "You're so sweet."

"And I have very good manners," he said with a chuckle.
"See you in a little while, *cara*."

"Yes! And thanks!" She hung up. "Antonio's going to have
Uncle Jacob's men come get me. I'll be safe."

"I never thought I'd see the day. Pirates. Mobsters. Drunk
bosses." Tilly just shook her head. "And this seemed like such
a quiet place to work when I started."

"At least it's not boring," Jackie pointed out with a grin,
just as her uncle Nick came out of his bedroom, dressed for
sailing and still smoldering.

Gaby had run out of curses, but not out of tears. That Nick
could misjudge her so badly broke her heart. She'd thought,

hoped, that he knew her better than that. She had to remember that his attraction to her was physical, not emotional. He didn't want women close. Well, not close except behind closed doors. That was even more depressing.

"You need a change, *ma chérie*," her grandmother said a few days after the birthday party, when Gaby went to visit her. "And I have an idea. Why not go and stay with your cousin Clancey in Jacobsville for a week or two? It would get you out of the city and away from the problems here. And she has been urging you to visit her."

"I haven't seen her for two years," Gaby began, reluctant to leave the city. Stupid reason, too, because her blind-as-a-bat former boss might drop by. *As if*, she thought irritably.

"Then this is a good time to become reacquainted, no?" her grandmother persisted. "You can take your knitting and make things for the forthcoming baby."

Gaby sighed. It wasn't a bad idea; of course it wasn't. "Keith's in jail," she began.

"His friends are not," came the quiet reply. "Clancey's husband is a Texas Ranger," she added pointedly. "You would be safe there. Also, you would be near your great-aunt Rose. I know you have little contact with her, but she is at least another relation."

Gaby's big, worried pale blue eyes met the older woman's, her feelings almost tangible.

"My darling," her grandmother said softly, "a man who cares for a woman will not permit mere distance to separate them. *Tu comprends?*"

Gaby drew in a long breath. "He won't care that I'm gone," she said quietly.

Madame Dupont doubted that, but she didn't say so. "In which case, is it not better, the distance?"

"Yes. Of course it is," Gaby had to agree. She managed a wan smile. "I'll phone Clancey tonight."

Madame smiled tenderly. *"Très bien!"*

It had been two years since Gaby had been to Texas. She was still uncertain about the wisdom of leaving the city, but her grandmother had been very persuasive.

As she walked down the concourse at the airport in San Antonio, a slender, dark-haired woman, obviously pregnant, stepped into her path and hugged her warmly. "Gaby!" Clancey said, grinning. "You look terrific!"

"You're the one who looks that way," Gaby teased, her eyes on her cousin's swollen belly. "Is it a girl or a boy?" she asked.

"Yes," came a drawling deep Texas voice from behind her. She turned and laughed. "You must be Colter," Gaby said. "I'm so glad to meet you."

"Same here." Colter was tall, drop-dead handsome, dark-haired and dark-eyed. He smiled at Clancey tenderly. "You two ready to go home?"

"Yes. It was a long flight," Gaby confessed. "There was an electrical fault and we sat on the runway at O'Hare for a couple of hours. Thank goodness for air conditioners. How's Tad?" she asked as they left the airport.

"Growing like a weed," Clancey said. "He'll be so glad to see you. First it was meteorites. Now it's fossils and ancient pottery." She rolled her eyes. "He'll bore you to death."

"Not likely," Gaby replied with a smile. "I love those things, too!" she added, without reminding her cousin that she took her bachelor's degree in anthropology, minoring in archaeology, and that she was the child of archaeologists.

It wasn't a long drive down to Jacobsville. There was an airport in Jacobsville, of course, but since Colter worked in San Antonio and Clancey had been in town waiting for him to get off work so they could fetch Gaby at the airport, driving was quicker.

"How's Grandmother?" Clancey asked. "Well, I've always called her Great-Aunt Melly," she amended. "God knows exactly how we're related, anyway, it's such a tangle of relationships!"

"Please don't ever call her Melly to her face," Gaby pleaded, laughing. "One of our other cousins in France did, and he was actually given a room in the servants' wing. A vindictive woman, my grandmother," she added, shaking her head and smiling fondly. "Just as well it wasn't the dungeons!"

"Dungeons?" Colter asked, still unfamiliar with that branch of Clancey's family.

"There's an estate in France," Gaby explained. "*Grand-mère* visits there in the fall when the grapes are harvested."

"Grapes?" Colter was still puzzling.

"Gaby's grandmother owns one of the premier vineyards in France," Clancey told her husband. "Dupont wines are some of the oldest and most famous in Europe."

"Okay, now I get it," Colter chuckled. "So, dungeons?"

"Her estate dates to two centuries before the French Revolution," Gaby explained. "*Grand-mère* has never had anyone actually put in the dungeons, of course. However, that doesn't stop her threatening people with them. She has a rather dour sense of humor."

"And she's a wild woman," Clancey recalled. "Honestly, didn't they pull her out of a race car in Paris one weekend, cutting circles at some amusement park?"

"Oh, yes," Gaby sighed. "Then there was the parachuting thing."

"Parachuting thing." Colter was obviously fishing.

"She was taking a skydiving course," Gaby explained, suppressing a chuckle. "When they gathered after a jump, one of the younger male students remarked that my grandmother was far too old to be doing that. He added a rider to the effect that her children should have her put in a home because she was obviously lacking, mentally. My grandmother and the young man still had their parachutes out, of course, because it was just after the skydive. The young man was chuckling at something another skydiver said when *Grand-mère* suddenly dropped him with a karate move, wrapped him in her parachute and stuck a glove in his mouth. There were minor assault charges—dropped, of course, after a substantial contribution to the victim's favorite charity. He did apologize when he was told who she really was. He sent flowers, which she tossed into the kitchen sink disposal unit. He also sent candy, which she had melted and returned. As her coup de grâce, she sent him a present—a handsome ottoman that she'd had stuffed with dead shrimp." She shook her head while her companions roared. "She makes a very bad enemy." She couldn't help joining in the uproarious laughter. Her grandmother was one of a kind. "She's studying the tango right now. Which reminds me, she's going to be taught it by one of the more socially prominent crime bosses of Detroit," she added.

"Your grandmother lives an exciting life, I gather?" Colter asked.

Clancey cleared her throat. "I believe Gaby's is only a little less exciting lately? Great-Aunt Rose mentioned something about the Mafia and you being beaten up...?"

Colter was really laughing now. "What a family!"

"Don't look so smug," Gaby chided with twinkling eyes. "It's your family, too, now!"

Supper was a riotous meal. Clancey's little stepbrother, Tad, followed around the ranch house by no less than three cats—

one of them Colter's red Maine coon cat, Miss Kitty—was telling them all about his latest video game.

"Do you play, Cousin Gaby?" he asked.

"No, sorry," she replied, liking the boy. She glanced at Clancey. "Do you still play the guitar?"

"Does she!" Tad exclaimed. "They actually offered her a job playing it at Fernando's, the Spanish nightclub over in San Antonio!"

"I just play for my own amusement," Clancey said. "But not so much right now, if you see the reason…" She indicated the size of her stomach and beamed at her husband.

"He plays, too," Tad said, pointing at Colter. "You should hear him!"

"Later, young fella, later," Colter said. "Your cousin's tired. She's had a long week." His eyes narrowed. "I hope they keep that polecat who attacked you in stir until his trial comes up."

"No worries there. His family is wealthy—well, his father is," Gaby amended, "But his father's disowned him. He'll probably stay in jail until his case is called." *Case.* The word reminded her of Nick, who was an attorney. It made her sad. She missed him so much.

"Now, what's this about the Mafia?" Colter asked.

"The Mafia!" Tad exclaimed, all eyes.

"He's hung up on the *Godfather* trilogy," Clancey said, rolling her eyes.

"I was attacked by the former boyfriend of my boss's niece," Gaby said, simplifying things for Tad. "Her new boyfriend has an uncle who's…well, shall we say, a little outside the law." She glanced at Colter and grimaced. "Sorry."

"Oh, no worries, so long as they don't come blazing into my jurisdiction," he chuckled. He studied her. "Was it any of Cousin Mikey's people?" he added, because most people in Jacobsville, a very small town, knew about local FBI Senior

Agent Paul Fiore's cousin, a crime boss back in New Jersey.
Mikey had married a local girl and visited his cousin occasionally. Gaby's great-aunt Rose knew him, because Mikey
had lived at the same boardinghouse she did for a while, during which time he was courting Bernadette, whom he later
married.

"Well, not really," Gaby said. "But Mikey knew somebody
in New Jersey who knew the big crime boss in New York
who had a connection to a crime boss in Detroit who was
on speaking terms with another crime boss who belonged to
the Outfit in Chicago…"

"Stop," Colter pleaded, holding his head. "I'm getting a
headache."

"You never get headaches," Clancey teased, nuzzling her
head against his.

"But anyway, they were sort of watching out for me when
Mr. Everett wasn't."

"Mr. Everett?" Clancey asked.

"My grandmother's bodyguard, Tanner Everett," Gaby
explained.

Colter sat up. "Tanner Everett?"

"Yes. You know him?" Gaby asked, surprised.

"I know of him. His father, Cole Everett, owns a huge
spread called the Big Spur, up around Branntville, next door
to King Brannt's ranch. Those two have two of the biggest
ranches in south Texas. The Everetts had two sons and a
daughter and the Brannts had a son and a daughter. Tanner
and his father are estranged, from what I was told."

"Yes," Gaby replied sadly. "He has to meet his mother away
from the ranch. It's been years, and his father still won't forgive him for not staying at home and learning ranch management. Tanner had another set of priorities."

"So I've heard," Colter said. "We have several former mercs

here in Jacobsville. Tanner was involved with one group of them before he went into private security."

"I've heard Cal mention him," Clancey added.

"Cal?" Gaby asked.

"Cal Hollister. He's a police captain in San Antonio. I used to work for him," Clancey said.

Gaby looked confused.

"Cal wasn't always a cop," Clancey said helpfully.

"He's our friend," Tad added.

"Mine, too," Colter said with an affectionate smile at his wife. "Well, at least, now he is. I have to admit to a little jealousy before Clancey married me. Hollister's not bad-looking and he's been around the world a time or two." He grins. "Still gets outshot on his own target range by Detective Lieutenant Rick Marquez's wife, though," he added with just a little lingering malice.

"What I miss, living in the city," Gaby said, shaking her head.

"You have no idea, and I mean that," Clancey told her. "We should take Gaby up to Fernando's on Friday and introduce her to Cal," she added suddenly, beaming.

"That's not a bad idea at all," Colter said, immediately following his wife's lead.

Gaby, listening to Tad's excited commentary about how he'd defeated a boss in his video game, missed the whole conversation. Which wasn't really a bad thing.

Nick sailed out onto Lake Michigan, enjoying the late-spring warmth. He was wearing sunglasses and his natural tan was darker than it had been in a long time, from the many days he was on the lake. He glanced at his crew, four friends who loved yachting as much as he did.

Once, he'd participated on a team that competed for America's Cup, the epitome of yacht racing. His team had lost, but the experience stayed with him. He loved the wind in his hair, the feel of the polished wooden deck under his feet, the thrill of speed. There was plenty of traffic on the water, but he always kept his eyes on the space around him. If he missed something, his crew wouldn't.

He thought of Mara, who hated sailing. She was going to be nothing more than a footnote in his life now, he supposed, after their recent argument. He was tired of her moods, her other lovers, her grasping greedy nature. She was the sort of person who loved life in the fast lane. She'd never stick with a man who lost his fortune. She'd leave him flat and hare off after new game.

Gaby was her exact opposite. He grimaced, recalling what he'd said to her last weekend. It had been a shock, to find her in a couture gown, dripping diamonds, dancing with a man old enough to be her father. Worse, a man he knew to be a multimillionaire. While Nick was independently wealthy, due to a legacy left him by a forgotten great-uncle on his mother's side, outside the huge fees he commanded as a trial attorney, he wasn't in the older man's class. Poor Gaby. Beaten up by Jackie's nasty boyfriend, then accused of exploiting an old man for his money. He was sorry and ashamed for the things he'd said. But he couldn't unsay them. Soon, he was going to have to talk to her.

He didn't know what to say. He was sure that she hadn't meant to be underhanded when she came to work for him. She'd been surprised when he met her at the door that first day they met and accused her of being late. When he mentioned the job he had available, Gaby had simply stepped into the shoes of an applicant, probably without thinking very hard about the complications she was creating in both their lives.

She'd been assaulted by a friend of her grandfather's. One

of Nick's own attorneys, in the firm he'd founded, had represented the unsavory man. Nick himself had turned down the case, but he'd been overseas with an investigator, working a case that had international suspects. He hadn't paid much attention to what was going on in his own law firm while he was away.

Gaby's grandfather was a sleaze, a man out for anything he could get, whatever price his family paid for it. He was mercenary and cold and selfish to an unbelievable degree. Poor Gaby, who'd been sold like a slice of meat to a foreign diplomat to pay her grandfather's gambling debt. And if it hadn't been for Madame Dupont, she'd have been raped. No wonder she was so wary of men, so afraid of anything intimate.

But she'd lain in his arms as soft as a kitten, her pale blue eyes lost in his, her body singing as he touched her. He closed his eyes and groaned silently at the memory. How difficult that must have been for her, after what had happened. He'd thought it was a boyfriend who got too amorous. He'd had no idea what the truth was. Now that he knew, he wished he could go back and relive those precious moments. He'd have made different choices. Better choices.

He spun the wheel to avoid another boat with an obviously inebriated man at the wheel. He noted the make and model of the yacht and pulled out his cell phone. People like that caused tragedies. He wasn't going to let the man get away with it.

Not too many minutes later, the harbor patrol stopped the boat. Nick nodded his head in silent approval. He might have saved a life. It was the only bright spot in his day. When he got back to the apartment, it was empty. Gaby was gone. Jackie was at her new friend's house. Tilly had gone home, leaving a note about his supper in the fridge that would need reheating.

He sank down onto the sofa with a sigh. His life was falling apart. Here was his future, here in this cold, empty apartment.

Jackie would eventually marry or go to college or get a job or go back to her mother. Tilly might stay. Maybe. But Nick would come home to a life without love in it, a life without a family, a wife and child.

Samantha. He closed his eyes on a groan of misery. His baby girl. Would he never forget the horrible, anguished sight of her little face as Glenna jumped? Would he never stop hearing their screams?

He got up and poured himself a whiskey and tipped it down his throat. It wouldn't stop the memories. Nothing would stop them. Maybe another family would, but he was afraid to take the chance. He was afraid to love again, to have a child he might lose again, to face a future that could repeat itself.

It was a bad time to remember Gaby's tender smile at the little girl in the elevator. She loved kids. It stood out a mile. She even loved Nick's impossible niece. The girl had toned down since Gaby's arrival. She'd softened. Become less belligerent. She'd even developed a sense of humor. Gaby had said that all Jackie needed was someone to love her. Nobody really did. Except Gaby.

He poured himself another drink. Even though tomorrow was Saturday, he planned to bury himself in work to avoid thinking about the past. Gaby was part of the past now. He could still see her shocked, sad face when he'd accused her of unspeakable things; Gaby, who had a heart as big as Chicago, who'd do anything for the people she loved.

Well, at least he knew where she was, he consoled himself. She'd be with her grandmother. Maybe he could call over there, just to ask how she was. There might be a maid or a housekeeper who answered the phone who might tell him before Madame Dupont asked the name of the caller and slammed the receiver down in his ear. He took another sip of his drink, got up and went into his study. He had no appetite for food. He'd drink his supper and try to go through case files. It might get his mind off Gaby, at least temporarily.

Jackie came home to the apartment, leaving her escort at the door. "Thanks a lot, guys," she said, grinning at her two escorts, one short and chubby, one tall and somber.

"No problem. Jacob says we got to keep an eye on you," the taller one said with a grin. "Nobody's going to mess with you while we're around, kid."

"I know that. Thanks. Good night."

"'Night," they chorused.

Jackie smiled as she locked the door behind her. She and Antonio found so many things in common. It was really strange. Her background was Scottish and Dutch; his was Argentinean, but they were like two halves of a whole, especially when they danced together.

She moved toward the living room, doing the slow walk that was a hallmark of tango. Just as she reached the sofa, she heard muttered curses coming from the study. She winced. She'd hoped her uncle had already gone to bed. It was very late. But then, he was a workaholic. Probably there was some big case he was handling. It took a lot of work. He had a whole firm of attorneys, and it also included paralegals, trial specialists, psychologists, a bodyguard, a former skip tracer, even a private investigator. He surrounded himself with people who became invaluable at rooting out tiny facts that might save a client's freedom, or his life.

Nick came out of his study, looking older than his years, with bloodshot eyes and new lines in his face. He could have used a shave, too.

"You look awful," she said before she thought.

He glared at her.

She cocked her head. "Need to talk?" she asked unexpectedly.

"No." He hesitated. "Yes."

Her eyebrows arched.

"Maybe," he amended, and scowled.

"Do you have trouble making decisions?" she asked with a straight face.

A deep laugh escaped his throat. "Yeah. Recently, anyway. You had supper?"

"No," she confessed. "Tonio and I danced and danced. I forgot the time and they'd already eaten. Did Tilly leave you something?" she asked hopefully, because he might share it and she was hungry.

He smiled. "She did. You hungry?"

"I'm starving," she confessed.

"Me, too."

He followed her into the kitchen and went toward the coffeepot. He filled it with water while she was preheating the oven.

"Whew!" Jackie remarked, because it was close quarters where the stove and the cabinets met. "The fumes are enough to knock a person out."

He turned, coffeepot in hand. "What fumes?"

"You been drinking?" she asked, glowering up at him.

He turned away and started making coffee.

"Uncle Nick?" she persisted.

"I only had four highballs," he muttered.

"Four?" she exclaimed. "How are you still vertical?"

"Cast-iron stomach," he said without cracking a smile.

She laughed. "Okay."

He grinned at her. It was the first time in years that the two of them had had any sort of rapport. Jackie felt less like an intruder, and Nick decided that she wasn't such bad company after all.

They ate the supper Tilly had left for them, talking about everything under the sun.

"Your mother called while you were out," he remarked.

The smile on her face turned down. "And?" she asked uneasily.

"She said she's coming to stay for a couple of weeks. Maybe longer."

"Did her boyfriend die?" Jackie asked coolly.

"Not yet," he remarked. "You never know, though. He dumped your mother for an aspiring actress who's ten years younger."

"Poor Mom," she replied, sipping coffee and feeling no pity at all. Her comment was droll in the extreme.

"She was bawling," Nick said. "First time I've heard her cry in years." He studied his coffee, steaming in the cup. "She asked about you."

"That's a first," Jackie muttered coldly.

He sipped hot coffee. "She said she'd made a mess of her life, and of yours." He put down the cup. "Our father did a number on both of us," he said curtly. "Beatings, verbal abuse, and he was almost never sober after he got home. I always thought that our mother just gave up and died when she saw the hopelessness of how we were living. She loved him, in spite of his failings. She'd never have had the strength to leave him." His lips made a thin line. "And he threatened to kill her, and us, if she ever tried it. She might have risked her own life. She'd never have risked ours. She was the sweetest woman I've ever known," he added softly, smiling at the memory. "Always worried about everybody but herself, loving and gentle and kind." His eyes went to a painting on the wall. "She was like Gaby," he said, deep in thought.

Jackie's heart bumped in her chest. He cared about Gaby! She could hardly believe it. Her uncle was a man about town.

He'd had girlfriends as long as she could remember. Mara was just the last in a long line. But he never got serious about anybody, he never really cared about any of them. But when he said Gaby's name, it sounded soft and full of wonder. He'd gotten stinking drunk after he'd said those things to Gaby at the party.

She stared at him with sudden insight. He was in love with Gaby. And he didn't even know it!

FOURTEEN

Fernando's was full on a Friday night. Colter had reservations for himself, Clancey and Gaby. They'd left Tad at home, because he'd pleaded that his new video game was so much more important than flan and couldn't he be excused? Colter's sister, Brenda, was spending the weekend with them anyway, and she was more than willing to babysit.

So the three of them sat at a ringside table, eating the house special—fish in a jalapeño sauce of the owner's own creation. Onstage, a handsome dark-haired man was playing a flamenco on a guitar while his wife, dressed in a beautiful red dress with a long ruffled skirt, wearing a red rose in her hair, danced.

"This is great," Gaby whispered to Clancey.

"Aren't they terrific?" Clancey asked. She smiled at her husband, who caught her hand in his and held it tight. "We had our first real date right here," she added in a whispery tone.

"The first of many," Colter agreed, clasping her hand closer.

The dancer finished with a flourish and the guitarist stood, bowed and led his wife offstage.

"What a super performance," Gaby remarked.

"What are you doing here?" came a deep, curious voice from behind them. "I thought you had company this week."

"We did, and here she is," Clancey told her friend Cal Hollister. She grinned at him. "Hi, boss, long time no see. Why don't you ever come visit?"

"Too many bad people trying to destroy my town, that's why." He stared down at Gaby curiously. "The houseguest?" he remarked with a smile.

He was handsome. Drop-dead handsome. Light blond hair that looked like spun gold in the lights overhead, with dark eyes and a sensuous mouth. If it hadn't been for Nick wrapping her heart up in mothballs, she could have fallen for this man big-time.

"I'm Gaby Dupont," Gaby introduced herself.

"Cal Hollister," came the smiling reply.

"Look. He's smiling," Clancey said to her husband. "He never smiles unless he's going to fire somebody."

"I do not," Cal said with mock haughtiness. "I smile all the time."

"Once in a blue moon, usually when you've just been on television uplifting the virtues of the San Antonio Police Department," Clancey retorted.

"No respect," Cal told Gaby. "I get no respect from her, and she worked for me for— Oh, my God," he whispered, and the color drained out of his face. His eyes were on a young woman, blonde, with her long hair in a bun. She was wearing no makeup at all. Medium height, somber, quiet, a good face. Not beautiful but serene and gentle.

Gaby was fascinated by the way Hollister looked at the newcomer, as if he were seeing a beloved ghost.

"Years," he said almost to himself. "It's been years. And she hasn't aged a day."

Clancey and Colter exchanged worried glances. They knew about Hollister and this woman, Gaby surmised. There must be a history there, one that wasn't spoken of.

The young woman had gone to the desk. She waited, smiling at the server, who went away and returned almost at once with food in two plastic bags. The woman thanked her, smiling, and turned to leave.

The shock on her young face was the equal of what was briefly visible on Hollister's. She stared at him. Her big dark eyes were sad for seconds, and then blazing with hellfire, as if she wished him on a spit roasting over hot coals. She didn't speak, or nod, or even acknowledge him. She turned and walked out the door.

As she went, Gaby got a glimpse of a pistol in its holder on the woman's rounded hip.

She wanted to ask questions, but it would have been cruel. Hollister looked as if he were made of stone. He'd closed up, put up locks and bolts, all in a matter of seconds.

He turned to the others. "I guess I'll see you guys around," he said, and forced a smile for the women.

"Nice to meet you," Gaby remarked.

"Sure. Same here." He wasn't really hearing her, or seeing her. His expression was almost identical to the one Gaby had seen on Nick's face when he told her about his late wife and his little girl.

"That poor man," Gaby said when he'd gone out the front door.

Clancey was shocked at her cousin's perception. Gaby didn't even know about Cal and that unknown woman. Clancey wasn't sure, but she knew Hollister had loved and lost a woman long ago. He'd married a woman he didn't love, he'd told her once, to get even with a woman he did love. The marriage had been a terrible one. His late wife had been on drugs and alcohol for almost the whole of their married lives. Since her death, Hollister dated nobody. People thought he was still mourning his wife. Clancey knew better.

But Gaby was a stranger. How had she divined the truth about Hollister so quickly? It was a remarkable thing, the empathy she felt for him, as if she knew he'd been hurt, and very badly.

Clancey promised herself that they'd talk about that when they got home.

But by then, they'd talked about so many other things, that the blond police captain and his lost love were the last things on anybody's mind. They sat around in the living room, talking and laughing.

Gaby liked her cousin. She always had. Clancey was gentle and kind, although she had a temper. It was nice to see how happy she was with her husband.

On the other hand, Gaby was in mourning for the man she'd lost. Nick would certainly have figured out by now that Gaby had come to work for him with ulterior motives. It would make him even more cold toward her than he already was. He thought she was a woman who'd do anything for money, and that after she'd lived in his apartment, worked with him, listened to his darkest secrets—he hadn't known her at all. So why was she wasting her time missing him?

"Want to tell me why you look so sad?" Clancey asked as they sat in the kitchen over cups of hot chocolate while Colter and his sister watched a program in the living room.

Gaby smiled sadly. "Old story. Girl finds guy, girl loves guy, girl loses guy." She shrugged. "I just wanted to find out if my grandfather was going to hire his firm to represent him again. My grandfather's trying to get his law license back, but to do that, he needs to have the charges against him dropped. We've heard rumors that he's got new witnesses who'll swear that he was falsely accused."

"Your grandmother has photos," Clancey reminded her.

"He'll claim they were Photoshopped."

Clancey put a small hand over her cousin's. "And you'll have witnesses who can prove they weren't," she said firmly. "Your great-aunt Rose says he hasn't got a ghost of a chance."

"She knows?"

"Well, when your grandmother phoned her, she had to tell her the whole miserable story. They're related by marriage," she was reminded.

"Well, Great-Aunt Rose is family, I guess."

"Absolutely, even if she avoids us all like the plague," Clancey chuckled. "I don't think she ever spoke to me in her whole life until a couple of weeks ago. Talking to your grandmother must have really affected her."

"How did she meet a mobster?" Gaby asked suddenly.

"He was living at her boardinghouse while the feds found enough proof to clear his boss of a murder charge. Long story short, another crime boss in New Jersey was trying to frame his boss in order to take over the territory. He lost. It turns out that the guy had a whole lot of enemies, and he ended in a bad way." She laughed. "There was even some gossip that Marcus Carrera got involved."

Gaby frowned. "Why is that name familiar?"

"Well, he's pretty famous in mob circles. And he was in the newspapers a few years back when he helped the feds send a couple of really bad people to prison. But you may have heard of him from Great-Aunt Rose, because Mr. Carrera's wife, Delia, is from Jacobsville. She used to do sewing repairs at the local dry cleaner's. She taught quilting, and Mr. Carrera won international awards for his own quilts."

"He quilts?" Gaby exclaimed.

"Yes, he does. They have two sons and they live in the Bahamas. Mr. Carrera owns casinos all over, but he has a big one on Paradise Island, where their house is. They come back here from time to time to visit friends."

Gaby was frowning. "There was something my grandmother told me just recently—yes, now I remember! One of our distant cousins still owns a beautiful villa on the Riviera and his wife is also from Jacobsville. She was a Copeland before she married Connor Sinclair. He's our cousin.

"I met him once, years ago, when he was in Chicago. He came to talk to my grandmother about some property that another cousin owned. He was thinking about starting a vineyard of his own. He was drop-dead handsome," Gaby chuckled. "That was long before he married. I was still in school."

"I know that name," Clancey said with a smile. "He owns all sorts of aircraft companies. They said he used to do his own test flights."

"I'll bet you a nickel he isn't doing them now he's married," Gaby teased. "And certainly not since he and Emma had two little boys."

"That's a bet I won't take." Clancey studied the other woman's drawn face. "Want to talk about the man in your life?"

Gaby grimaced. "Former man. I do. And I don't. It's a raw wound."

"So we won't rub salt in it tonight," Clancey promised. "Would you like to go tourist in San Antonio tomorrow? We can come home with Colter at lunch."

"I'd love that. We could go and look at the Alamo. Or visit the hotel where Teddy Roosevelt organized the Rough Riders." She noted Clancey's raised eyebrows. "Or we could visit some stores that sell baby clothes…?"

"Now you're on!" Clancey said, and grinned.

"Couldn't you fly out there and bring her home?" Nick asked Mr. Everett, having tracked him down with the help of a private detective. He wasn't going near Gaby's grandmother under present circumstances.

Everett finished his breakfast and sipped coffee while he stared at the man across from him at the table. "I can't do that unless she wants to come back. Her grandmother says she's having a very nice time helping her cousin buy baby things."

Nick's face tautened. He looked away.

Everett put his napkin down. "You can live in the past with your ghosts, or you can live in the present," he said very quietly, not intimidated when the other man glared daggers at him. "Gaby is unique. She doesn't want a career or the life of a socialite. She's the sort of woman who'd never leave a man she loved, even if he lost everything he owned. She'd dig her heels in, get a job and do anything to support him."

Nick's eyes were black with anger. "Who told you?"

Everett just looked at him. "I don't dig into people's private lives. Not unless it's in the line of duty. In this case, it was. You could have been anybody, and Gaby was going to live under the same roof with you. Her grandmother was concerned."

Nick backed down, just a little.

"I have tragedies in my own past," Everett added, his voice quiet and somber. "I don't talk about them. But I try not to look back. All we ever have is right now, this minute, this second. Yesterday is a memory. Tomorrow is a dream. The present is all there is."

Nick frowned. His eyes narrowed. "You did merc work," he recalled. "For a reason?"

Everett hesitated. Then he nodded, a quick jerk of his head. "I hoped I might catch a bullet." He laughed coldly. "I was too good at it. Lost an eye and and got a few scars. That's about all."

Nick took a deep breath. "I got a part-time job as a volunteer fireman, while I was working on the docks, for the same reason. I didn't die, either. I wanted to."

"Gaby had a friend who went to London to live. Her friend had a little girl, about two. Gaby begged to babysit her, anytime her mother needed someone. She loves kids."

Nick just stared at him. "She has issues."

"She carries scars, just like the rest of us. The difference is that she doesn't let them lock up her life. She's optimistic and funny and people love her. Even people who don't want to." He wasn't looking at Nick when he said that. Deliberately. "She's overdue for a little happiness."

"Well, of course she is, but why is she looking for it in Texas?"

"Her mother's people have a ranch in Jacobsville. The family still owns it, although there's a manager taking care of it. Gaby's staying with a cousin whose husband is a Texas Ranger."

"How long for?" Nick asked without wanting to, and stared into his coffee cup.

"Not really sure," Everett commented. He pursed his lips and he had to hide a smile. "Now that she's met the San Antonio captain of detectives who lives near Clancey and her husband, she may not want to come back too soon."

Nick's head jerked up. "What captain of detectives?"

"Cal Hollister," he said. "Of course, he didn't start out as a cop. He was in one of the groups I signed on with. Hell of a fighter. Handsome guy. Blond, blue-eyed, handy with firearms. Afraid of nothing. I hear that she and Clancey and the Texas Ranger were with him at a restaurant in San Antonio a couple of nights ago."

Nick was smoldering. He finished his coffee. "Nice talking to you," he said, and got up without another word.

Everett watched him leave with twinkling eyes. He pulled

out his cellphone and pushed in some numbers. "Yes, it worked," he said, chuckling. "I'd bet real money that he's on the next plane to Texas. No, of course not. I wouldn't dream of warning her!"

Nick stormed around the apartment stuffing things into a bag. "Tilly's going to live in until I get back," he told a fascinated Jackie. "You tell Uncle Jacob that I'm going to Texas and you'll be here with just Tilly. He'll make sure you have somebody watching your back."

"Okay, Uncle Nick."

"One more thing, don't open that door unless you know who's on the other…"

Somebody was leaning on the doorbell.

"Oh, hell, what now?" Nick fumed as he went to open the door.

His sister was standing there, thinner and frail-looking, all the misery of the world on her pretty face.

"Hi, Nick," she said, and her lower lip trembled. "Got a spare room for a couple of days?"

He didn't say a word. He just held out his arms.

Miranda looked older, despite her skillful makeup and trendy clothing. But she was different somehow. She sat in the living room with Nick and her daughter, drinking coffee.

"I've been soul-searching," she told them quietly, and a laugh faltered in her throat. She looked at her daughter with the same dark eyes and winced. "You've had a hell of a life, haven't you?" she added sadly. "I'm so sorry. I've been wrapped up in myself for so long…" She bit her lower lip. "I know why you asked to come here, Jackie. I wish I'd believed what you told me. I was blind."

Jackie just stared at her. "You never believed me. You didn't the other times, either."

Miranda averted her eyes. "That's true."

"What other times?" Nick asked shortly.

"Other times that we won't talk about right now," Jackie said with odd maturity and a smile.

Miranda looked taken aback. She frowned. "You sound so grown-up," she said with a little laugh.

"It's the Mafia influence," Jackie said simply. "I'm hanging out with a gang boss's nephew. He has bodyguards tail me wherever I go, so that my ex-boyfriend doesn't get to me."

Miranda sat with her mouth open.

"Jackie will have to tell you about it," Nick said, interrupting what looked to be a sudden interest on his sister's part in her daughter's life. "I have a plane to catch."

"But I just got here," Miranda said. "Where are you going?"

"To Texas," he said shortly, rising. He looked at his watch. "I'll miss my flight." He kissed Miranda and smiled at Jackie. "You can keep each other company until I get back."

"Who's in Texas?" Miranda asked.

"My former administrative assistant," he said. "She's trying to get mixed up with a police captain." He scowled. "I wish I knew somebody on the bench in south Texas. Maybe I could get a restraining order…"

He walked to the front door, picked up the bag he'd dropped there and walked out, still muttering to himself.

"Police captain?" Miranda asked, her eyes as wide as saucers.

"It's a very long story," Jackie said. "I expect you're tired."

"Not that tired. I'll make another pot of coffee. Doesn't Nick have a cook?"

"Yes, Tilly, but she has Sundays off." Jackie got up. "I'll make the coffee."

Miranda blinked. She followed the younger woman into the kitchen. "How are you mixed up with the mob?"

"Well, it's like this," Jackie began, and while she made the coffee, and then while they drank it, she related the recent events that had turned her life upside down.

"But mostly it was Gaby who dragged me out of trouble," Jackie finished. "She was kind even when I gave her hell." She grimaced. "I'm sorry she's gone. I hope she'll at least let Uncle Nick apologize before she lays his head open with a blunt object."

"She doesn't like him?"

"I think she loves him," Jackie said with a mischievous smile. "In fact, I think he likes her, too, or he wouldn't go rushing off to Texas when he heard she was seeing the handsome police captain in Jacobsville."

Miranda sat back, stunned. "I never thought I'd live long enough to see Nick want to get married again."

Jackie stared at her. "Again?"

Miranda nodded. "I don't think he knows that I've even heard about it. He never told me. But he had a friend that I met on a plane, several years ago. We got to talking and he mentioned what a tragedy Nick had survived. I asked him and he told me." She smiled and shook her head when Jackie asked what it was. "He's very private, even though he's my brother. I wouldn't dream of gossiping about it." She sighed. "It's why he never remarried, why he plays the field. So he's going to Texas to save... What's her name?"

"Gaby," Jackie volunteered, smiling.

"What's she like?" Miranda asked.

"Funny and sweet and naive in a lot of ways. Uncle Nick said she was like his mother."

Miranda pursed her lips and whistled. "I've never heard him compare any of his women friends to Mom," she said. "That's a first. And he isn't the type to date innocents, you know."

"I do know." She grinned. "That's why I called Mr. Everett and asked him to lay it on thick with Uncle Nick about the police captain. I overheard a phone call that Uncle Nick made to a private detective. He was looking for Mr. Everett. I knew how to contact him, but I'd never told my uncle."

"Why would you know?"

"He's Gaby's grandmother's bodyguard."

"Her grandmother has a bodyguard?"

"Oh, yes. She's one of the richest women in Chicago. Well, I guess Gaby's rich, too. The family owns vineyards in France. Gaby says that Dupont wines are world famous."

"Good grief, I had one with dinner not a week ago in London." She stopped, swallowed tears and stared down into her cooling coffee. "A lifetime ago."

"What happened?"

"Rory dumped me for a little blonde," she said simply. "I looked in the mirror afterward and realized why he dumped me." She laughed hollowly. "I'm not a young woman anymore. Oh, I can have face-lifts and go to spas and buy expensive cosmetics to cover it up. But I'm never going to be young again, even if I look young."

"It seems like an awful waste of time, all that effort to cheat people who think you're one thing, when you're another. Besides, you sort of earn gray hairs, don't you?" Jackie asked without venom.

Miranda smiled sadly. "Fifteen. And you know more than I do."

"I grew up too fast," Jackie said. "And then there was Keith." Her voice dropped. "He said he loved me. I was ready to do anything he wanted. Then Gaby got Mr. Everett to do some checking and found that Keith had a prior for assault on a very innocent girl, sort of like me." She flushed. "She saved me from something terrible. I was awful to her, when she first came to work here."

"I really would love to meet her."

"I'd like that, too. Maybe Uncle Nick can bring her home with him," she added.

Miranda looked doubtful. "I've never actually heard Nick apologize for anything," she said.

"Maybe this will be a famous first," Jackie replied. She grinned. "I want you to meet Antonio. He's teaching me how to tango! And his great-uncle Jacob is teaching Gaby's grandmother how to do it!"

"Oh, my goodness," Miranda exclaimed. "You're learning the tango? It's horribly difficult. I always wanted to learn, but it's too complicated."

"Not to worry," Jackie said. "Gaby and Uncle Nick can both do it, so can Uncle Jacob and Antonio. Plenty of instruction available—all you have to do is ask!"

Nick got off the plane in San Antonio and stood on the concourse wondering what the hell to do next.

He had no idea where Gaby was, who her cousin was, where her cousin was. All he knew was that a captain of detectives in San Antonio was trying to date her.

He took a cab to one of the luxury hotels downtown and checked in. Then he sat drinking coffee in the restaurant's dining room, trying to remember if he knew anybody in San Antonio in legal circles.

He drew a blank. He hadn't done much in Texas. There had been a case several years back. He'd defended a woman whose husband had faked his own death and tried to kill her to keep her from finding out that he was running away with a local dental assistant.

But as he recalled, that case had ended rather abruptly and he'd had no time to get acquainted with legal and law enforcement circles in the city. His most recent case had been the one in Chicago, where a millionaire's wife was trying her best to kill him and he thought his own attorney was persecuting her unjustly. He'd just survived a third attempt on his life when he got out of the hospital—his wife had accidentally backed over him. Twice. He shook his head. The man was going to die, and he'd never believe his wife was responsible. At least, Nick told himself, if she succeeded in offing her husband, he'd have the woman up for felony murder even if he had to hire two detective agencies to prove it.

He finished his coffee and went outside. It was late spring. The city was already warm. He liked the atmosphere of it. Despite the tall buildings and the lush palm trees and the traffic, it had the look of a small town.

Well, he wasn't going to find out much today. He'd get a good night's sleep and in the morning he'd find a local detective and set him to find Gaby's cousin. He had enough information to accomplish that much, at least.

Meanwhile, since he was here, he might as well do a little sightseeing. It had been years since he'd had a holiday.

He strolled along the famous River Walk and browsed through the Mercado. He spotted some pretty things he could get for the women back home. Not Mara, of course—she wouldn't be seen dead with anything that didn't come from a couture house even if it was outdated. But then, Mara was the past. He had no intention of looking her up again.

Tomorrow, he decided, he'd come back and buy presents for Jackie and Miranda and Tilly. For now, he wanted his hands free. The Alamo was close by, and he'd never seen it except in travelogues and movies. He turned toward it.

There were several people walking around the historic building. He vaguely remembered a movie with John Wayne that was built around the legend of this place. He noted that there were guided tours, as well. With nothing better to do while he tried to decide on his next step, he wandered around with a group of strangers listening half-heartedly to the history of the Alamo.

He stuck his hands in his pockets and wondered how those men had felt when they were barricaded inside during the ferocious battle with what must have seemed like the entire Mexican Army at the walls.

In the fields beyond, Santa Ana and his regiments were camped. He recalled that Santa Ana was greatly revered in Mexico after the war finished, just as Daniel Boone and William Travis and many others were revered here. Atrocities were committed, factions were divided against each other. History, he decided, was a tricky business. At least the law had guidelines that owed nothing to emotion. In any case, it was a big mistake to judge the past by the mores of the present. He'd learned that from his history courses, if nothing more. He paused at the entrance to the Long Barracks, where the last stand was fought. He could picture the carnage. A trial lawyer, with most of his cases involving violence, he had a pretty good idea of what the area would have looked like during the siege. It wasn't a sight for squeamish eyes. The fever of battle must have been high on both sides.

However, thinking about emotion brought him back to Gaby and the things he'd said to her at her grandmother's birthday party back in Chicago. He shouldn't have attacked her without knowing why she was seemingly doting on the elderly yacht builder. She was wearing a fortune in diamonds, and he'd been certain that she'd been fawning on the man who had given them to her.

He'd judged her by the women in his life. Women like Mara, who didn't care who or what a man was, so long as he had money and social value. He knew better. Gaby had never been the sort to rush after wealth. Jackie was right. She kicked around in blue jeans and loafers, not fancy clothes. God, he wished he'd never let Mara push him into going to that birthday party! If he hadn't, Gaby would still be in his apartment, in his life.

Now here she was in Texas, with people he didn't know, getting involved with another man. He could have kicked himself.

Tomorrow, he promised himself, he was going to hire that private detective and track her down. He didn't know what he was going to say to her, but he knew he'd think of some way to apologize, no matter what it took.

He was proud; he hated to be in the wrong. But he knew that unless he was willing to back down, Gaby would be out of his life forever. He hated the thought of losing her. The bedroom she'd occupied was barren, like his life, like his heart. He missed her. So did Jackie and Tilly.

Miranda would like her, he mused. Gaby really was very much like their mother. A gentle, sweet woman who nurtured those around her.

He turned the corner and walked right into a pregnant woman. While he was apologizing, another woman moved forward, blue eyes blazing.

"And just what the hell are you doing in San Antonio?" Gaby, her eyes shocked, her face reddening with temper, demanded furiously.

FIFTEEN

For a space of seconds, Nick was speechless. He'd just been thinking about Gaby, and she appeared in front of him from out of nowhere. It was a shock to find her here like this, unexpectedly.

Beside her, a very pregnant Clancey was trying not to grin. Her cousin Gaby was mostly shy and she never raised her voice, much less cursed. This big, tall, handsome man with thick wavy black hair and dark eyes and olive complexion was obviously tongue-tied. Also obviously interested in Gaby, or he wouldn't be here. She had to hide a smile as Gaby put her hands on her slender hips and gave him both barrels.

"What, did you think I might be down here adding another millionaire to my collection?" she was demanding. "And just how did you find me? I know my grandmother didn't tell you where I was!"

Nick glared at her. "I hired a private detective," he shot back, without blowing Everett's cover. Not that he liked the man…

"Where I am is none of your business!" she raged.

"Yes, it is," he shot back. "You left without a forwarding address and one of your bags is still in the closet of the room you were in!"

"And you came all this way to get me to move a bag?" Gaby exclaimed.

Clancey had to turn away. She could barely contain the laughter.

"You still owe me a week's work, too," he continued, unabashed. "Some assistant you are! I wonder how you can live with yourself!"

Gaby was fuming. "You accused me of being a gold digger!" she raged. "You said I was playing up to an old man to get him to give me expensive things! I don't need anybody to give me money—I'm rich! My grandmother owns a vineyard in France and I'm her only heir! She gave me the diamonds for my birthday! They belonged to my great-grandmother!"

"I didn't know," he began.

"You didn't ask!" she retorted. "You are the worst boss I ever had in my life, and I wouldn't work for you again if you offered me the Eiffel Tower!"

"I can't afford the Eiffel Tower," he mused. "How about a nice meal at one of the better restaurants in Paris?"

"I'd choke trying to sit at the same table with you!" Tears were forming in her blue eyes. "You...you...!" Words failed her. But it didn't matter.

She stopped in midsentence, because before she could get the words out, Nick had her up in his arms, off the pavement, cradled against his broad chest, and he was kissing her as if the world was about to end.

His head was spinning. He couldn't manage words to convince her to come home, but he could show her how he felt. Only seconds into the kiss, her arms went around his neck and with a choked moan, she gave him back the kiss with all the pent-up misery of the past few days.

He held her in his arms, right there on the street corner, with traffic and pedestrians hiding smiles while he made the most of his opportunity. Gaby, in his arms, holding him, kissing him back. It was like the sweetest dream he'd ever had.

"I hate you," she choked out when he lifted his mouth from hers just long enough to look into her soft, accusing eyes.

"Come home and do it in comfort," he whispered deeply, and kissed her again. "My sister came home. You can have a chaperone. I'll get Uncle Jacob to loan us somebody to help out."

"Nick," she groaned.

He buried his face in her throat, where her loosened chestnut hair was bunched up under his fingers.

She slid her fingers through his cool, thick hair and just let him hold her, oblivious of people coming and going around them.

"Oh, dear," Clancey murmured as a squad car pulled up beside them and stopped.

Nick lifted his head and looked into the eyes of a San Antonio police officer.

Gaby followed his gaze to the car, out of which a blonde woman in plainclothes emerged. She cocked her head at them and smiled.

"Hi, Detective Rogers," Clancey greeted the older woman with a grin. "You working or just riding around with Gunn there to keep an eye on him? Hey, Gunn!" she called to the driver, a San Antonio patrol officer in uniform.

He chuckled. "Hey, tidbit. We're on our way to a meeting."

"Which is why we're here. I hate meetings," Rogers said with a pulled-down mouth. "The captain hates them, too, but Gunn and I were able to plead an emergency and get out of it. So, guess what, you're our emergency!" She glanced at Gaby, still held high in Nick's arms. "Kidnapping?" she asked hopefully.

Gaby grinned. "Not yet. But if I can borrow some hand-cuffs...?"

"Have mine. Damned things don't work right anyway," Rogers scoffed.

"This is my cousin Gaby Dupont from Chicago," Clancey introduced them. "And he's..." She hesitated with raised eye-brows.

"Nick Chandler," Nick replied genially. "I have a law firm in Chicago. She works for me," he added, indicating Gaby with his head, because his arms were busy holding her off the ground.

"Worked for you," Gaby said curtly. "I quit!"

"Well, I didn't agree that you could quit, so you still work for me," he countered. "I can look the statute up in a lawbook when we get back home." He grinned at her. "They teach us stuff like that in law school," he added helpfully.

Gaby was in no mood for quick forgiveness. "I am not going...!"

"Jackie misses you," Nick interrupted. "She was quiet for ten whole minutes last night, in fact."

Gaby blinked. "Ten minutes? Is she sick?"

"No."

"You didn't leave her alone, with Keith on the loose?" she persisted.

"Uncle Jacob has people watching her."

"We have an uncle Jacob?" Clancey wanted to know.

"He's an honorary uncle, but he's interested in my grand-mother," Gaby volunteered. "He's teaching her the tango." She looked a little worried.

"It's okay. He locks his pistol in a drawer while they're dancing," Nick assured her.

"Is he a cop?" Rogers wanted to know.

"No, he's a crime boss from Detroit."

Rogers's eyes were like saucers. Clancey chuckled. "We have interesting family ties," she pointed out.

"Uncle Jacob isn't family, though, not really," Gaby said.

"If he marries your grandmother, he will be." Nick scowled. "I can see the headlines already. I don't have any mob bosses in my family."

"He won't be part of your family," Gaby said firmly.

He was studying her with pursed lips and twinkling eyes. "Want to bet on that?"

Gaby blushed furiously. "Will you put me down? We're about to be a tourist attraction!"

"The last time I put you down, you ran halfway across the country," he pointed out. "I'd need some assurances that you won't do it again. Certainly not until we've had time to talk."

"I don't want to talk to you," Gaby shot back. "You accused me of being a gold digger!"

"You were dripping diamonds and smiling at one of the richest men in Chicago," he muttered. "I thought you were just another college graduate with very little money."

"All this is very interesting, but Gunn and I have a meeting to go to. Nice to see you Clancey. And you two should get a room, for God's sake," she told Nick and Gaby. "This is a nice, respectable Western town with great people and superior moral fiber..." She ended with a curse of some heat as two people approached the street corner.

"Will you put the damned gun down and talk to me?" A handsome blond man was raging after a young woman with blond hair in a bun and her pistol exposed at her side.

"I have not pulled a gun on you!" the blonde woman raged.

Rogers was grinning. So was Gunn. And Clancey. Seeing their usually imperturbable captain out of control was going to feed the gossip mill for days.

Gaby recognized the police captain from Fernando's along with the blonde woman who'd glared daggers at him the night before.

"Five minutes," Cal Hollister said with evident exasperation.

"I wouldn't give you five seconds," the blonde woman threw back. She noticed, belatedly, a group of people standing together. There was a uniformed police officer, two women— one heavily pregnant—and a man with a woman cradled in his arms.

She stopped and stared. So did the police captain.

"Well, what a nice surprise, sir," Rogers murmured dryly. "Gunn and I were just about to cite these lovely people for public indecency."

"For what?" Nick burst out. His gray eyes flashed fire.

"Ha!" Gaby exclaimed. "Maybe they'll arrest you!"

"I'm going back to the ranch," the blonde woman said curtly, flushing a little as she nodded toward the group of strangers and made her way across the busy street when the light changed.

"Damn!" Hollister cursed. "Damn!"

"And that's a misdemeanor, sir," Rogers told him. "Cursing in public...?"

He turned to Rogers. His eyes were blazing.

She held up both hands. "Gunn and I are just leaving, right, Gunn?" she prodded.

"Oh, yes, ma'am!" Gunn rushed around the car to the other side and got in.

"And you'll notice that I don't have a single cigarette on me, sir," Rogers added with a blithe smile.

"No doubt they're in Gunn's pocket," Hollister said hotly. "And if I find one, you lose the bet."

Before anybody could ask what the bet was, there was a sudden gush of water under Clancey.

"Oh, my God," she cried, "my water broke! My water broke! What do I do?"

It was almost a wail.

"We get you to the nearest hospital," Nick said gently, putting Gaby down carefully.

"Put her in back. I'll ride with her," Hollister said at once, guiding Clancey into the back seat. "It's okay, honey, you're going to be fine. I'll call Banks. He'll meet us at the emergency room entrance."

"Got to go! And get a room!" Rogers called back as she dived into the passenger seat as Gunn was putting the squad car in gear.

"Now what?" Nick asked.

"The hospital! I have to go to the hospital! Clancey's my cousin and it's her first baby," she exclaimed.

"No problem." He held up a hand, and a cab barreled toward them.

"How do you do that?" she exclaimed.

He just grinned as he put her into the cab. "Luck," he explained once they were in the cab. "It's how I win cases in court."

"I expect knowing the law very well helps," she said, feeling awkward because of the way he'd kissed her. There had been utter desperation in it, as if he expressed in the kiss all the feelings he couldn't quite admit to. It had been a revelation.

His hand curled into hers as the cab flew toward the hospital.

"It's her first," Gaby said uneasily.

His fingers slid in between hers and tightened, comforting. "She'll be fine."

She looked up at him. After a minute, she smiled. So did he.

★ ★ ★

For a first child, its birth was almost immediate, something the doctor imparted to a beaming Colter Banks as he was led from the waiting room back to the delivery room.

Nick was having a hard time. It brought back memories of his own child, of Samantha's birth. Pain lanced through him.

Gaby sensed it. She reached for his big hand and locked her fingers into it. She looked up at him with soft, caring eyes. He got lost in them. He took a deep breath and seemed to relax.

Banks was back shortly, grinning from ear to ear. "It's a boy!" he exclaimed. "We wouldn't let them tell us—we wanted it to be a surprise. Son of a gun, a boy!" His eyes were full of dreams.

"What are you going to name him?" Clancey asked.

"Jude Dalton Banks," he said. "The Dalton is for Clancey's late grandfather. He taught her to play guitar." He didn't add that her grandfather had been murdered, or that he'd helped find the killer. "She's doing great. Hey, want to come see my son? They've got him in the nursery!"

Nick was almost rigid. Gaby contracted her soft hand around his big one. "Come on," she said gently.

He'd wanted to find an excuse not to go, but Gaby was smiling at him. He sighed and went along with her.

There was only one blue blanket in the nursery. Colter smiled at the nurse, who laughed and picked up the little boy, bringing him to the window.

"He's precious," Gaby said softly. "You lucky man!"

"Lucky, yes," Colter said. "I want to buy him a toy store," he murmured on a chuckle.

Nick was having a hard time. Gaby moved closer to him, comforting him. He drew in a long breath and slid his arm around her shoulders.

"Congratulations," Nick told him.

"Thanks. Now I want a daughter who looks just like Clancey," Banks said, with an ear-to-ear grin.

The nurse was putting the little boy back in his crib.

"I'd better get back to Clancey. They'll have her in a room shortly if you two want to wait?" he added.

"Of course," Nick answered for them, and Gaby nodded.

"See you later." Banks went back the way they'd come.

Gaby looked up into Nick's tormented eyes. "It was half a lifetime ago," she said softly. "You can't go back, Nick. You have to live in the present."

He didn't answer her. She tugged at his hand. "I'm hungry," she said simply. "There must be a cafeteria here somewhere."

"A cafeteria." He'd been lost in horrible memories. He looked down at her. "Yes. Coffee would be nice."

"Coffee and food. Have you eaten?"

He shook his head. "Not much since supper on Friday. And I had four highballs with that."

"Four…!"

He scowled at her. "You left."

She flushed. "You know why."

"I'd have apologized if you'd stayed around for a few hours more," he said heatedly, but keeping his voice down.

"And how was I to know that?"

His eyes stared straight down into hers. "Because you know me, right down to my big feet. You know me, Gaby. And I know you."

She swallowed. Hard. She lowered her gaze to his broad chest. She felt his fingers curling slowly into hers and her heart threatened to beat her to death. She felt so much emotion that it seemed to electrify her whole body. So this was love, she thought with sudden realization. And she looked up at Nick with all that emotion in her soft blue eyes.

He was feeling something similar. His heart raced in his

chest. He'd fought involvement, avoided kids, avoided any thought of a woman in his life who might be impossible to forget. He would never forget Gaby. If he lost her, he'd mourn her for the rest of his days. Forever.

He opened his mouth to speak, just as a tall, handsome blond man came around the corner. He spotted the two of them and smiled ruefully.

"They ran me out until they get Clancey into a room," he told them. "I'm starved. You two going after food?"

"We are," Gaby said, smiling as she clung to Nick's big hand.

"There's a nice cafeteria here," Hollister told them. "I've spent a lot of time here in recent years on cases, before I made captain. Now I just sit at a damned desk and talk to outraged civic groups." He sighed as they walked toward the elevator.

"It's a worthwhile profession," Nick said, glad to have something to take his mind off the baby. "You catch crooks."

"And you defend them?" Hollister mused.

Nick laughed. "I was an assistant district attorney for years before I became a defense attorney and founded my own law firm. We take select cases. Usually," he added, with a rueful glance at Gaby. "I can afford to be choosy about my clients."

"Nice to know you're not helping drug dealers get back on the streets," Hollister chuckled.

The cafeteria was just beyond the elevator. All three of them walked in and got in line.

"Right now I'm trying to keep one of my clients alive," Nick replied. "His wife has tried to kill him several times. The police are persecuting her."

"Is she? Trying to kill him?" Hollister asked.

"Very definitely. He's a millionaire and she waited tables before he found her," he said simply. "She's inventive about murder weapons. The last one was a car. She accidentally backed over him. Twice. Lucky for him that he knew how to do a breakfall."

"We had a guy who accidentally shot an acquaintance. Thirty-six times. He had to reload several times."

"Accidentally?!! Was he acquitted?" Gaby asked.

Hollister chuckled. "Not in San Antonio, he wasn't."

"Now, now," Nick mused as he chose fried chicken over beef. "We don't let people get away with that in Chicago, either."

"Sorry. It was the mob reference," Hollister added, tongue in cheek.

Nick sighed. "Well, if Jackie ends up married to Antonio, I guess she could do worse. At least I'd never have to worry about her going out at night alone. Which reminds me, her ex-boyfriend is on the loose. His father forgave him and bailed him out," he told Gaby grimly. "Which means, you have protection when you go out, too, when you come home."

"He'll be after Jackie again!"

"And maybe you," Nick added, quietly grim. "We'll see if your Mr. Everett has some free time to tail you. I'm sure your grandmother would approve."

"Everett?" Cal asked. "Tall guy, good-looking, bad attitude, Texas accent, missing an eye…?"

"The very same," Gaby laughed.

"We worked together for a while," he said. "Good man to have in your corner in deadly situations," he added.

"I found that out myself," Gaby said. She looked at Nick and raised her eyebrows. "Only my grandmother and Mr. Everett knew I was here in Texas," she murmured.

He shrugged. "I tracked Everett to a restaurant and pinned him down," he confessed.

"Oh? Why?" she asked.

He sighed and made a face as he pulled out his wallet and paid for his and Gaby's lunch.

"Why?" she persisted when they were seated at a table with the trays put aside.

Nick stared at her. It felt like coming home. His eyes were warm on her face. "I told you," he teased. "You left a bag in your bedroom closet."

She gave him a look of patent disbelief.

"I need the space," he continued. "Miranda brought ten suitcases with her."

Her face tautened. "Miranda?" Was that a new woman in his life? Had he replaced Mara with someone else?

He saw that expression and felt joy well up inside him. "Miranda is my sister," he said softly. "Jackie's mother."

She let out the breath she'd been holding and hated the flush that swept over her high cheekbones. "Oh."

"Banks was hoping for a little girl," Hollister said between bites. "But Clancey wanted a boy." He chuckled. "I guarantee this won't be their only child. They both love kids. Her little brother's lived with them since they married."

"He's sweet," Gaby remarked.

"They both are. Clancey was taking care of him all by herself. She worked for me until I was promoted. She had to walk to work, and it was too far to get to my new precinct, so she got a job with the Texas Rangers as Colter's assistant." He shook his head and chuckled. "It was open warfare for the first few months."

"They didn't like each other?" Gaby asked, laughing.

"Not one bit. Then Clancey got a chest infection and Colter had to take care of her. I would have, but I could see which way the wind was blowing. Clancey and Tad were kind of like my family," he added softly. "I was married, but my wife died years ago and I have no family left alive."

Gaby wanted so badly to ask him about the blonde woman he was arguing with when Clancey went into labor, but it seemed presumptuous.

"I gather that you're not married?" Hollister asked Nick.

He was sipping black coffee. "I was," he said tautly. "I... lost my wife and child, a long time ago."

Hollister winced. "Sorry."

"Life goes on," Nick said heavily. "It has to."

"How is Jackie?" Gaby asked.

"Thriving. She's taken charge of her mother and seems to be the more adult of the two." Nick chuckled, glad of the change of subject. His dark eyes twinkled. "She misses you."

"I miss her, too," Gaby confessed.

"You were right, you know. The only thing wrong with my niece is that nobody loved her. Not until you came along."

"That's not true, Nick. I know you love her."

"I do, but I didn't realize it, not until things came to a head." He finished his dessert and put down his fork. "We don't know how much people mean to us until we lose them, sometimes."

Gaby wouldn't have touched that line with a pole.

Nick looked up at her. "And you still owe me two weeks' notice," he said easily. "Breach of contract. I could take you to court."

"You wouldn't dare," she said haughtily.

He just grinned.

Hollister chuckled.

Gaby sighed and finished her own dessert.

They were fetched by a strutting Colter Banks shortly after second cups of coffee and led to a private room where Clancey was sitting up in bed nursing a tiny little boy.

She looked up, beaming. "Isn't he wonderful?" she exclaimed, looking at her husband with eyes brimming over with joy. "Colt, we have to let Tad come and see him!"

"I'll go home and get him directly," he promised her with a smile. "I did phone home. He was over the moon. He said, and I quote, 'Now I'm not the littlest kid in the house anymore!'"

They all laughed.

Hollister sighed. "Well, honey, I can see that you're well taken care of, so I'll go back to work and face the music." He made a face. "I've got a committee meeting at three," he added curtly. "I hate committee meetings. I'm going to go and find Rogers and make her sit in on it."

"That is not nice," Clancey pointed out. "And she'll get even."

"Not unless I'm driving the ranch truck and you teach her how to remove the rotor," Hollister pointed out.

"I'll get on that first thing tomorrow," Clancey replied gleefully. "By then, she'll be out for revenge."

Hollister just laughed.

"Are you going back to the ranch with your cousin's husband?" Nick asked Gaby when they were outside the hospital.

"I...well, I hadn't thought about it." She hesitated.

He linked her fingers into his. "I can get us both on the next plane to Chicago," he said softly. "The apartment has four bedrooms."

"I have an apartment of my own," she reminded him.

He turned her around and looked down into her worried eyes. "Your grandfather hasn't got a ghost of a chance of overturning that verdict," he said out of the blue. "No reputable attorney in the city would represent him."

She caught her breath audibly and bit her lower lip. "I'm so sorry," she said. "About not telling you the truth in the first place." She looked at his chin instead of his face. "You said I was late and I thought, well, if I worked for you, maybe I could find out what sort of person you were before I had to ask if you were going to take his case again."

"And what sort of person am I, Gaby?" he asked quietly.

She lifted her shy eyes to his. "You're the sort of man who'd think nothing of risking his own life to save people he loved. You roar around like a lion when you lose your temper, but you're strong and steady and dependable and you never quit on anybody you care for."

There was a faint flush on his own high cheekbones. "I quit on you, though, didn't I, Gaby?" he said sadly.

"You didn't know me," she said simply.

He caught her hands in his and held them, staring at them instead of at her face. "But I did. I knew you the first time I saw you and hated it. I could take Mara or leave her, and mostly I left her. I couldn't…touch her, after you moved into my apartment," he confessed tautly. "I didn't want her, but I kept her around. She was like a shield and I needed one." He drew in a breath and met her eyes. "I didn't want ties ever again, Gaby. And you know why."

She nodded. "You didn't want to love again, to care again, to risk losing a child again."

"Yes."

"I can understand that," she said, her voice soft and comforting. "It was a horrible tragedy. But you can't live in it, Nick. You can't live in the present if you're locked up in the past."

His teeth ground together. "I see her face. I hear her screams!" His eyes closed.

She stepped closer to him and slid her arms around him and pressed close. "And she's safe, now. Nobody can ever harm her again. She's playing with other children in fields of wildflowers, laughing," she whispered. "She's all right, Nick. And so are you."

His fingers dug into her back involuntarily as he held her bruisingly close and buried his face in her throat.

"It's all right now," she whispered, rocking him. "Everything is all right."

After a minute he dragged in a breath and lifted his head, averting his face until he regained the control he'd almost lost.

"Nothing is all right, unless you come back with me," he bit off.

She hesitated.

He cleared his throat and looked down at her. His eyebrows lifted. "I'll sue," he threatened. He grinned.

She burst out laughing. "Oh, all right. But if you accuse me of being a gold digger again…"

He held up a hand. "I'm reformed. Honest."

She cocked her head and stared up at him.

"Okay, I'm sort of reformed," he added after a minute. "But we can't rule out sudden bursts of helpless irritation. I mean, I am who I am."

"Infrequent sudden bursts of helpless irritation," she persisted.

He shrugged. "Okay."

She smiled. "Okay."

SIXTEEN

Nick had left his car at the airport, so he drove Gaby back to her apartment to leave her suitcase and pack a few things to take with her to Nick's.

He wandered around the apartment, discovering things about her from the photographs and books and keepsakes scattered around it.

"What in the hell is this?" he asked, picking up a resin cast of a skull that resided on a shelf of her bookcase.

"It's *homo erectus erectus*," she said. "An early version of modern man. It's a cast from a skull that my parents found on their last dig. This is them," she added, nodding toward a big portrait higher up on the bookcase.

He picked up the framed photo and looked at it. He smiled. "You look like your father."

She smiled. "I do, don't I?"

"Books on orchids," he mused. "And bonsai trees."

"I've always wanted to grow both, but I don't have a green thumb."

"One of my clients has them. But he has an elaborate setup with sun spectrum lighting and automatic waterers." He glanced at her and pursed his lips. "We could put one of those in a corner of my office in the apartment. It's plenty big enough."

She glanced at him. "Oh. Well. Yes, that would be nice," she stammered. "I was thinking I might do it here one day."

He moved to stand in front of her. His big, warm hands framed her face. He bent and kissed her, very softly. "You look pretty in blue," he remarked, smiling as he studied her clothes. She was wearing blue jeans and a knitted blue sweater, her hair perched atop her head held with a blue silk scrunchie. "You don't dress like a wealthy woman."

"I don't have to," she said. "I'm never going to be the kind of person who does well at social things. I love the ballet and the opera and symphony concerts. But teas and committee meetings..."

He chuckled. "I like opera and symphonies, as well. Ballet, not so much. I guess I could get used to it," he added thoughtfully.

She didn't understand what he was saying. He was having trouble trying to put into words what he wanted, what he was feeling. It had been many years since he'd felt any such things.

"We should probably go," he said after a minute, moving away from her. "You'll like my sister, I think. She's going through a bad patch. Her lover dumped her for a younger, prettier woman. Jackie's looking after her."

She smiled at him. "Does she look like you, your sister?"

He chuckled. "She looks more like Jackie."

"Is she nice?"

"Usually," he replied. "And she doesn't shout and throw phones at the wall," he added, tongue in cheek.

"I guess foul tempers don't run in the family so much…?" Her voice trailed away.

He pulled her into his arms and kissed her. "Pest. Let's go."

He picked up her suitcase and she followed him to the door. "I'm not sure…" she began.

He turned, bent and kissed her again. "Yes, you are." His dark eyes smiled. "Come along."

She went with him and wondered if she was out of her mind.

Miranda was welcoming. She looked like an older version of her daughter, and she seemed fascinated with Nick's obvious affection for the young woman he brought home with him. She'd never known Nick to look at any woman that way, especially not Mara.

Nick had a call from a client and went into his office to take it. Miranda and Jackie sat on the foot of Gaby's bed in the third guest room, watching her unpack.

"Uncle Nick went nuts when you left," Jackie said with a smug grin. "He got drunk, he threw things." She chuckled. "Well, he does throw things, but it's the first time I ever saw him that hungover. He felt guilty."

"I thought he knew me better than that," Gaby said on a sigh. "I'm mostly afraid of men. I wouldn't know how to attract somebody just for what he had."

"Uncle Nick said he just flew off the handle. He does that," Jackie said on a laugh.

"Yes, he does. There are reasons, you know, my darling," Miranda said, gently smoothing back her daughter's hair. She sighed. "You have no idea what our childhood was like. Our father drank to excess, all the time, and he beat us."

Gaby looked horrified. "You, too?" she exclaimed.

Miranda nodded. "Me, too." She drew in a long breath. "I

was very pretty when I was young, like my sweet girl here," she added, nodding at Jackie. "I didn't have anything. Nick was just starting night school to study law and there was a very rich man who wanted to take care of me. So I let him. It was nice to have anything I wanted, to be pampered, given things, to buy pretty clothes, go on exotic vacations." She grimaced. "I sort of fell into it. When he got tired of me, one of his friends came along and I took up with him. I've gone from man to man for a long time. Not that I do it for money anymore. I have more than I need. This last one was a gigolo, but I didn't know it. Not until it was too late."

Gaby sat down on the bed, too. "We all do things that seem shameful in retrospect," she said gently. "I pretended to be an administrative assistant, when the real reason I came here was to find out if your brother was going to represent my grandfather again." She folded her arms around herself. "He sold me to a foreign diplomat when I was sixteen, to pay off a gambling debt. My grandmother discovered it just in time." She shifted restlessly. "He wants his law license back, so he's found some witnesses to swear that I lied."

"There are photographs," Jackie reminded her, and she looked indignant. "If he tries to mess with you, Uncle Nick will take him apart in court."

"Indeed he will," Miranda seconded, outraged for this gentle woman who looked so innocent. "I've never met your grandmother, but I certainly know of her. She's one of the wealthiest women in Chicago."

"And one of the sweetest," Gaby replied. "My parents were archaeologists. They died together on a dig. My grandmother raised me, with no help at all from my grandfather. He was so greedy. All he ever thought about was money. He had none, but he convinced my grandmother that he was rich. She married him, so infatuated that she didn't question anything he said. By the time she realized what a sad excuse for a human being he really was, it was too late. Her generation didn't believe in divorce. She stuck with him, although they mostly lived apart. And then when I turned sixteeen he wanted to have a party." She stopped. "I've been afraid of men ever since. Well, except for Nick," she amended.

"Uncle Nick wouldn't hurt a fly," Jackie said. "Although, he's not so easygoing around men. There was this bar fight when I was just ten…!"

"There were a lot of bar fights before you were even born," Miranda laughed with twinkling eyes. "Nick takes after our maternal grandfather. He was a union boss. They don't come much tougher."

"Nick's had a hard life," Gaby said softly.

"He's been living in the past until now," Miranda told her. "But I think he's beginning to see the light in the tunnel. He doesn't drink, you know," she added. "Not to excess, anyway. For him to get drunk, well, that's definitely not Nick."

"He felt really bad about misjudging you," Jackie told her. She smiled wickedly. "And then I had Mr. Everett tell him about the handsome police captain in San Antonio that your cousin introduced you to."

Gaby caught her breath.

"So then he packed a bag and canceled all his appointments and said he was going to Texas," Jackie chuckled.

Gaby flushed. She felt reborn. New. Whole.

Miranda and Jackie exchanged mischievous glances.

Nick came to the door. "What is this, a committee meeting?" he asked gruffly. "And what are you all plotting?"

Three sets of eyebrows lifted.

He glowered at them. "You were talking about me, weren't you?" he demanded. He looked at Gaby and his eyes softened. "That police captain seems to have a female in his life already. Shame." His smug little smile belied the last word.

Gaby glared at him. "He's a friend of my cousin's. I hardly spoke to the man."

He grinned.

Tilly came to the door, surprised to find four people in Gaby's room. "I was going to make dinner…"

"Make it for four," Nick said. "I'm not going anywhere tonight."

"Four it is," Tilly said. She smiled to herself as she went back into the kitchen.

"So, am I working for you again?" Gaby asked Nick while the other two women were talking in Jackie's room.

He took her small waist in both hands and drew her gently against him. "For now," he murmured, looking at her pretty mouth. "I guess you know that I'm only interested in you because you're rich," he said outrageously.

She laughed softly. "And I'm only interested in you because you're rich and you have a yacht," she pointed out.

"Nice to know we're both mercenary," he mused, bending to brush his mouth softly over hers.

She lifted closer and felt his arms drawing her intimately close.

"You love babies, don't you?" he whispered into her parted lips. "Your eyes were almost glowing with hunger when you looked at Clancey's little boy."

She shivered a little with feeling. "Yes," she whispered. "I'm sorry, about what happened to you…"

He kissed her hungrily. "I can't live in the past with my little girl," he said. "Even though I'll never stop missing her or blaming myself for her death."

She drew back and put her fingers against his firm, warm

mouth. "You can't go on blaming yourself. You didn't know that your wife had mental issues, Nick. Nobody could have anticipated what happened. It's not your fault."

He drew in a long breath. He looked his age, just briefly. "I suppose not," he said finally. "It's just the memory of her little face…"

She pulled his face down to hers and kissed him with more enthusiasm than skill. "Stop looking back," she whispered. "It's over. It's all right. She's playing with a basketful of kittens in a flowery meadow, and she's fine."

He kissed her fiercely. She made him feel as if it was fine, as if Samantha was finally at peace. He lifted her against him. His mouth devoured hers. "I want a baby…" he ground out.

Her arms tightened around his neck and she kissed him back with such fervor that for a minute he thought seriously about laying her down on the carpet and doing what would come naturally.

He shuddered a little as he forced himself to ease his mouth away from hers, although his body was so hard that she knew how much he wanted her.

She touched his mouth with her fingertips, fascinated with him, with what he'd whispered to her. It was probably just something that he blurted out in the throes of sensual hunger, she told herself, and her face lost its wonder and began to tauten with sadness.

"No," he whispered, kissing her tenderly. "I meant what I said." He lifted his head and looked into her wide, pale blue eyes with joy possessing him. "I want a baby. Don't you?"

She shivered. "More than anything!"

He pressed his lips to her forehead. "I'll be difficult at first, you know. I'm not used to living with anyone."

"There was Mara," she began with a flash of jealousy.

"Mara was an infrequent lover. I never stayed with her at

night, never wanted to. And since you moved in, I haven't wanted her at all. That's over. Finished."

She smoothed her fingers over his chest, feeling the thunder of his heartbeat. "My grandmother won't like it," she said softly. "She's very conventional…"

He was laughing. "Do you think I'm offering to live in sin with you?" he asked with some amusement. "Jackie would stop talking to me and Tilly would burn every meal she put in front of me. Not to mention that your grandmother has a former hit man teaching her to tango."

She laughed, too, at the absurdity of what he was saying.

"It has to be marriage," he said quietly, and felt as if he'd just come from a dark place into the light. "And soon," he added, one eyebrow going up as he pressed her hips into the swollen contours of his own.

She cleared her throat. "Okay. But you have to remember that I don't know much about that, and I have my own little terrors…"

"You won't have them anymore," he said softly. "And I promise that I'll treat you like priceless porcelain. Okay?"

She sighed and laid her cheek against his broad chest, all her dreams coming true in this unexpected way. "Okay."

His chest rose and fell quickly. "But remember that I'm only marrying you for your money," he drawled.

"And you remember that I'm only marrying you for your yacht."

They both dissolved into laughter.

"What's so funny?" Jackie wanted to know as she and her mother rejoined them.

"We're only marrying each other for our respective fortunes," Nick told them.

"No, I'm marrying you for the yacht," Gaby corrected.

Nick grinned down at her. "Do you get seasick?"

"Let's find out," she replied.

He laughed, feeling his body slowly recover from her proximity. He'd waited until then to release her.

"You're getting married?" Jackie exclaimed. She hugged Gaby hard, and then her uncle. "This is super! You'll be my aunt!" she told Gaby.

"Built-in family," Nick added with a grin. "Just add wedding ring."

Miranda hugged her, too. "You'll do well together," she said, smiling at them. "I'm going to stay in Chicago, so I'll get a place of my own. Jackie can live with me, if she wants to," she added quickly. "I've made a lot of stupid mistakes," she told her daughter. "But if you can forgive them..."

Jackie hugged her. "Just hush. I'd love to live with you. And I'll be a great babysitter," she added with a sly look at Gaby, who blushed. "Not to mention that you'll have great protection, because the mob follows me wherever I go. Speaking of that," she said, turning to her mother, "I'm going over to Antonio's. His family's having a special dinner so they can meet me. I'm sorry to leave you when you just got here."

"Go on," Miranda teased. "Have fun. I'll help Tilly in the kitchen and be available for wedding plan consultation. Not that I've ever been married, but I've been involved in a number of other people's weddings," she said.

The doorbell rang. "I'll get it," Jackie said.

She looked through the keyhole first, pursed her lips and opened the door. Two men stood there. One was middle-aged, short and innocent-looking. The second was tall and drop-dead gorgeous with dark eyes and hair and olive skin.

He gave Miranda, who was sitting on the sofa, a look that combined interest with surprise, taking in her nice figure in the slacks and cashmere sweater she was wearing, and the long, wavy black hair and dark eyes and pretty face.

"Hi, guys, come on in," Jackie greeted. "This is Mole." She indicated the short man. "And that's Angel." She nodded toward the taller man.

Miranda was staring at him. "Angel? Are you sweet?" she teased.

He pursed chiseled lips and his eyes twinkled. "It's Angelo. Everybody calls me Angel." He didn't add why. It had nothing to do with a heavenly nature, either.

"Angelo."

"Who are you?" he asked with a smile that would have charmed snakes.

"Miranda," she replied.

He cocked his head. "You married?"

She shook her head. "You?"

He shook his head.

"Jacob said to bring you and anybody else you wanted along to dinner," Angelo told Jackie. He looked at Miranda. "It's good Italian food. My mama does the cooking for Jacob's household. So," he said, "you coming along?"

"Come on, Mom," Jackie coaxed. "You'll love Uncle Jacob."

Miranda hesitated.

"Go on," Nick told her. "If Tilly cooks too much, we'll have it for dinner tomorrow."

"Let me change my clothes," Miranda said, and suddenly looked years younger. She almost ran back into her bedroom.

The others smiled at each other.

It was quiet in the apartment after Miranda and Jackie left.

"You worked wonders with Jackie," Nick told her. She was curled up in his lap while Tilly put the finishing touches on dinner. "She'd never have talked to her mother at all, the way she was when you first came here."

"She's a sweet girl. All she needed was love."

"I noticed." He kissed her forehead. "She's changed."

She sighed and curled closer. "Do you really want to marry me, Nick?"

"I really want to marry you." He sighed. "I'm hard to live with sometimes."

"I noticed."

He chuckled at her throwing his favorite phrase back at him. "I'll try to lose my temper less."

"Not on my account," she replied. "I think you're terrific. I lo…like you, bad temper and all."

He drew back and looked down into her soft eyes. "That isn't what you wanted to say."

She grimaced. "Well…"

He nuzzled her nose with his. "Want me to say it first, do you?" He smiled. "I love you. I didn't even know it until I walked into that room and saw you dripping diamonds and standing with another man—I wouldn't have cared how old he was. I was so damned jealous I wanted to punch him out."

"Really?"

"Really."

She sighed. "I hated Mara."

"She was no competition at all. I didn't want involvement. I went around with women who didn't want it, either. And now here you are, all domestic and stuff, wanting babies."

She flushed. "You want one, too," she said defensively.

He chuckled. "I want several," he corrected. "I'm greedy."

She smiled, her heart in her eyes. She felt reborn. "I want several, too."

He drew her close and bent to kiss her in a way he never had before. It was soft and tender and caring, saying things with a kiss that he would never have been able to put into words, even with his oratory skills.

She looked up at him then, fascinated. "Wow," she whispered.

He smiled. "Wow is right."

Tilly stuck her head around the door. "There's food," she said, eyebrows raised. "I mean, if either of you are hungry. I cooked for four people and two of them escaped."

"They only went to have supper with the local mob," Gaby teased.

"Same difference," Tilly huffed.

"We'll be right in," Nick assured her.

He stood up and pulled Gaby up with him. "Rings, first thing tomorrow."

"Don't you have court?" she asked, remembering the court docket in his office.

He grimaced. "Yes. Damn. Well, rings after court. We can get a marriage license at the same time." He groaned. "Your grandmother will want to kill me before she agrees to let us get married, and then she'll want a society wedding with all the trimmings."

"We can have a very quiet civil service at the courthouse and then a society wedding with a member of the clergy," she said.

He laughed. "Dear heart," he said, "that's exactly what I was hoping you'd say."

She grinned. "Were you, now?" She reached up and pulled his head down to hers and kissed him hungrily.

"Food!" Tilly called again.

He wrinkled his nose as he drew back. "Spoilsport," he muttered.

"It's getting colder," Tilly insisted.

Nick took Gaby's soft hand in his. "I suppose we should eat something. After Tilly's gone to all the trouble to feed us."

"Just what I was saying to myself, Mr. Chandler," Tilly piped up.

He and Gaby looked at each other and laughed.

★ ★ ★

In the middle of the meal the phone rang. Nick had forgotten to turn off his cell phone. He picked it up reluctantly and answered it.

"Yes?"

Gaby was watching his face as she sipped coffee. It went from irritation to shock to wide-eyed surprise. And then he let out a breath and shook his head. "Well, I'm damned," he said to the person on the other end of the line. "How's he taking it?" He laughed. "No surprise. No, I'll go by and offer condolences. What hospital is he in? Same as last time. Sure, but he'll be safe there this time. Sure. Thanks for calling me. You, too."

He hung up. "Well!"

"What happened?"

"Remember my client, the one whose wife has been trying to off him for weeks and he was furious because he thought we were unjustly persecuting her?"

"Oh, yes," Gaby replied.

"Well, she tried to push him off a roof. This was the second time she'd tried pushing him from a height, too, after she failed her first attempt! She took him up to watch a meteor shower, got him close to the edge and pushed. He fell onto a ledge and she went all the way to the street. He's got a broken wrist. She's at the morgue."

"Talk about getting your just deserts," Gaby said.

"Yes. He's heartbroken. He knows she never meant to push him off. In fact, he's convinced that she knew they were both off-balance and going over the side, so she pushed him to the ledge to save his life. He's mourning her. She was so brave, he said." He rolled his eyes. "My God, the things we learn about people."

She just smiled. "He'll be safe now, at least."

"Let's hope he chooses better next time," he replied. He took her fingers and curled them into his. "Like I did."

She smiled with her whole heart.

Gaby insisted on taking Nick to her grandmother's apartment the following night. He was reluctant.

"I'll bet you ten to one she's put out a contract on me already," he muttered as they stood at her grandmother's door. "And she's got just the guys to handle it."

"She won't hire a hit man. Honest." She pushed the doorbell.

The maid, Celeste, met them with a smile and led them into the living room, where Madame Dupont was sitting on a delicate antique chair by the window, dressed in a pretty pink couture gown that made her look younger than she was.

She got to her feet as they entered.

"*Grand-mère*," she said softly, holding Nick's hand tight, "Nick and I are getting married."

He waited for the explosion.

Madame moved in front of him. She was shorter than Gaby, with the same pale blue eyes. She looked up at him with those eyes narrowed.

"You treat my granddaughter well, Mr. Chandler, or I shall have my new friends dig a very large hole and find a rosebush to put over you!"

Nick burst out laughing. "I believe you."

Madame grinned. She held out a hand and he kissed it with great courtesy.

"Jacob is teaching me the tango. He threw out my former instructor, called him a charlatan, and said that if he ever returned, he would never return." She laughed delightedly. "They say Jacob is a bad man, but to me, he is the soul of chivalry. I adore him!"

"That's what you said about the sheik you met in Dubai…" Gaby began.

"He was a passing fancy," the older woman replied with a wave of her hand. "The arms dealer was a great deal more serious, but, then, how can I wait twenty years for him to get out of prison? Life must go on, you see."

Nick's eyes were howling with laughter. The little woman was nothing like her public image. And now he could see for himself where Gaby got her zany sense of humor.

"Celeste, bring coffee and some of those little tea cakes, would you?" she called to the maid.

"We can't stay long," Gaby said. "Nick is trying a case in Superior Court and he has to get up very early."

"You are living with him?" her grandmother asked coolly.

"With him and his sister and his niece and the cook…" Gaby replied, her eyes twinkling.

Madame Dupont laughed softly. "Shame on me, for what I was thinking. You must forgive me. I was brought up in a more restrictive environment."

"As was I," Nick replied. "I'm as old-fashioned as Gaby is." He glanced at Gaby and laughed. "In other words, no messing around before we get married."

"Nick!" Gaby exclaimed, flushing.

Her grandmother thought this was hilarious and laughed until tears rolled down her cheeks. "Mr. Chandler," she said after a minute, "welcome to my family."

"Madame Dupont, it is my honor," he replied, and meant every word.

"But it's a secular ceremony," Miranda complained as they walked into the ordinary's office in the courthouse.

"My grandmother wants a huge society wedding with everybody who's anybody in Chicago to attend," Gaby said with resignation. "He—" she indicated Nick "—will break out in hives if he has to wait six months before we can get married."

"Imagine the embarrassment if I start scratching myself in the middle of a summation," Nick added his two cents' worth, tongue in cheek.

Miranda laughed. So did Jackie.

"Okay," Miranda said. "Your grandmother does have a point," she said to Gaby. "Plus it gives us all an excuse to buy beautiful dresses to wear to the wedding."

"You two will be my matron of honor and maid of honor, respectively," Gaby told them. "If you would be so kind…"

They both exclaimed at the same time, aglow with delight.

"Don't wear black tights with a beret and combat boots," Gaby told Jackie, with a mischievous grin.

Jackie made a face at her and laughed. The Jackie of her first few days in Nick's apartment might have done exactly that. But not this new, more mature Jackie, who had reached a lovely accord with her much-absent mother.

Nick's fingers closed around hers as they went into the office and the ordinary spoke the age-old words of the marriage ceremony.

Gaby looked up into Nick's eyes and said her two words with her whole heart in them. Nick did the same. The rings they'd bought earlier in the day, simple gold bands, were put into place. They were pronounced man and wife. And Nick kissed his new wife with such delight that Miranda and Jackie just sighed. And so they were married.

That night, Nick and Gaby flew to Cancún, where they were to spend their honeymoon. It was very late when the plane got to the airport, and even later when they went through customs and passport control to get a taxi to their hotel.

Gaby was in tears, because she was tired and nervous all at once.

Nick took her in his arms and rocked her. "We'll have a nice sleep and then we'll go play in the sand. We're both worn-out, my darling. We have the rest of our lives together. No need to rush it. Okay?"

Tears were stinging her eyes. "Okay." She looked up. "You're not mad?"

"Silly woman." He kissed her tenderly. "Let's have room service send up a wine and cheese tray. We'll nibble on something delicious and then go to sleep."

She hugged him. "Thanks for understanding."

"I can be patient." He said it with twinkling eyes and a smile that made her blush. But she smiled back.

SEVENTEEN

Gaby was wearing a pale yellow gown, a silk one with white lace inserts, that fell to her ankles. She'd wanted so badly to feel up to a wedding night with Nick, and she felt guilty that she was too tired to do anything about it.

He was wearing just pajama bottoms, also silk, and he looked so sexy that her heart flipped over just looking at that broad expanse of olive skin under thick curling black hair that wedged from his collarbone down the middle of his flat stomach.

"You're so gorgeous," she said softly.

"Isn't that my line?" he teased. "Beautiful Gaby. I've hardly ever seen you with your hair down. I love it like that."

She smiled. Her chestnut hair was curving around her shoulders, thick and soft with its red highlights shimmering in the overhead light before Nick turned it off.

"Come on. Bedtime." He got under the covers and held them open for her. She climbed in beside him and pillowed her head on his chest. It felt like heaven. She sighed and curved one small hand into the thick hair on his chest. "You feel nice."

"You feel nice, too, angel," he whispered. "It was a long flight."

"It was. The hotel is wonderful. And the beach. I love Chicago, but this beach is extraordinary. I can't wait to get into the water."

"Time enough for all that. We're here for a week." He stretched. "No loopy clients, no fuming judges, no rabid defense attorneys...just blissful peace and a beautiful companion."

She smiled. "Nick, I think…"

"Hmm?" he murmured.

He looked down at her. She was already sound asleep. He smiled and closed his eyes. Gaby in his arms. Heaven.

Gaby opened her eyes to the thick scent of strong coffee. "Oh, my," she murmured drowsily.

Nick was sitting beside her on the bed, chuckling, with a cup of coffee in his hand. "Wake up and have some coffee."

She looked up at him with wondering eyes. This was her husband. His thick wavy black hair was tousled on his head and there was faint stubble where he hadn't shaved yet. His chest was bare and sensuous. He looked like every woman's dream.

She stretched sensuously, her breasts straining against the lace that covered them, and little hard peaks formed quickly as he stared at her.

His breath came more quickly. He put the coffee cup down slowly on the end table. She arched again, moving under the covers.

He slid them away. His big, warm hands slid the straps of

her gown slowly down her body, watching her the whole time, his heart beating him half to death. He didn't want to frighten her, but his whole body throbbed with hunger. It had been a long time since he'd had a woman and he was ravenous for his wife. He had to go slowly. She'd been traumatized as a teenager. It would take patience. He prayed that he had enough.

The fabric came away from her pretty, firm breasts, creamy and mauve-tipped, the nipples hard with desire.

He bent and brushed his mouth over them tenderly. He heard her gasp. He smiled as he did it again, taking the firm little breast inside his lips to tease the nipple with his tongue. Her breasts were very sensitive. She arched and began to moan.

He slid onto the bed beside her, his mouth slowly insistent as he moved the gown away from her hips, down her soft thighs. One hand was under her back, lifting her toward him, the other smoothed between her legs and up, up, to a place that had never known a delicate, tender touch.

She gasped as his thumb found a tender spot and began to trace and tease it. She shivered, moaning. His hand turned, became more intimate, more probing.

Something was happening to her, something she'd never felt in her life. She arched toward his fingers, her eyes half-open, looking at his hard, taut face.

"Nick…" she began, and suddenly she was crying out, sobbing, as a wave of pleasure hit her and washed over her, swamping her, tossing her. She felt her teeth grinding together as she arched and shivered, pleading with him for more, more!

His mouth invaded hers hungrily as his body moved onto her. She was ready for him, surprisingly quick, when he'd expected her to need much more time than he'd given her. She wrapped her long legs around his and arched with every quick thrust of his body, shivering, sobbing, as the pleasure became so much more than she thought she could bear.

"I…can't…" she cried out as her nails dug into his back and she went taut all over, shuddering as if in convulsions as the ecstasy overcame her.

"Nick," she sobbed, trying to get even closer. The little flash of pain when he went into her was only a wisp of memory as she endured a fulfillment she'd never expected to be so unbearably sweet.

His hand was under her, welding her hips to his as he drove into her, feeling her satisfaction, blinded with the joy of his own. They shivered together in the silken aftermath, sweating, clinging, as the room sailed once more into sharp focus.

"Oh," she whispered finally.

He lifted his head. His face was more relaxed than she'd ever seen it, his dark eyes soft with love and pleasure. "Oh?" he whispered back, smiling.

She traced his mouth with her fingertips. "It was the first time." She sought the right words. "Isn't it supposed to be uncomfortable and…well, you know." She flushed.

He chuckled. "Are you complaining?"

She pulled him down on her, burying her mouth in his damp throat. "I love you so much," she whispered. "Is that why it was so good?"

"Probably. I won't mention my amazing and unmatched skills in the bedroom…oof."

She'd punched him. "Shame on you."

"Now, now," he coaxed. "All those educational experiences were just leading up to this. And where would you be if I'd spent my youth learning how to knit or cook?"

She laughed with pure delight. One long leg moved, and her toes traced a pattern on the inside of his muscular leg.

She felt him shiver. "I won't say another word about it." She moved under him. "Nick, do you think we could…"

He only laughed, because they certainly could.

The honeymoon was wonderful and far too short. They lay on the beach together, built sandcastles, walked hand in hand through the surf at dusk and dawn, and learned each other in many sensual ways. By the time they went home to Chicago, they were as comfortable with each other as couples who'd been married for many years.

Four months later, Madame Dupont had arranged the wedding of all weddings, a spectacular affair with every noted politician, every famous actor and actress, every socialite in the city in attendance.

Gaby was nervous. "It's too tight, isn't it? Everybody will see!" she moaned.

Her grandmother just patted her on the shoulder gently. "It doesn't matter, my darling. Everyone already knows that you and Nick were married months ago in a civil ceremony."

"It will show," Gaby sighed.

Madame Dupont laughed. "Your child will be born into love. And so it does not matter if your pregnancy is noticeable, yes?"

Gaby hugged her. "No. Of course not. I'm being emotional."

"Are you ready?" Miranda asked, as she and Jackie, both wearing lacy pink dresses came into the room. "You look marvelous, Gaby!"

"I look pregnant," Gaby chided, laughing.

"Pregnant suits you," Jackie said. "And please notice that I'm not wearing black."

"A sacrifice well noted," Gaby teased. She hugged both

of them. "Half the important people in the country are out there. What if I trip and fall on my way to Nick?"

"Half a dozen people will pick you up. Jacob first, I expect," Madame Dupont mused, tongue in cheek.

"Great-Uncle Jacob's sweet on her," Jackie teased the older woman. "He told Antonio so."

Madame Dupont actually flushed. "Well!"

"And my grandfather is hiding out in Aruba, we hear," Gaby mused, with a pointed look at her grandmother.

"Jacob only mentioned some things that could happen," she said with an innocent look. "He made no actual threats." She smiled and her eyes danced with mischief.

Gaby laughed wholeheartedly, along with the others. She did look lovely in her white gown with its acres of silk and white handmade lace, a couture garment with no sleeves and lace-patterned straps that led to a softly plunging neckline. The waist was a little tight, but hardly noticeable. Besides, there was a fingertip veil pulled over her face, pinned into the exquisite looping hairdo high atop her head. She carried a bouquet of fleur-de-lis, white roses and freesia, and she wore her family diamonds, along with the magnificent diamond engagement ring Nick had bought for her.

"I feel pretty," Gaby teased, singing the first lines of a popular song.

The others grinned.

"There's your cue—let's get going," Jackie teased as the organ began to play.

Gaby walked down the aisle, head high, heart racing, as Chicago's best and brightest watched. Flashes from a dozen smartphones went off as she stared at Nick, who was half-turned, watching her walk down to him.

He was as excited about the baby as Gaby was. They'd had long talks about it. He'd finally realized that living in the past was impossible, especially with a wanted and loved child on the way. He and Gaby were closer than ever.

She stopped beside him. He took her hand in his and looked down at her with such love in his eyes that she flushed.

They were going to be so happy. She didn't have to say it. He knew. The words were in his dark, loving eyes.

★ ★ ★ ★ ★

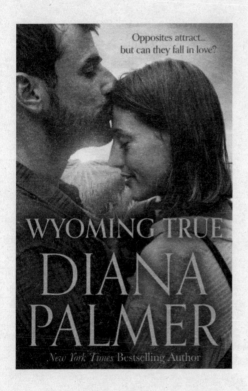

MILLS & BOON

THE HEART OF ROMANCE

LET'S TALK

Romance

Follow us:

📘 millsandboon

📷 @millsandboonuk

🐦 @millsandboon

I9 ·